The Last Time I Killed Him

Him

April Savage

SPLASH TIDE
PUBLISHING

Contents

The Immortali Curse of the Broken Heart

I mmortality comes at a price for the heart. When the curse has spent ages hunting love and is forsaken, it renders upon itself, and death's malicious grip flees them. To die with a broken heart is the most painful death of all, as the one stricken with grief never rests, and the one last to fall never forgets.

1

Scotland, Iona Abbey Raid, 795 A.D.

Erik dumped the bucket of water over his thick blonde braided hair, closing his eyes to the refreshing coolness. He did not mind his leathers and trousers getting doused; he had worked up a sweat shoeing the horses for the week's rampage. He shook his head, his tall, thin frame casting shadows down the alleyway behind his horse barn, where he worked.

He heard loud voices shouting in their Scandinavian tongues and meandered past the alley, wiping the water from his unshaven face to see what the commotion was about. He turned to see Liv peeking out from their house, watching as the village leaders convened in the street.

It was a quaint Viking town on the edge of the cliffs. A forest of solitude rested around them for hunting and shade and Pine and Beech timbers for keeping warm in the bitter winters. The stone houses were quaint, but his village was comfortable. He lingered closer to the street, noticing Liv had joined him.

Liv was a petite blonde-headed beauty, or so he thought, although she stayed to herself and seemed very quiet. He nodded at her, wiping more water off his scruffy face. "Liv." He nodded.

Liv widened her eyes at him and nodded back. "Erik." She pulled at her long-sleeved tunic dress, dusting off fresh herbs to her apron tied around her waist. "What is my father plotting this time." She mumbled.

They always had some conversation as they had grown up together. Liv always seemed interested when he shooed horses or made swords. He thought she just liked the smell of the horses and hot iron. Most of the time, she wanted to stay to herself, hauling water or growing herbs for the stews.

The street was filled with bustling bodies of Vikings fully armed, shoving long spears and battleaxes in their pouches and sheaths. They strapped bows and arrows to their backs, and small black feathers loomed over their brutish heads. The round wooden shields strapped toward the rear of their saddles dotted them in rainbows of colors.

Liv hollered out. "Papa?!"

Erik recognized Liv's father, the village elder. He had braided his beard down to his chest and wore his leather tunics, readying his round shield to attach to his horse. He turned as he recognized Liv's voice, his wrinkly face lighting up at her, marching to them.

"Are we going to battle?" She fretted.

"Ah, my girl. Ready your horses. We go to Iona Abbey to raid it. They have gotten gold and silver from the rich rulers passing through. It will feed us for a year, maybe two. We will also get new furs and cloaks for the winter."

Erik gasped. "The priests there are good people."

Liv's father, Ira, laughed. "We need the riches for supplies. Our seer says a harsh winter is coming that could be our demise." He lunged over and patted Erik hard, pulling him away from Liv to his horse.

"Some say these priests have the power of curses," Erik warned, whispering. "Ancient relics. I have heard the tales from my parents."

Erik held his breath as Ira breathed in his face. "Curses do not exist, and those riches collect dust. It is better to use them to care for ourselves. We must be able to survive. Do you not want grandchildren one day?"

Erik opened his mouth to say something, but nothing came out. At this point, he had never considered marrying, and he was only seventeen.

Ira stopped walking with him and stood face to face, glaring in his eyes. "Our people, our way of life must go on. It is how we survive in these times. One day, our great-great-grandchildren will survive differently. It is up to us to ensure they can be born by surviving ourselves."

Erik huffed.

"Prepare your weapons, cloaks, and rations. Then saddle up. We ride by midday." He gazed past Erik's tall, slender frame to his daughter Liv. "You are coming. We need every hand to carry the booty out."

"But what about mother and the others..."

Ira shooed her. "Girl, listen to me. I want you and Erik to ride together and help. You both will get to know one another." A twinkle in his eye made Liv panic, and the color drained from her face. "You know the seer stays with the older women to care for the village."

Erik glared back at her, his eyes wide. "Shit." He whispered.

Ira patted Erik on his shoulder and pulled his horse up the street away from them, the other men of the village waiting on him with rations to attach to their saddles. "We will be back in three days if all goes well. That will give you two plenty of time to know one another."

Erik nodded and headed into the stables, his eyes craning to watch Liv.

Ira breathed heavily. "Atta boy." Ira pointed to Erik, motioning for Liv to follow him.

Liv clenched her jaws. "Papa!" She complained.

But Ira just smiled and turned away from them both as they stood there watching the dozens of Vikings linger in the street under cover of forest to head to the coast. Liv sighed.

"Here we go again." She questioned.

Erik scoffed at her. "Yeah, carry as much as we can hold on the way out."

Liv followed Erik into the stables, gazing around at the horses. She pulled out a horse and took a deep breath. "Let us get on with this then." But inside, a frustration swelled inside her.

Erik sighed. "Indeed."

B y nightfall, they had reached an encampment and had a soft fire going among the solace of a Birch glen. They warmed up sourdough loaves and white carrots for their evening meal. Liv sat there on her butt, leaning against a fallen tree with a wooden plate of wild greens, bread, and carrots, sipping on spring water from her bone vat. The warmth of the fire kissed her hands as she pulled her wool cloak tighter around her frame.

She was not the only woman there. Other women had come with their husbands, but they were older than her by many years. She and Erik were the youngest there, only seventeen. In her village, they were to marry by age twenty, so she sat there, itching inside of frustration because of what her father had said.

You two will get to know one another. Liv knew what that meant. She did not like it. She shooed, blowing loud as Erik plopped next to her, stuffing his face with bread. "Good evening to you, too." He rolled his eyes, crunching on a carrot.

"You see what father is trying to do, do you not?" She whispered, her eyes on fire like dead coal. "We are of age."

Erik pursed his lips, his long braided blonde hair flowing down his back, his tight braids sticking up on his tanned head. He glared at Ira, who sat around the opposite end of the fire, laughing at stories the elders were telling everybody.

"Our traditions will make us marry. You want to escape?" He eyed her from the side, his eyes twinkling.

Liv gasped. "Do you?" She nodded her head *yes*

Erik laughed at her, this thin, scruffy face beaming in the firelight. "I love doing what I do. I want to shoe horses and be a bladesmith. I love our home, the village, the woodlands. It is beautiful."

"I want to travel. I want to get out of here." Liv complained.

Erik ate more bread, shrugging. "Then go. I release you." He laughed.

"I cannot go. My father is the village leader, and I have heard him talking about marrying me off. To you." She scoffed, her eyes wide.

"And I just released you," he whispered in her face, shoveling another piece of bread in, his lips spreading in a smile.

"They have been saying that since I arrived at fourteen." He rolled his eyes. "You are your own person. I release you to escape me."

Erik then gazed down at her, half smiling. She noticed a dimple on his cheek, his eyes crystal blue. Erik had not shaved, so his face lit up with blonde stubbles. He pointed to a row of Vikings sitting on benches with their wives, arguing with one another. One of the women slammed cold ale in her husband's face, and they continued arguing even as he rubbed it out of his eyes.

"Look at these old miserable fools. Even your father leaves for time to escape your mother's pestering. I do not want this."

Liv stopped chewing the bread in her mouth, swallowing a lumpy mass that felt lodged in her soul. Her eyes went from one couple to another, bickering, slamming things down, complaining. The couples who were not complaining sat quietly, ate, and ignored one another. Her eyes went to her father, who was still laughing at stories with the men who continued to be oblivious to the relationship chaos behind them.

"I would rather die." Liv sighed. "I do not want to live like that."

Erik sat his empty plate down, leaning back against the log and stretching out his long legs, watching them. "My parents were happy together, but they chose one another. My father put my mother's happiness above tradition."

Liv gazed up at him, crossing her arms and sighing. "You were fourteen when Papa found you."

Erik cleared his throat. "They died happy, even as illness took them. I would rather live a short life and be happy than live a thousand lives and be miserable."

He paused, sighing, and continued staring across the fire at everyone. "Time matters not. It is how we live it."

Liv gazed upon his strong face for a moment, holding her breath. She sighed heavily, and they sat together in the darkness as the fire pressed ember-laden shadows upon their weary faces, their eyes upon the chaotic marriages across the fire.

"Your people need to learn that," Erik mumbled, his arms crossed over his chest atop his fur.

They watched across the glen as the Viking couples bickered and moaned at one another as Ira, with his elder warriors, continued to tell stories and fill up on ale.

"They do," Liv whispered. She turned away from Erik, her back facing him, and tried to sleep.

Erik watched her turn, but his eyes lingered up and down her body. Her long blonde hair spilled behind her in braids and knots. Then, he turned his head away from her and held his breath.

B y dawn, the Viking party had crested over the plain through the woods, and the pristine blue sea sparkled under a tangerine dawn rising.

The salty spray from the sea kissed their suntanned, scruffy faces, dousing them with hope of riches and splendor. Ira paused on the winding trail, his eyes watching the abbey's rising tower kiss the morning light, spreading shadows across the emerald fields.

The L-shaped stone abbey, with its slender arched windows, was not lit by candles yet. Ira motioned for a third of his party to veer around the abbey by the seaside, and another third behind him veered to the left around the field. Liv and Erik sat horseback behind them all, watching and waiting.

Their party of fifty men and women was formidable, and the monks likely would not fight back. A round stone well lay feet away at the arched doorstep, its pebble-lined road inviting to travelers. Or so it seemed.

Ira took his party of twenty, and they raced down the hill toward the entrance. The abbey formed a rectangular fortress with pristine views of the sea and a quiet courtyard nestled in between the stone. Ira dismounted his horse with his Vikings as Liv and Erik watched outside while the men gripped their plank to open the door.

Liv watched her father pause at the door, listening, and then it opened without them tearing it down. On the side of the abbey, a flickering flame suddenly lit up, and it caught her eye. She leaned back on her horse and glared at it for moments on end before shouting was heard from inside the abbey.

"That is the signal. Your father has taken it." Erik climbed down from his horse.

"This was too easy," Liv questioned, following him in as the other riders emerged from around the abbey on the seaside.

Liv's eyes melted from the flagstone floor to the arched stone-beamed ceilings. A wall the length of the abbey was arched and opened to a great hall that led outside to a courtyard. She froze at its beauty, ignoring the face of a monk sitting on the floor guarded by her people, watching her. The monk was bald and wearing a brown tunic to his ankles, his gray eyes wide and bright.

She noticed him and widened her eyes as he blinked. He looked at her face and then watched Erik's expression, as he was fascinated with the abbey's architecture. She melted around to watch her father and the others skim the abbey, pulling out silver and gold relics and piling them up in the middle of the floor before the monk.

Ira watched his Vikings bring out more monks from the courtyard, and they were made to sit against the wall and watch them pillage and loot. The clanking and chatter of her people rose in the air around them, and she sighed, stepping away from them to explore the back aisle behind the building. Liv froze as the couple arguing last night held armfuls of precious metals coming from the courtyard.

"We are not burning this..." Liv worried.

The old lady scoffed. "We are not barbarians, dear!"

Her husband joined her side by side, smiling. "Why would we do that?! No point in burning it when more rich fools keep bringing the goods here."

Liv watched them march off together, talking and laughing about the goods they would buy for their household with it. It seemed odd the only time those two got along was when their arms were full of riches. She meandered down the great hall, the stone arched pillars kissing her face with spreads of light the shape of the openings. Her heart beat fast in her chest, and her knees gave out, so she sat down upon an opening and gazed out into the yard until something sparkly caught her eye.

She pulled herself through the opening and marched to it, her eyes on a slender silver engraved cylinder as wide as her hand. Inside it laid a burgundy Jasper stone. Rivets of black swirled in it, enticing her. It was as long as two hands, and engraved with runes that she could not understand. The stone sunk inside the shaft, and Liv could not see how it was made, or where it ended.

As she gazed upon it, she noticed some of the runes were smooth and missing, and she was curious to see if other runes were missing on it. It looked like whoever created this beautiful artifact had not finished carving its runes. As she went to pick it up, Erik grabbed it from the other end. Their eyes met one another, and they stood together facing each other.

The runes shimmered in the morning light as if the sun had kissed it from the inside out. The brightness of the blast catapulted them both away from each other, leaving the shaft lying in the grass.

Erik hit the wall in the courtyard, but Liv was flown back through the pillars and slid on her side down the hall. She hollered in pain as she landed on her hip, twisting to sit back up and wondering what had just happened.

The ground shook beneath the abbey, and thunder echoed in the heavens. Ira and his Vikings froze from carrying the goods out, and everyone grew silent, gazing up at the vibrating ceilings. The sixteen monks they had secured sitting against the wall gazed up, eying one another in silence. Ira noticed their gazes and stopped before them, his arms full of silver candlesticks.

"What was that." He demanded. "Is this ground weak?"

A younger monk belted out, his eyes on the ceiling. "It is now."

The old monk shivered. "The Imortali curse. It has opened."

The room fell silent as everyone waited to see if there would be another quake or thunder, but nothing happened. Ira stared at the wall of monks sitting on their bums, his eyes going up and down their faces as if a shock wave pelted them from the inside out.

"What is this curse you speak of?"

The elder monk spoke up, his voice as old as his face. "The Immortali curse of the broken heart and chaos."

A Viking piped up behind Ira, his arms full. "I have chaos every day with my wretched wife!" He roared in laughter on his way out.

The Vikings roared in laughter with him and continued to carry loot to their horses, but Ira was not laughing. His mother was a seer, and he had heard stories his whole life.

"You monks are strange." Ira scoffed. "But we will let you live because we love your treasures and stories!"

"It is not something to take lightly! No doubt one of your own has opened it, and now it is too late." The monk warned, his white beard dancing on his chin.

Ira turned his back to them, side-eying him for a moment. His eyes shifted to the hall behind the windows, then to the ceiling beams and the cracked wall by the corridor.

Liv pulled herself back up, moaning, while Erik was on his knees, stretching his back. "I told you to let it go!" He hollered.

But she did not answer, so he rushed to her from across the yard and lunged through the pillars. Liv let him pull her up with her forearms, and they crept through the pillars again together.

Liv felt queasy and lightheaded. "Something hit us."

They glared at the runes as they helped each other walk back over to it. It shimmered crimson as if a light breathed inside it, and it was on fire. They stood there gazing upon it, questioning if they should pick it up again. Erik stepped back, noticing the grass was catching fire where it lay as if embers had burst through the soil, but it was not spreading. Then, the ground cracked at their feet, and another rumble roared around them.

"We should leave this relic here." Erik swallowed, stepping back.

Liv gasped, her eyes lighting upon it. "No. Our village needs this wealth to help us survive the harsh winter. Look at the silver and the fine jewel it possesses!" She bent down to grab it again, but Erik lunged down and grabbed the other end again. They pulled against one other, and the runes burned in crimson, searing into their hands.

"Let it go, Erik!" She screamed at him, her knuckles white.

"You let it go and leave it be. It has a curse upon it!"

She pulled again, her hand slipping, gripping it with both palms. Erik pulled on the shaft again with both hands, but they were going nowhere with the relic.

She gritted her teeth at his face. "I will never marry you!"

Erik clenched his jaws. "Good."

From inside the abbey, the quake rumbled. The monks' glared to the cieling, their faces drawn and drained of color. Ira froze as the dust from the ceilings snowed down upon them. His ears perked to shouts coming from behind the wall where the courtyard lay. He moseyed out there with several of his Vikings, their eyes wide to the spectacle of Liv and Erik.

"Enough!" Ira screamed at them, and then silence filled the abbey again.

"We are bringing that treasure with us. Erik will carry it." Ira demanded.

Erik let it go, raising his hands. "I do not want it! It is cursed."

Liv pressed it against her chest, her fists clamped around it, her heart flittering as it touched her. She grimaced; her stomach burned.

Ira sighed. "Give it to him." He turned away just as Liv begrudgingly handed it over, but Erik stepped away to keep from touching it, his eyes as wide as silver coins.

"Told you both you would get to know one another." Ira marched off, laughing at them.

Liv watched Erik take it, sliding it into his satchel. When he lifted his hand back up, he pulled at Liv's arm as she walked away. "Liv."

She froze at the urgency in Erik's voice and turned to see him gazing at his right palm. Her face suddenly drained of color as she held her left hand against his. They faced one another, staring at the runes carved in their palms.

"What have we done?" Erik's voice was stern, filled with dread.

Liv's eyes were wide, and nothing came out as she opened her mouth to speak. "I do not know. There is dark magic on this." She whispered, a fire filling her guts deep inside. They stood there gawking at their palms and then met one another's stares as chills rushed up their spines.

"What have we done." She whispered in his face. Erik met her stare, his eyes roaming all over her face, his back full of tension.

Liv backed away from him and turned to go but kept glaring back at Erik. A hot anger rose within him as he followed her out, his heart beating wildly, his eyes hard upon her.

When Ira reached the monks, he paused at the elderly monk. "What is the silver relic? I saw the runes."

He gasped. "Who touched it?" He whispered.

Just then, Erik marched around the corner with Liv, the shaft sticking out of his satchel. Both of their palms had indentations of the runes on them. The monks chattered among themselves, and a younger monk who looked in his early twenties next to the older man rolled his eyes and shook his head. He was bald and tanned, and his brown eyes wavered at the young Vikings.

"You must leave the relic here, or a foreshadowing will follow you! We must secure it here so the curse cannot breathe!" He pleaded.

"You may take any other treasures. Just leave that one so we can secure it again to prevent catastrophe. Please, I beg of you." His soft, rolling lowland tongue echoed.

Erik stood frigid, listening to them. Liv froze at the door, her back stiff, craning her neck to see the young monk warn her father. Ira pulled his long sword, pressing the tip end of his blade under the monk's chin. The monk leaned further into the wall to escape the blade, but it was too late.

"What is your name, monk," Ira demanded.

"Halfdan."

Ira removed the blade, peering down upon him, gritting his teeth. "There is no such thing as curses. I have heard these stories all my life from my crazy mother. There are only treasures that bring hope to my people. You would do well to remember that."

Ira marched out, preparing his Vikings to leave with the booty. Erik stood there watching his people go, his eyes on the monks. As Erik walked by them, he lunged the relic out of his satchel into Halfdan's lap and bolted out of the abbey before his people saw what he did.

"No. No. No." Halfdan gritted his teeth and watched Erik strut out. He flailed against the wall like hot coals had touched him.

The old monk sitting beside him gasped. "You are commanded to guard over the weakest of them til the curse lifts."

Halfdan gasped and covered it with his cloak, his face red. "Damnit!" He moaned.

The monks beside him patted him on the shoulder, shaking their heads in concern.

Erik followed on his horse behind them all, but a restless anger rose within him. He had remorse for the monks, as they did not deserve the raid. His parents would have never done that to innocent people. He would leave the Vikings and disappear forever if he knew where to go.

He clenched his jaws at Liv, who glared at him from behind. She rolled her eyes and raced away to follow closely behind her father and the elders. Erik saw the monks look as if they had all seen an ancient spirit, as if something had awakened from the ground there in the abbey. As Erik followed behind, the air moved heavily around them, and something followed them home.

2

Betrovement of Death

Dahlia sat outside under her covered porch on her fur-skin stool, a sliver of wood plank table before her. Behind her on the wall were stacks of leather-bound books and parchments. She grabbed a handful of Birch and Dandelion, plopped them into the stone mortar and grinded with the pestle. Alongside her, a fire pit roared with an iron kettle, and she eyed it, waiting for the steam to fester.

She took lambskin cloth and put the herbs in it, wrapping it up to form a ball and tying it closed with jute. When the steam billowed from the kettle, she poured the piping hot water over the herbs in a bowl, filling it and letting it steep. She pulled a chunk of honeycomb from a bone jar and plopped it into a cup, her ears perked up to the road vibrating.

Summer was ending soon, but it did not stop her from pulling her wool shawl over her tired shoulders in her old age. Her long blonde and white hair braided down her back was also braided at her temples. Her green eyes lingered on the Vikings, with Ira in lead, coming back with a haul of booty. The village came out, and the wives who stayed rushed to their husbands, shouting joyfully at the sight of the treasures.

Dahlia noticed two drawn faces that were not joyful, Liv and Erik. As she poured her hot tea into her cup, she contemplated their circumstance as a foreboding filled the air in the town like a fog had dropped in suddenly. Dahlia stood on the edge of her house, gazing at the village on her little gentle slope overlooking everything. She sipped her tea as Erik, the boy the town had adopted, marched past them to his stables, his shoulders slumped as if he carried a heavy weight upon them.

He gripped the reigns and pulled his horse, and then she froze, noticing the runes carved into his palm. Her eyes melted upon her granddaughter Liv, who rolled her eyes at Erik and then stomped off to her own house. As she disappeared into the doorway, she gripped the trim. She, too, had runes carved into her hand.

Dahlia spit out her tea.

T he fires filled the village that evening, and songs and stories were heavy in the air. Stars twinkled overhead like the abundance of wealth they had just pillaged from the abbey. Ira stood at the pillar of the village, drinking his ale and laughing with the elders as they lined up on their seats to feast on the wild game and vegetables. Sourdough bread and stews cooked on the fires for anyone to help themselves. The aromas of fresh herbs and seared meat enticed Erik, but he stayed in the dark alley with his horses.

Ira gloated about the pillage. He laughed, telling stories of the monks' faces. He even made jokes about how Liv and Erik argued and that it symbolized something more than just differences. Erik froze when Ira called for him.

"Come on, son." He called him.

Erik widened his eyes and sighed. "Shit."

Liv stood aside her mother on the side of the fire pit, and her face contorted with the steam, her eyes a malicious fervor at him.

"Liv, come." He commanded, and Liv walked out to him and stood aside Erik.

"Today, we celebrate a great victory of wealth for our people! The booty will provide for our way of life for two Winters!" The villagers hoorayed and hooped and hollered.

"With that blessing upon us, I announce that my only heir, Liv, will marry Erik. His people are coming from across the sea to celebrate with us! They will share the wealth and bring us much-needed weaponry and supplies."

"No," Liv whispered, knowing she could say nothing. It was too late.

Erik stood there staring at her, his face hard and stricken as the town behind them cheered and stuffed their faces with food and ale. He clenched his jaws at her face as Ira pulled their hands together and made them hold them. Liv's hands shook in Erik's palms, and the runes itched. He gripped her hands hard to keep them still, and Liv clenched her teeth at his firm grasp, her eyes folding to his. Just as Liv pulled her hands away from his, Dahlia appeared at the end of the lane.

"So, the test begins, does it?" She meandered up to Liv, eying her hand, and gazed upon Erik's.

"What are you blabbering on about, ma?" Ira complained, rolling his eyes at her. "We are not believing your seer nonsense."

Dahlia laughed. "Of course not, my son. Of course not. However, since Erik hails from the Baltic tribe across the sea, they will want to ensure he is a man worthy of our heir. He will want to return with them and endure a series of trials. When he is done and comes back a man, then he may marry Liv."

Silence filled the street, but Dahlia spoke again. "That is custom, and it will be honored." She warned.

Erik gawked at her, his heart pulling a dull ache within him.

Liv sighed.

Dahlia gazed upon her stubborn son, and he huffed. "Indeed. I had forgotten about the old ways. Let us see what the elders say when they arrive."

Dahlia nodded. "So be it."

Erik felt her stare at his hand, so he pulled it away from Liv and stuffed it under his cloak. He and Liv followed Dahlia as she meandered back up the street to her house, and Ira shooed them off to enjoy the festivities.

Dahlia stepped on her porch and pulled out an unusually thick leather-bound book, searching for a page. "You two have done it now." She blew at them. "You have done it now."

Liv and Erik stood on her porch, eying their hands and each other. "What did we do?" Liv asked, worried.

"What did you do with the relic?" She asked them.

Liv glared at Erik. "I do not know what he did with it."

"How do you know of a relic?" Erik pondered.

Dahlia sat down, reading an entry in the book of runes. She eyed him, silent and stiff, until he answered.

"Gave it back to the monk."

"Of course you did." Dahlia rolled her eyes. "Could have just been you two, but now you must contend with the monk until the curse breaks."

"We did not open a curse." Liv swallowed.

"Why are there runes on your palms? Engraved into them." She sighed heavily, turning the book so they could see runes like the ones on their hands. "There are five lines, five relics." She rolled her eyes.

Silence.

"The summoning begins, one chasing, one fleeing." She sighed. "A lot of things will happen..."

"I warned Ira not to go to that abbey. The monks there have mysterious, cursed ancient relics if messed with. He is getting lazy in his old years and wants to pillage closer to home."

"No one else has said anything about these," Liv complained, gazing upon her right palm.

"They cannot see them," Dahlia warned.

"I do not understand what this means." Erik sighed, trying to decipher the symbols dancing on the pages.

"What did the relic look like? Did it have a stone?"

Liv thought a moment. "It was a cylinder with runes over it, yet missing some. It was silver with a red stone and black lines through it."

"Did it give off a light?" Dahlia fretted.

Liv gazed at Erik, and his eyes grew wide.

Dahlia flipped to another page and sighed. "The Imortali curse. The curse has chosen you two..." Dahlia sneered, turning the book back around to find something else. "It is a cruel curse..." She mumbled. "A curse of the heart takes its time."

"What does this mean?" Liv questioned.

Dahlia pressed her fists into her hips at them. "Do you care for each other, yes or no?"

Liv gawked, but Erik held his breath at her.

"Stubborn. That will be fun for both of you throughout the ages as you both hunt and flee one another." Dahlia pestered them.

"Hunt?" Liv belted out.

"I am not stubborn." Erik chirped.

"Sure." Dahlia sighed. "I believe you."

Liv widened her eyes and gawked at Erik, shaking her head. "She does not." She whispered.

"That monk will be coming on the look for you, both of you. He is also bound to the curse as well, to guard over you both if that is even possible. He will be the final piece..."

Dahlia froze, and her eyes widened as a strange voice appeared behind her house. "I am already here, seer." Halfdan jumped up on the porch to join them, a satchel on his back and a palm full of fresh bread.

"Where did you come from? How did you get here!" Liv gawked at him, gazing around.

"Your mother gave me bread; the stew is quite good too." He shoved the rest in, his pale face clean-shaven, his brown eyes sparkling back at them as thick as his Scottish accent. "Ira sent me up the road here to you."

"He let you come into the village?" Erik wondered. "He drinks too much." He rolled his eyes.

Halfdan pursed his lips at them. "They are all too drunk. Besides, it would do them no good to kill me. I would just come back, seeing how we are immortal now."

"Now let me take a good look at you..." Halfdan eyed both Liv and Erik up and down and huffed. "Betroved. This curse keeps getting worse and worse."

"We are not marrying." Erik scowled.

Halfdan laughed at them, his dark brown eyes lit up. "Whatever you believe."

Liv and Erik gasped as Dahlia found an entry in the book. "Ah, here it is, dear monk. Immortality comes along with whoever lays their hands upon the relic and whoever receives the relic after touching it. Its power feeds off their love and pain, and," She froze, sitting down as her breath had gone out of her, "catastrophes."

Her eyes melted over the book, and then her gaze raised to Liv and Erik. "It has the power to take down kingdoms, destroy our world. The reics attached to this curse must break."

Then Dahlia scoffed. "Oh, why did my ancestral seers have to complicate curses?! They were just bored and wanted to play with humanity!" She scoffed.

Halfdan sighed. "Yet here we are, bored to tears."

"Perhaps they hated their husbands." Liv rolled her eyes.

"Where are the relics?" Erik demanded. "I do not want to live like this forever. I just want to live simply and be happy." Erik complained.

Everyone gazed at him, and silence filled them for endless moments before Halfdan chimed in. "Yessss, I just wanted to be a simple monk minding my own business and doing the Lord's good work, and your barbarians went and ruined that now, so here we are."

"I do not want to marry him," Liv demanded.

"Would be miserable." Erik agreed.

Liv cupped her hands at her stomach and fidgeted.

Dahlia and Halfdan leaned over the book and began reading passages, mumbling amongst one another before he raised and shrugged his shoulders. "This curse is incomplete. It will take me some time to gather any other relevant parchments that go with it."

"No doubt drunk when my ancestor made this curse." Dahlia sighed. "You are immortal now, Halfdan and my ancestors never made curses easy to break."

"How do we break it," Erik whispered, clenching his jaws.

"By finding the relics, but then after, well..." Dahlia froze again, and Halfdan cleared his throat. "There should be a map or something..." Dahlia pressed through the pages.

"Does this mean I can get out of here to find the relics?" Liv blasted out; her face lit up.

They all glared at her before Halfdan sneered. "This is not a game, dear child. Your life is now on the line, bound to Erik."

"I am not a child, and you look merely a couple of years older than me, monk."

Halfdan pursed his lips. "I am twenty-two."

"I am seventeen." She gritted.

"A child." Halfdan huffed.

Liv growled, storming off the porch back up the street to her house.

Halfdan sighed heavily. "This will be one of the worse curses to break ever."

Dahlia agreed with him. "Tea?" She stood up to put the kettle on.

"That would be lovely, thank you." Halfdan agreed, smiling.

They turned to stare at Erik, and Dahlia cleared her throat. "Oh, where are my manners? Erik, would you like some tea."

Erik narrowed his brows. "I would like not to have been chosen for this curse."

Dahlia plopped down in her chair, gazing up at the tall blonde-headed Viking lad and sighing at his face. "I need you to go freely with your people when they come. We need you both separated so Halfdan can work with Liv to find the relics. Once they find them, you must to the abbey so Halfdan can break the curse on you both."

"What."

"You will, in time, hunt her to keep her from getting them, Erik. That is what the curse does. It will control you in the end. The relics must be found and destroyed. In the meantime, while she seeks them, you both will be drawn to one another, hence why it is a cruel curse." Dahlia warned.

"I do not understand this witchery," Erik complained, his face hard.

Halfdan stretched his satchel out and pulled a parchment. "I found what I could at the abbey about this relic." He stretched it out, and it showed the relic itself, and a map of the Baltic Sea, Estonia.

"It appears there is a dagger we need to break the relics against the runes."

Erik sighed but did not answer.

Halfdan huffed. "I have a lot of research to do."

Erik stood there watching them act like chums getting tea ready while the book of curses and the runes on his palms unnerved him. And

the only way to break it had something to do with Liv, who stormed away from him. He watched where she had gone, and sudden shivers raced up his spine.

L iv stood on the hill overlooking the brook as it spilled into the forest, the shadows of the trees towering over her. She cupped her fur pelt tighter around her shoulders and stood with her back to the village. She thought about what had happened at the abbey and what her grandmother and Halfdan had told them.

"I know you follow me." She belted out, craning her neck to see Erik linger up to her.

He pressed into her, his sword dangling at his lanky side, his long cloaks blowing behind him. "How did you know it was me."

"I smelled horse dung."

He pursed his lips at her. "I had to shoe the horses today." He sighed. "You should try it."

Liv half smiled and then dropped it. "I gathered herbs, dug up carrots."

They stood on the hill together, their backs to the village, their faces hard, staring into the forest. Beyond the forest rose a mountainous plateau, kissing the horizon even in the darkness before them. Liv pressed her palm up again and sneered at it in the dark. Erik gazed upon it, his heart fluttering with an urge he could not describe.

"What have we done?" She spoke, a nervous twitch in her voice.

Erik stiffened his shoulders, his eyes hard into the forest as if some distant land called him. But it called them both. He clenched his strong jaws and narrowed his eyebrows under his blonde crown of braids.

"We break this curse together." He breathed.

"You leave with your people tomorrow." She whispered.

Erik turned his head and gazed into her face, his eyes soft, lingering on her high cheekbones. "My people are your people." He whispered back to her.

Liv reached into the folds of her layered dress and pulled out a parchment. She opened it up and showed it to Erik. "I need you to begin hunting the relics. You are going there anyway, and we can begin to break this together."

Erik gawked. "You have stolen a page from your grandmother's most sacred book." He took the parchment and studied the map and relic.

"I have the other maps. Each page shows what these relics are, where they should be, and how to get there. I will study more about this curse with Halfdan's help."

Erik took the parchment and held onto it. "I will do it."

"Will you come back?" She wondered.

Erik craned his neck and stared down at her. She would have met his stare, but it was hard, riddled with determination, and she could not look at him. She took a deep breath and gazed upon the rolling lands while Erik remained drowned in her face.

D ahlia moseyed out to the porch in the morning, sipping her hot tea. Her eyes fell upon Halfdan. He was leaned over asleep in his arms on her table. She paused, sighing. They had been up all night studying the curse and any other parchments she had managed to keep throughout the years.

She sat her tea down at the table's edge, picked up the leather-bound curse book, and slammed it down by his head. Dust flew up around them. Halfdan lunged up and fell out of the chair, laying flat on his back, gawking at her. "Damnit." He moaned.

She leaned over him, her wrinkles kissing her pale face, her eyes lit up by laugh lines, while her long gray hair spilled in braids down her thin shoulders. "Tea?" She asked.

Halfdan sat up, his eyes wide at her. "Please."

She set the kettle on the fire behind them and watched Halfdan turn the pages again, sighing to himself.

"I did not tell her." Dahlia sighed, waiting for the water to get hot. "I know you found the parchments that are not in the book of my seer ancestors. I know you studied them, and you know the consequences."

Halfdan craned his neck to stare at her from the side, his back to her, his face clenched. "I know they are not ready for this." His eyes clenched as hard as his face, and he rubbed his bald head. "I find it interesting you also did not tell them how the curse will lead them to one another, the battles, the pain, " He turned to face her, his eyes wide. "Their heartbreak. This curse is a cruel one of the heart."

Dahlia poured him tea, meeting his eyes with teary eyes. "I did tell them. I said one hunts and one seeks. I carry much sorrow for them." She cleared her throat, reaching over to grab her cup. "They must learn to be stronger to break this together."

Halfdan scoffed. "Ah, but they do not break this together, do they?" Halfdan questioned her. "One seeks, one hunts, that is the way of it. The curse does not want the relics found. It needs to feed upon them to grow stronger, only pulling them together to hinder them from breaking it. It lives and breathes, does it not?"

Dahlia sipped her tea, though it had gotten cold. "They are the last hope. We must rid the world of this curse once and for all. Many kingdoms have already fallen from this heart-wrenching chaos, and that is why it was hidden. I warned my son not to raid the abbey, I did."

Halfdan agreed. "It was not hidden as well as it should have been. We should have sealed it in the stone, but the elders kept it with all the other treasures."

Dahlia stared down the road. "Erik and Liv are strong, they will prevail. One day."

Halfdan sighed into her face, clenching his strong jaws. "The world is not ready for this." He whispered.

Dahlia poured the tea for them. "I will be dead and gone, so this is all on you, dear monk."

She handed the cup to Halfdan, his eyes wide and mouth gaping open. "Typical seer pushing the curse your ancestors made upon the monk."

Dahlia shrugged her shoulders. "We are Vikings, what did you expect?"

D ays later, Erik stood on the shoreline a day's ride north of the village. On the horizon, he saw three Viking Knarr's, cargo ships from his people. Erik recognized the wider hulls, although shorter than longships, could bring more cargo. These were operated by smaller crews, too, and Ira became excited thinking about the wool, wheat, furs, and weapons they would be getting. Not to mention the honey they needed, for ailments and medicines, especially through the winters

Erik stood aside from Ira and Liv, the silence between them breathtaking. Behind them, the village elders and families had made temporary encampments to enjoy festivities and trading of wealth and supplies. The fires were already burning wild game, and stews cooking in pots over the open fires. The air smelled sweet and savory, and a pang hit Erik's heart.

He would travel with them across the sea to his parent's homeland, where they would begin grueling training to make him a man. Dahlia and Halfdan stayed back at the village, reviewing the book of rune curses and filling their stomachs with her herbal teas and freshly baked bread.

Erik missed it already. Supposedly, he was now immortal, but something pulled at him from deep inside. Ira waved them off and their stories, dismissing his own seer elder, his mother. Liv and Erik did their best to maintain their composure before Ira, although it came out as if they were annoyed with one another.

"I hope you never come back," Liv told Erik, crossing her arms over her chest.

Erik scoffed, laughing. "I hope you never get to leave."

Ira patted them both on the backs, smiling. "Sounding like a married couple already!"

"Tonight, we feast and trade goods! You go to be a man with your people in the morning." Ira told him.

"How long will I be gone?" Erik asked, watching the ship's coast closer to the coastline.

Ira paused. "I do not know."

"Then why betrove me to Liv?" He questioned. "What if I never return? What if I die? How will you know?"

Liv perked up, her eyes wide at Erik, but Ira huffed at them both.

"Yes, how would I know, Pa?"

"I know you do not want to marry. That is too bad." Ira patted him on the shoulder. "You two are the only ones left in the village old enough to marry. It is time for you to stop fighting it. If it takes you ten years, Liv will still be here. She will wait for you."

"I will not wait for him!" Liv gawked. "You are saying I am not marriage worthy."

"Perhaps if I never return, then you need to wait til the young ones grow up." He huffed, "then you will be old." Erik smiled.

"I feel ill," Liv complained.

Ira stepped away from them to join the crowds at the fires, and Liv closed her eyes, allowing the salty breeze to bite at her thin, pale face. Erik stood beside her, both shoulders slumped, their heads pounding. Erik towered over her short frame, his slender yet muscular body casting a shadow upon her.

"Will you find me again?" She asked him, still gazing out at sea.

Erik gazed upon her but then turned, clenching his jaws.

Liv sighed. "We felt something at the abbey, a powerful force."

"We did." He replied.

"If this imortali curse is true, then we cannot die until..."

"Until we find the relics and break it together." He bit.

They lifted their palms and gazed upon each other's runes, the silence filling them with dread. "I am sorry you must go. I know you want to stay," Liv whispered to him.

Erik swallowed. "I am sorry you must stay. I know you want to go."

She picked her palm up and gazed upon the runes again. "Perhaps one day we will be free to live as we want."

Erik gazed upon her, the sun lighting her face like angels had kissed her. Her blue eyes sparkled like the sea before them. He turned to stare at the ships getting closer, and a part of him felt torn inside.

"Will you stay until I come back?" He asked.

Liv thought a moment. "If you do come back, there is nothing here but endless shooing of horses for you."

Erik laughed at her. "I thought you enjoyed the smell of horse dung?"

She laughed with him.

That night, Liv and Erik sat around the fire together. They passed the stew, the bread, and the ale. They ate honeycomb and sipped hot herbal teas, telling stories of ancient times and laughing at each other's stories of battles and pillages. When the stars twinkled like fires had lit up the heavens, they gazed upon a dark sky that blanketed them with hope.

At dawn, they stood on the shores while the ships loaded with treasures, and Erik pulled his wool cloak over his shoulders. Liv watched him pick up his satchels, strap his broad axe to his back, and his long sword sheathed at his side. He paused before entering the water to jump on the smaller boat carrying him to the ship.

Liv watched him, her eyes wide and face tired from not sleeping. But everyone was tired. Erik turned one more time to go, his eyes lighting on her face. He turned around, and they rushed into each other's arms. He bent down and kissed her, their lips meeting in a passionate embrace. Their mouths open and breathing into one another.

They shivered from the cold of the sea, shivering inside from the harshness of reality. They stood there and kissed in the morning light among a sea of treasures. They clasped one another in an embrace of passion while Erik pulled her tighter against him, and she clutched his strong arms against her waist. He gripped her face in his palms and pressed his head against hers, and breathed on her skin.

"I will come back for you."

And then he was gone. Liv was left alone standing there on the shore, questioning the madness of why he had to leave and why she had to stay, not knowing when he would return, if ever. Her whole world had just crumbled because now she was forced to wait, bound by a curse that tied them both together by fate.

Dahlia and Halfdan had come the night before, and stood on the plateau overlooking the sea as the ships sailed away. Liv stood pressed into the sand, her face in the wind, watching Erik.

Halfdan stared at Dahlia. "You sent him away."

Dahlia sighed. "He is the hunter in this curse. I saw how he followed her last night and the obsessive glare in his eyes. It has already begun. She is the one who will flee him when the time comes to search the relics."

"Else, he would not have left?"

Dahlia shook her head. "They would die here together in the curse and destroy our way of life. Chaos will follow them. They must keep going."

"So it begins." Halfdan sneered, his face hard.

In the evening, as the three Viking Knarrs sailed on, their cargo was not as heavy since they traded with Ira's village, but the treasures they took still did not belong to them. Erik awoke to an unsettling feeling as the ship rocked back and forth as if some hand from a nameless god was playing chess with them and knocking them over. A fierce wind belted against the brace, snapping it in half.

The riffs pulled off the sails, and the bowline ripped out. The Skor pulled apart in the hull, and the ship started taking on water. Lightening hit the mast, pulling the halyard down, and the men lost at sea.

3

50 Years Later

The field rolled out, and headstones stuck up in solitude spread across the village plains for miles. Liv gazed upon the last headstone, and the deaths pummeled her empty heart. She had only aged a few more years, so she looked like she was in her early twenties. That was something Halfdan discovered later, and it unnerved her to no end.

She and Erik would continue to grow and look older in their immortality, with it peaking in their mid-thirties. If they had not made amends by then, they would walk the earth as immortals for eternity. Liv did not want to walk around looking like a seventeen-year-old anyway. Dark clouds billowed behind them for miles as a warning of a storm approached. Liv sighed, thinking the road looked lonely to travel even with Halfdan with her.

"Everyone is dead." Halfdan rolled his eyes.

Fifty years ago, they had gotten word that Erik's ship had gone down, and everyone was lost. She knew he was immortal like her, so she waited, hoping he would come back for her. But he had not come.

Since that day, her grandmother, the old seer, had passed, along with her parents and everyone else in the village. Halfdan sighed, walking up behind her with his satchel on his back, the old leather-bound rune book stuffed in it.

"He is not coming back. I implore you to leave this place." He begged, his brown eyes severe. "You will never break the curse waiting here like this. Erik has been on the move, and we must move to find the other relics. We have wasted fifty years toiling here, shoeing horses, and gardening."

"He is supposed to bring me back the first relic..." She whispered to herself.

Liv sighed again, gazing upon the graves that seemed to spill out in an endless abyss before her. "Why didn't he come back?" She questioned. "I thought he cared for me."

Halfdan sighed again. "I do not know. Perhaps something happened. Perhaps he still searches for it while you are lingering on here in your sad state."

Liv gasped at him, pulling her cloak over her arms. "So be it."

She turned to walk toward her house to gather her satchels and saddle the horses, but a shadow moved among the trees and caught her eye. She froze, pulled her long sword, and waited aside Halfdan, whose eyes were as wide as his bald head.

A tall, slender man on horseback meandered out from the grove the Birch trees. He wore a satchel on his back, an axe and a bow and arrows stuck over his head in their sheaths. He wore thick, wool trousers, and a leather breastplate matched his black boots to his knees. His black stallion matched his ensemble. Its ebony mane was so dark that it looked like purple had kissed it.

Erik froze at the sight of Liv. His tanned, slender face starkly contrasting the drab lands he had once called home. He leaned forward atop his steed and paused for a moment to glare at her. She looked tired and wore the same attire she had worn, but it was newer.

Erik bit his tongue. "Shit." He mumbled.

Liv opened her mouth to say something but froze, watching him.

This tall, handsome warrior trotted over to her on his magnificent stallion. Erik slid off his horse, his eyes gazing around to the empty village and the field full of tombstones.

"Have you stayed here this whole time?" He gasped, his long cloak flowing behind him as if he were a king. "You look sad."

Liv gawked. "How can you say that to me?! We received word you had perished at sea. I waited here for you. Of course, I am sad!"

Erik laughed at her, rolling his head back, his laugh an assault to her heart. "For fifty years?!" His laughter was much deeper and louder than she ever remembers him being. "You! The one who wanted to leave so badly!"

"Why are you just now coming back?" She demanded. "Did you find the relic?!"

Erik shook his head. "No."

Erik pulled his horse to her, his blue eyes wide and bright, his face older and mature, his body more defined and muscular. "I came to see what became of you. My parent's people have all gone too, or left to travel the world."

He eyed her up and down, half smiling at her. She had changed too, and grown more mature. Liv hauled off and slapped him across his face. Erik jerked back, blinking his eyes against the stinging burn.

Halfdan grimaced. "This is going to be a long curse, isn't it."

"How dare you dismiss our feelings! After the moment we had on the beach before your demise!"

"It was the right thing to do, to kiss you before I disappeared forever." He gawked at her.

"You did not mean it?!" She gasped. "You played with my heart?"

He grabbed his cheek, sighing. "It is good I did come back, or you would have sat here and rotted. Now maybe a fire will light under your ass to leave." He pointed in her face and then turned to pull his horse up the road. As she gawked at him, her mouth wide open, then he turned and bowed to her. "You are welcome."

"Where do you think you are going?" She demanded, crossing her arms.

Erik did not look back at her. He boarded his horse and shouted. "Wherever I want!"

"We still have to end this curse!" She bellowed.

Liv watched him disappear up the road, her face a rageful red. "Well then, we shall leave too." She turned to walk back to her house.

Halfdan sighed, throwing his head to the skies, his mouth wide open. "Finally!" He rolled his eyes, his arms in the air as if arguing with the clouds. "The fire under the ass has been lit!"

H ours later, they were traveling by horse, their satchels packed, axes and swords swinging on Liv's back. She learned from a young age to fight and protect herself, but she was thankful Halfdan had to join her. They traveled South out of Scotland. Behind them lay the village, its rolling plains, and wooded beauty. She gazed upon Halfdan, who sat with the book opened on his lap atop his horse, reading.

"I was right. This is interesting." He mumbled.

Liv rolled her eyes. "What is interesting, pray tell."

"The curse continues to pull you both together. So, no matter where you go, you will end up together again." He huffed. "No wonder he came back. He had no choice but to be drawn to you."

Liv widened her eyes at him. "Fifty years later? What is it to be? Every fifty years, we will have a run-in and accomplish nothing but my abject hate for that man! And no closer to finding the relics. I believe he did not even try."

Halfdan did not seem to hear her and continued laughing to himself. "There is hope yet to break this so I can still enjoy life." Halfdan sneered.

But then his face changed, and Halfdan huffed. "Hmm." He widened his eyes and closed the book, his heart beating wildly. He would need to do more research because if what he just read was true, they were in for dangerous times ahead.

"We need to find a place that holds ancient documents, Liv. We still have much about this curse we do not know."

Liv turned her head to peer back at the road. The village she had known all her life was gone, and her family was gone. As she turned to peer straight ahead on the path laid before them, an uneasiness rose within her, and her heart ached. She would take her time exploring the woodlands for the next many years, veering away from the sea. The sea is where her people came from to take from others. The sea is where a part of her died inside.

4

The Kingdom of the West Saxons, 878 A.D.

Erik stood gripping his long sword, with his broad ax and shield strapped to his back and a bow in his left hand, ready. He waited aside King Alfred, the king of Wessex. He was part of his royal bodyguard, and a fierce protector of the brave man. Erik blinked the soft rain out of his eyes, his long blonde beard braided down his face, his blue eyes piercing the enemy lines for miles.

Before them, for miles, were the thousands of Viking soldiers. They had taken their fortress town, Chippenham, the kings home. They had taken their supplies and food, attacked them mercilessly, and even drove them to the Somerset marshes. Erik helped Alfred spearhead the harassment of the Danes from their fort while the king assembled an army to take back their kingdom.

Erik was not surprised to see Vikings raid against the kingdom he had come to love. He just wanted to settle somewhere peaceful for a while, whereas the Vikings came to Edington to quite literally conquer. Erik loathed them. He loathed them taking what was not theirs to take, and he would fight to the death to keep the home he had come to love from being destroyed by them.

King Alfred rubbed his hands through his beard, and his eyes focused on the invaders as his army alongside Erik challenged the Danes at Edington. His dark hair was disheveled around his slender face, but his drive was adamant.

Over twenty thousand of his men there, their shields ready and on foot. Alfred raised his sword, and Erik followed in pursuit, blasting the front line of the Vikings with arrow after arrow. He pressed into them, catapulting the front lines and knocking them back until bodies laid on the path before him with shanks through their heads or hearts.

When Erik's arrows were spent, he pressed his arm into his round shield. He catapulted into the front line with his men and king, and slaughtered them with his long sword and axe. As the line became a whimper for the Vikings, he chased them with Alfred to their fortress, Chippenham, pinning them in to face certain death.

The quaint market town lay on a crossing of the Avon River, its walls rising on the plain to form a formidable lodge, its royal Vills spread out into multiple estates kissing the stone town. Erik looked forward to feasting again in the wooden hall with the ragtag family he had come to love.

While Erik led a group of his men to secure the surroundings of Chippenham, he sighed. They would either starve to death inside, or come out to face the consequences of their choices to invade their territory. King Alfred marched through the warriors, their arms high in the air, gripping bloody swords, spears, or axes, nodding to them.

They had won. They would wait it out to see how long they could last inside once supplies ran out. For now, Erik was free of burden and war and could work at being at peace. Or so he thought.

Three weeks later, there was grand feasting and celebration as King Alfred accepted the retreat of the invaders. Their leader, Guthrum, was baptized. Summer had come, but the gentle breezes blowing off the river settled the town into a restful state of joy. On the eleventh day of feasting celebration, Erik meandered down a lamp-lit road by Wedmore.

The square tower rose above the field, its arched windows echoing a time he remembered at the abbey in Scotland. He paused gazing upon it, and his heart was heavy suddenly. People were lingering inside the church, and he smiled at the families conversing with one another. They had sustained loss of life over the past couple of years but came out victorious. They didn't give up.

Erik sighed. One day, his king would die, and everyone he had grown to know around him during the years of helping them fight against his own, the Vikings, would die. What would become of this town? He turned away from the church and noticed two horses tied to a stone inn behind it. It caught him off guard and a sudden weight in his gut made him freeze.

An engraved saddle had a particular fur pelt laid across it. Erik marched behind the church pathway and glare upon these horses and the two people who had just paid the inn keeper.

"Shit." He widened his eyes, gazing upon Liv, and something broke in his chest, and a fire lingered there.

Liv pulled her grandmother's seer pelt off her saddle, rubbed her face, and nodded at Halfdan, who was also exhausted. They had spent many years camping in the forests, living off the lands, hiding.

Liv was good at surviving all these years, especially with Halfdan's vast knowledge of basically everything. She marched inside the inn and plopped down at the table across from Halfdan as the innkeeper served them bread, cheeses, and fruits with seared root vegetables. Liv sipped on her hot herbal tea, her eyes craning to the door suddenly as a looming shadow beamed in at her. She nearly choked, recognizing Erik barge in, heading straight for her.

Halfdan recognized him, but he wasn't smiling. "Ah, look who it is, the disappearing Viking. It has been one hundred years this time. Well done." Halfdan sighed. "I so enjoy seeing my very life pass before my eyes, over and over."

Erik sat there staring at them, his face lit up.

"You look like hell." Erik gazed at them while Halfdan sipped his ale, gawking at Erik's battle scratches and bruises.

Halfdan huffed. "I could say the same for you."

Liv jerked back in the chair, her face pale, her eyes wide. "What are you doing here?"

Erik cleared his throat and stared at her face, mesmerized. His long beard hung down his chest, and his long, blonde hair was braided down his back. He wore leather body attire and was fully armed. Liv swallowed at the sight of him. Though he had bathed and dressed in clean attire, Erik's head was bruised and he had scrapes on his hands. Liv was sure he had other injuries but he was not showing them.

"What are you doing here? Did you not know we have been at war? You could have been killed or taken." Erik stared at her, gawking.

Liv crossed her arms. "You left me for fifty years. I could have been killed or taken then."

Erik took a deep breath and motioned the bartender for an ale. Then he turned to gaze at her face, his jaws clenched. Liv froze at his firm glare he gave her, her eyes wide. She pursed her lips, and Erik gazed at her blonde hair cascading down her back in ribbons of curls. There was something different about Erik, something stronger, and a pang hit her guts.

"I have ways to survive. I am not a weak woman." She sipped her tea, stuffing her mouth with bread.

"We lived in the woods like mad people possessed with afflictions." Halfdan sneered. "The Vikings were afraid of her, to be honest."

"I learned that from my grandmother, okay?" Liv rolled her eyes at them, her mouth full of food.

Erik leaned back. "Hiding from me in the woods this whole time?" *Hiding from me*

Liv froze and eyed him from the side when he said that, chills darting up her arms.

"Very well. You both shall join me in feasting for the next day before we send our invaders off."

"Why," Liv asked.

"You in a hurry? Where are you headed?" Erik asked her.

Liv arched her back and glared at him, but Erik met her face with a clenched jaw. "You know this curse follows us. We cannot stay apart. We will find one each other one way or another, no matter where you go." He whispered, his voice deep.

Liv set the bread down on her plate and stopped chewing. She met his eyes and gazed inside him, and her heart fluttered.

"Surely you must have been thinking about me all these years I have been caught up in wars?" He blurted.

Liv huffed at him. "I thought about how you kissed me, then left, and I did not see you again for a hundred years because you chose to not come back as you promised and failed at finding the relic."

Erik's eyes rolled to her, his face firm, but then Liv saw a subtle smile emerge. "You will stay. I love it here. The king and I plan to secure the fortress and seaside for any other attacks. We will prevail. Then after, we shall see."

Liv sighed, sipping her tea. "We will not stay and wait for you. I need to keep going." she said, even though she had no clue where to go.

Erik swallowed. "Then I will follow there. Something will lead me where you go, just as something led you here, to me. Good timing, too. It is as if the curse protected you."

Erik took the ale the innkeeper brought him, and the plate of bread, cheeses, and root vegetables seared by fire, suddenly hungry. "It has been one hundred years, and one day, these people will all be gone too. I am happy to see you both."

"As told in the book of curses, we still have relics to find Erik. That is why we have come. I need to research documents here. I know the king has a vast library." Halfdan shoved the cheese in.

"You may have access to it, I promise you." Erik turned to Liv. "You will stay here with me."

Liv's eyes were wide at him, and her face scowled as if something had hit her. "Why would I stay? You lied to me and broke a promise. Why do you hinder our search to break this curse, Erik."

Erik sighed, glared into Liv's eyes.

"Erik." She whispered.

He sighed, setting the cup down. "Will you forgive me?" He leaned back in the chair, towering over her. "For kissing you on that shore and leaving," He stared into her, his face firm. "For not coming back while everyone around you died. For leaving you there, alone in your misery."

Liv swallowed, and her heart fell to her feet. "You are mad." She sipped her tea, rolling her eyes around the room to avoid his stare, but Erik did not falter.

Liv sat her tea down just as Erik lunged up from the table and grabbed the back of her neck in his palm. She raised her chin to meet his face in surprise, just as he swooned her back in the chair. He gripped the seat in his free palm to keep her from falling back. Liv grabbed his leather chest armor, her fingers clasping his bow sheath strap to hold on.

"What are you doing?" She whispered against his face.

He plastered her lips with a firm kiss, his mouth strong, his scent filling her nose. She grabbed his bulging forearms to keep from falling back and opened her mouth to speak, but it only gave Erik open-mouthed kisses. When he finished kissing her, he breathed against her lips, his eyes firm into hers.

She met his eyes, her face pale as if something had taken pieces of her heart, chewed it up, and spit it out. She clenched her jaws at him.

"I am sorry." He breathed against her lips, raising her back up. Liv watched him turn around and march out of the inn into the busy street of happy families celebrating their win in the war.

Halfdan raised his brows and gazed around the room as if trying to hear something, but it was just laughter and people talking around them. "Something is not right with this curse. Did he seem a bit off to you?"

Liv narrowed her brows, but all she could do was growl under her breath. She kept gazing out the door to the street, but Erik was gone. He just kissed her and left again, and Liv fumed. She bolted up from the chair and marched outside to her horse. Halfdan followed her suddenly.

"What are you doing?" Halfdan asked her.

Liz pulled her long sword from the saddle after pulling on her fur cloak. "Going to kill him."

"You cannot kill him. You are both immortal." Halfdan sighed. "Also, you do know that killing is wrong, correct?"

"I will not continue this any longer. Erik stalls, so I cannot locate the relics. If I kill him, he will stay down for a while, no?" She turned her face to him.

Halfdan widened his eyes. "Liv, it was fifty years the first time he came for you. Now it is one hundred. How do you know it will not be one hundred fifty or two hundred next time? We must all be together to break it."

"I cannot live like this." Liv eyed her sword. "I refuse to live like this."

"I am certain he does not want to live like this."

"Why did he kiss me and run off again?" Liv's face was grieved and hard. "He plays with my heart, again."

Halfdan swallowed. "I do not know."

"Then why are you here, Monk? Why are you cursed to stay by my side?" She demanded.

Halfdan shrugged. "He is faster, and I cannot keep up with him."

She glared at him, squeezed the hilt tighter, and Halfdan swallowed. "I am sworn to protect the weaker of the two!"

Liv gasped. "The weaker of the two?! Is it because I am a woman?" She growled. "This curse was made by a man, I know it!"

"I do not know. I am still researching the ancient text. I need to find a library. We must stay put here until I do, as King Alfred is known for his love of the written word and knowledge."

Liv huffed, and closed her eyes. "So be it, monk. Find a way to get those relics since the maps I have are bringing us no closer to breaking this curse."

"We still need him, and you must forgive him," Halfdan interrupted.

"The curse will break one way or another because I will break it." She bit.

Halfdan swallowed. "By forgiving him, correct?"

She stared hard-faced at him. "By forgiving him." She stormed off, her fist clenched around the hilt of her sword.

Halfdan swallowed, watching her go, and from within the shadows, Erik emerged behind the inn. "She wants to kill me now." He sighed.

"You keep kissing her and leaving, playing with her heart!" Halfdan huffed at him.

Erik bit his lip. "That is not what I am doing. I mean to keep her."

Halfdan gawked at him. "Keep her? That sounds familiar, Erik. Sounds like the curse talking. Why do you taunt her heart?"

Eric bit his lip. "I want to stay with her, but I cannot stay. I do not understand what is happening to me."

Halfdan sighed at him. "You know we must keep moving, Erik. You have three days while we are here. That is it."

"She will kill me now. The women of our village are vicious."

"And well deserved! You charlatan of women!" Halfdan complained.

Erik nodded. "I will talk to her."

"You promise you will not kiss her again, Erik?" Halfdan warned him, but Erik walked up the street to follow her, mumbling to himself.

"Erik!" Halfdan gritted his teeth, but Erik walked off.

Erik followed her toward the Wedmore church, oil lamps filling the street with an aura of uncertainty. Families still lingered, going in and out of the wooden estate house for feasting. It was late, but it did not matter. Revelry was in the air, and his home was happy. The smell of roasted game filled the air, and the fumes of flaming vegetables seared on open fires made his mouth water again.

The feasting would go on for another day, and then the Vikings who invaded would go away, and they could finally have peace. Yet Erik felt no peace, and a hunger he had deep inside for Liv would not be quenched either. He stopped in front of Wedmore, his back to Liv as she approached him from the darkness of the field.

He craned his neck to acknowledge her. "You come to kill me. It will not work well for you in the end."

Liv squeezed her hilt. "Why not?"

"I have died before, Liv." He took a deep breath and turned to face her as she pressed the tip end of her blade at his throat. She walked the blade across the skin on his throat as he lingered closer to her. "We are immortal. We have already lived over one hundred years."

"You lied to me." She gritted her teeth. "We must find the relics, Erik. Have you forgotten that a curse still binds us?" She pressed into him.

"I forget nothing." He belted out.

She seethed. "Then why do you stall me?!"

Halfdan rushed up the field and joined a slew of spectators. One older man sighed at them. "I remember my first love. She stabbed me, and then we married. I loved her so much."

Halfdan gawked, his eyes wide, pointing at Liv. "She will kill him."

Another older man piped up, laughing. "Oh, no doubt, she seems very vigorous."

A middle-aged woman crossed her arms, watching them. "She should kill him, probably deserves it." She walked off.

As spectators filled the road watching them, there was silence between Liv and Erik for moments.

"Tell me the truth, Liv." He whispered.

Liv's eyes watered up at him, her face clenched. "What truth!"

"You fear what will happen once you let me in." He warned. "You are afraid to live."

"I fear nothing but this abysmal existence. This lingering on and on for no purpose!" She belted out.

"We have a purpose!" Erik pleaded.

"I cannot live like this a moment longer!" She cried. "It is just you, me, and that monk for all eternity."

The crowd turned to stare at Halfdan, but all he could do was widen his eyes at Liv.

Erik sighed, his eyes focused on hers, his lips clamped as tight as his jaws. He loomed over her, intimidating her with his warrior attire, bulky muscles, and slender build. He could overpower her easily, and she would probably let him.

"Stay here with me, and we will break this together." Erik begged.

She quaked inside, pushing both palms tighter around the hilt. "We cannot break this together! I will not stay where you tell me."

"You think killing me in this moment will give you a purpose?" He pressed the blade against his throat. It cut the skin, and blood seeped out.

Liv pulled the blade away and stepped back. She twisted around like her father had taught her to do and lunged it through his heart, and Erik gasped and fell. "Yes." She pressed the blade through him so the tip end protruded out his back.

Halfdan threw his arms in the air. "Damnit! He should have kissed her again."

The people standing around surrounded them and began to holler. Halfdan could only watch them and sigh as Liv pulled the blade back out. Erik flopped over on his side, convulsed, bleeding out. Liv cried as he fell, her sword limp in her fist as blood poured from his chest. Her tears fell down her neck as she watched him close his eyes, and blood filled his mouth.

Liv slumped to her knees, her heart aching.

The older man leaned down and felt for a pulse, but there was none. "He's dead!" He screamed.

The men standing around lunged Liv up by her forearms, taking her sword. As more people and warriors came out from the feasting to see the commotion, the older man hollered at her. "You must pay for this! You killed Erik, one of our best warriors!"

Liv gritted her teeth at them, standing there being held against her will even as the old people and warriors decided what to do with her. Halfdan pushed through the crowds as people convened over Erik's body. He lay on his side, an open wound to his chest, blood spilling from his cold body. Halfdan glared at him, waiting for him to wake up, but he didn't. Everyone gasped.

Liv was pulled through the crowds straight up the street to the prison, her fate unknown, but she did not care. Halfdan sighed, watching them take her away, gazing back to Erik's body. A couple of warriors came out and picked his body up, and laid it to the side.

"Prepare the grave for this brave warrior. Taken out by a woman. Damn shame."

Another one sighed. "Yes. No doubt she loved him, and Erik did not feel the same."

"Perhaps he had another woman, and she found out?"

"Well, Erik was not like that! He was loyal and would be loyal to only one woman!"

"What should we do with her then?"

"Let her lie in prison. We will let the king know, and he will decide judgment."

Halfdan widened his eyes. "Ugh. Great."

The warriors pulled Liv through the crowd up the street, yanking her by her forearms. As they reached a great hall through a stone manor, they dragged her downstairs through a cavernous entrance into a dungeon cell. The two men handling her pushed her into it, and she slammed into the wall. Liv plopped down upon the dry straw, leaned her back against the wall, and cried into her arms all night.

5

Death's Kiss

Liv sat in prison for two more days while the feasting continued and the king remained oblivious to her crimes. It was a good thing too, because Halfdan could bring her plates of food from the feasting at least, so she would not go hungry. But she did not eat.

"They have dug the grave. It is a beautiful place under a big Sycamore tree." He wiped a tear from his face. "Such a beautiful place."

Liv glared at him from the floor. "He is not dead."

"It still hurts!" He pressed his bald head and long face into the bars at her. "I am leading the procession as the priest. I hope we do not bury him alive. That would not be pleasant."

Liv watched him storm off to begin the proceedings. She sat the plate down, still full of food, and let the rats take it. In the corner of her cell were empty plates. She had eaten nothing since killing Erik. Part of her wanted to get on her horse, and race away from him and Halfdan, and disappear forever. At least now she knew it was two days minimum before he would come back. Maybe.

Under a sprawling Sycamore tree, tombstones spread out on an open field outside the town. Erik's body was placed inside a grave. His sword lay in his palms, splayed over his body, and he was still fully clothed in his armor.

Halfdan stood, clearing his throat as the crowds gathered to pay their respects. His long brown wool robes hung on his short, thin frame. He shouted: "Dearly beloved, we gather here today," He paused suddenly.

"Damnit! Wrong one." He hollered and turned the pages in his leather-bound book. He cleared his throat again to speak but froze when Erik moaned, stretched out in the ground. The people froze, their eyes as wide as leaves. Halfdan bent over him to see Erik press his hand against his chest and moan.

Erik's eyes flew open, and he complained, "Aughhh."

The crowds and warriors gathered around froze, leaning over the grave to watch the horror. Sudden gasps and murmurs began to fill the field. Erik sat straight up, his long sword gripped in his clasp.

"She has a strong arm." Erik rubbed his chest.

People in the crowd screamed as he faced them, and the color returned to his tanned face. The people gasped in terror, but Halfdan hollered out to settle them "Valhalla," He paused, pointing to the sky, "has sent him back!" His eyes rolled from one person to another, and then he looked up as if speaking to the clouds.

"Valhalla sent him back." People started murmuring.

"Valhalla sent him back!"

"Valhallaaaaaaaaaaaa!" Some woman screamed.

"Clearly!" Halfdan hollered, his voice echoing. "Erik has more work to do in this life and has been freed from death! He has, therefore, not truly died. The killer may go free!"

The people cheered as Erik pulled himself out of the shallow grave. He pushed his sword into his sheath, his eyes roaming over the crowds for Liv.

"Where is she?" He asked Halfdan, who swallowed and pointed toward the prison.

As Erik ignored the crowds, his warrior friends shouted, "Go get that woman!"

"Your destiny awaits!"

"If you let her kill you again, that is on you!"

But Erik marched away from them, leaving the crowds gasping over an empty grave, even as a pang still hit his heart.

L iv lay on her side, straw in her hair, her head aching, her body weak from not eating. She was hoping she would starve to death, but she would just come back anyway. She could not even die properly. Somehow, she would always come back. She opened her eyes as a jingle vibrated the air, and the creaky cell opened.

She recognized Halfdan's voice, but it was Erik who leaned over her, very much alive. She lay on her side, arms splayed out, hair matted. Her eyes folded upon him, but held no strength of life.

She closed them again even as Erik sighed at her, and her awkward circumstance. "You happy now?" He sighed at her face, picking her up in his arms.

As she gazed up at his face, he lingered into hers. "I have you now." His face was stern, and his eyes lit up with a fire that pinged her heart, but she could not place it.

Still, she did not feel better. Erik carried her out of the cell, her limp, weak body pressed against him. A cool breeze hit her face, and she smelled flowering trees and herbs around her. It filled her with hope. It smelled of home. Erik carried her into a stone manor, where women waited to bathe her in a suite all her own.

He set her down gently, and she stood up, her legs weak, her body achy and tired from the cold stone floor. She turned to see a tub filled with hot, soapy water that smelled of roses. Her stomach turned as women brought food in.

Erik turned to go but then stopped. His eyes teared up. Liv faced him, too tired to fight back. She would have said something dreadful to him, but he sighed and marched out with Halfdan. As he shut the doors behind him, his shoulders slumped at her presence.

Hours later, Liv felt refreshed and had a new dress and cloak. Erik had ladies bring in a platter filled with cheeses, dried fruit, and seared meats. She had eaten and sat in the chair before an arched picture window, gazing upon the rolling hills. Liv braided her long blonde hair around her head and twisted it at her neck, and left a few braids hanging down her slender back.

Liv turned her face toward the door as heavy footsteps waltzed toward her. She craned her neck as the doors opened, and Erik barged in. She stood to face him, her eyes wide. Erik had new leathers, cuffs and more weapons in his sheaths. He had trimmed his beard so it was not as long, and it accentuated his strong jawline. His eyes lit up seeing her all cleaned up, and her eyes lit up seeing him as a man for the first time in ages.

"You cannot forgive me. Why?!" He demanded, his voice breaking. "I asked you to forgive me."

Her lips quivered. "You did not mean it."

He stopped walking toward her. "Do not presume to tell me what I meant or how I feel about you."

She craned her neck away from his enticing gaze to the summer fields, her eyes falling. "I cannot forgive myself." A tear fell. "I am responsible for our fate. It was me who caused this curse."

Erik sighed. "It was both of us."

She nodded, "We are bound by the curse." She faced him, her jaws clenched.

"It will take both of us to break this." Erik's voice shook.

She wiped her face. "No, it does not, you know this."

"I need you." He begged her. "I need you, Liv."

She scoffed. "I am not a relic, Erik! We are no closer to breaking it because of you."

Erik huffed. "We cannot continue chasing one another into eternity to do it. Stay with me."

She stepped back. "Do you care for me?"

Erik swallowed. "I do. I need you to stay with me until we break it together."

"How do we hunt the relics if we stay, Erik? I will not stay." She warned him.

"Everywhere you go, I feel you! I want to come for you! I was stuck in battles these last hundred years and could not find you." He paced before her. "I need you here with me."

"No." She crossed her arms.

He held out his palm to her. "If I do not care for you, why do the runes remain? They will not go away until we relent to each other. You can run no longer." He warned.

"That is not what the curse says, Erik. You stall me yet again. You are keeping me here for your own purpose."

Erik clenched his jaws. "I am protecting you."

Liv laughed. "I am a free woman. I shall go where I please."

"Free women do not hide in the woods. You have spent countless years hiding among the trees and the mountains. You are not free."

"I was hiding from you!" She yelled. "Keeping me with you here is not freedom."

He huffed. "We are not free because these runes remain carved into our souls."

Liv gasped. "What do you want from me?"

Erik paused, run his fingers through his long hair. "To stay near me so I can protect you."

"That sounds like a marriage of convenience, Erik. Neither of us want that, it will kill us both." Liv growled.

"So be it." He whispered.

She shouted at him, "There is no worse death than that!"

Erik huffed. "You killed me! I could still have you killed for your crime."

"Would it give me peace?" Her face was flat, and her tears dried up.

"Did killing me give you peace, Liv?" His face clenched.

"No. It broke my heart!" She gripped her chest and stepped toward him. "Living my life away from you will heal it." She marched by him to leave.

Erik grabbed her forearm and forced her to stop, pulling her into him. He narrowed his brows, his eyes hard. How he gazed upon her made her pause as if some strength had burst out of him through his face. She met him there, their bodies hot against one another. She froze in his grasp.

He clenched his jaws in her face. "I will find you. I will not let you go this alone with Halfdan no more." His eyes were hard as ice. "We break this curse together."

He let her arm go just as she lunged up and plastered a kiss on his lips. Erik froze for a moment but then pulled her in tighter by her forearms to him, their mouths open to inviting passion. Just as he thought he could cup her backside to pull her into his groin so she was flat against his chest, she pushed him off.

He stood there, his mouth still open, his eyes wide at her. She turned and wiped her mouth off, pursing her lips. "Next time, I will not warn you before you die again."

Erik clenched his jaws into her face, gritting his teeth. "Bring it onnnn." There was a deep edge to his voice.

"There are a thousand ways to die, Viking." She paraded away from him to the door, turning to bow.

"We have eternity." She raised back up and bolted out, leaving Erik standing there watching her curvy backside as she went.

"So that you know I come back stronger every time I die!" He yelled after her. "One day, you will no longer run from me!"

Halfdan had crept in to listen to them and sighed, his brown eyes wide. "You do? That must be new. I must write that in the book." He rushed to the library.

Erik stood there in the middle of the room, his head aching, and the taste of her kiss still heavy on his lips.

T hat evening the town square was busy, and the Lyres and flutes played alongside the harps. The feasting and celebrations were still ongoing, and Liv was drawn out to enjoy the music, a part of it reminding her of home. She pulled her fur tight over her shoulders and stood there alongside the road, watching the families dancing and eating. The children ran and played.

She promised Halfdan they would stay a few days so that he could research more about the curse and see if there were anything there in King Alfred's library. She hoped so because the last hundred years and more had done nothing for them. The music filled the night air, and she found herself smiling into it just as Erik emerged from the darkness behind her.

She gazed up at him, and her eyes fell upon the strength of his body armor and weapons, his long blonde hair braided down his back. He eyed her from the side. "It is not custom to leave a man once you have kissed him."

He looked at her, a gentle smile on his face. "Especially after killing him."

Liv scoffed at him. "Is that so? You must have another death wish, Viking."

He took a deep breath, glaring at her, and then stood before her and held out a hand. "Dance with me."

Chills chased her spine as she gazed at the runes. "No." She whispered, meeting his face.

Erik gazed at her lips. "Dance with me," he demanded again, his voice deep and beckoning. He was not smiling.

Liv could not deny his brazenness. She shook her head up at him. He clenched his jaws, his eyes hard. He pulled her hand out from her anyway, grabbed her around her waist, and made her dance. He lunged her against his chest. She sighed and let him take her hand. He gripped it with a strong grasp, pulled her against him tighter, and gazed into her eyes.

"You killed me. You owe me a dance." He glared at her face.

Liv met his tenacity, her eyes wide. "You owe me a relic. A dagger which you never retrieved."

Erik gazed around at all the other couples dancing and then melted back into her face, his eyes grazing over hers. "You will not let this go."

"Never. We had a promise to one another. You broke that."

Erik huffed. "I broke nothing. I could not find it and came back looking for you."

"I am forced to live out these days slowly while searching for relics I cannot find. I do not know how I will find them. The maps I took are not right."

Erik pursed his lips. "The curse is not hurting us, Liv. We are immortal. We have strength and courage, which many people will never see. Why must you hunt them?"

Liv thought a moment. "Because chaos follows us. The world will burn if we do not end this." She glared at him.

"But the world is not burning."

"But it was. You just got out of a deadly war." She reminded him.

Erik rolled his eyes. "There will always be wars, Liv. We do not need the relics. We can live as we choose."

He stared at her again, gripped her tighter around her waist, his fingers stretching over her backside. "We just need each other."

"Do you not feel that tug inside you? That something evil comes even as we dance here? Tell me you feel this curse pulling you, Erik. It is something dreadful I cannot understand right now." She begged him.

He sighed at her face but did not answer. They stood there and danced gently to the music, staring into one another and pressing against one another for endless moments until he spoke.

"You are still my people, you know." He whispered to her face.

Liv swallowed. "I will always be your people, but Erik," She sighed, but Erik interrupted her.

"We have a history only we are privy to. I do not want it to end this way." He begged. He clutched her hand against his chest and they sank into the furs. He clasped her against him tight as if he could never let her go, and she let him.

"I want this to end well." She hoped.

They stared at one another, their eyes lingering upon each other's faces. Just as Erik leaned into her lips, she closed her eyes and laid her head on his chest. Her eyes teared up. Erik wrapped his arms around her tighter and rested his chin atop her head, closing his eyes.

They danced until the music had stopped playing, the food was gone again, and Erik walked her back to the inn. Her face was cold from the night, and her heart was not full. It was heavy as if a stone wall had pressed on it. They walked in silence together, him looming over her in his warrior attire.

"Good night, Erik." She turned to go.

As she turned to walk into the inn, Erik grabbed her hand and yanked her back to him. She fell hard against his chest. He lunged against her lips and kissed her hard with an open mouth, and she met his kisses. Their deep-rooted passionate embrace filled them with a long-lost fire. Erik gripped her face in his palms and she wrapped her arms over his back, pulling him harder against her. They stood there lost in their open-mouthed kisses, even as the sun rose and dawn kissed them in crimson and tangerine orange.

Erik breathed on her lips, moaning like she had sucked the breath out of him. "Stay." He begged her, gripping the side of her neck with his firm palm. "Stay with me. Forever." He begged, his eyes on fire.

She whispered on his lips. "I do not want to live forever."

Erik pulled her tighter against him. "I need you more than these relics."

Liv pulled away from him. She swallowed as he said that, like something pricked her from the inside, and grew there.

Halfdan stood at the top of the stairs watching them, gawking.

"You two been out all night?" He rubbed his eyes.

Liv stared up at Halfdan, but she was not smiling. She pulled out of Erik's grasp, but he gripped her hand to stop her even as she turned to walk up the stairs. She met his face, and he would not let her go.

"Stay with me, Liv." He whispered, his face longing for her.

"I have to sleep." Liv moaned.

Erik let her go but sighed. Liv closed her eyes, and took a deep breath as she walked by Halfdan, her heart soaring. If she had let Erik pull her back to him, she would never find the relics. They would never break the curse. Erik stalled her, yet again, using her love for him to do it.

Halfdan noticed her face and stared down at Erik again. They were indeed beautiful together. Liv disappeared into her room, and Erik stood gazing at where she went. Erik turned to go, grazing his eyes back up the stairs to Halfdan, and then left. Halfdan's spine tingled, watching Erik's obsessiveness over her.

Erik would not let her go this time, and it would get worse every time. Liv would have to fight with everything in her to continue hunting relics. She may have to keep killing him over and over to do it. Halfdan's heart ached for them, knowing the curse would haunt them all until it was broken. But their broken hearts may kill them before the curse ever did.

6

Where the Curse Finds Them

L iv did not go to bed. She watched Erik out the window. He walked up the street to the manor where his room was, allowing her to creep into the library early. She pulled out parchments and scrolls. She yanked open the books and read stories until her head ached.

She knew Erik would look for her soon, but she had to find something. She froze when she found a story titled *The Immortali Curse of the Broken Heart*. She sat there alone and cried as she read it. The dawning of the tasks at hand haunted her.

She and Erik were living and breathing this curse now. He wanted her to stay with him, but that was the curse talking, not just his love for her. She had to find the relics, and the curse did not want them found. It strung their hearts along to live miserably with it. She ripped the next page out, stuffed it down her front dress, and crept out to join Halfdan for breakfast.

She sipped her tea and filled up on bread, cheese, and fruit. Halfdan eyed her with caution. "You seem unusually hungry."

Liv shoved the food in. "We have a long journey ahead of us, eat."

Halfdan sighed, watching her. "Hmmm. I still have research to do in the library today. We cannot leave til I find what I need to understand this curse more. I am looking for something that may explain this obsessive behavior from Erik and how to help break it."

Liv smiled. "Of course. So go to the library and I will rest until you finish."

"You will not," Halfdan rolled his eyes. "I am but a few years older than you and Erik, but I am not stupid. I see you plot things in your eyes. I know you, Liv."

Liv met his clean-shaven face and big brown eyes. "No, you are not stupid at all. You are the reason I have kept going. Thank you for at least trying to help me break this."

"You are like a brother I never had, you know that, right?" She added, smiling at him.

Halfdan smiled at her. "You know I am cursed too. You and Erik have this love-hate fiasco going on, but I am the one who ultimately breaks this for you both..." He froze as Erik walked in.

Liv widened her eyes at him. "What did you say?" Her eyes melted to Erik, who seemed to loom in on them from the door.

Erik walked into the inn and sat down with them. "Hungry, eh?" He glared at the food on Liv's plate.

"I spent countless years in the woods eating berries, herbs, and any vegetables we could plant. I deserve this food." She took another bite of the bread, and Erik laughed at her.

Halfdan smiled. "Not true. You also killed deer and birds. We fished. I did not like birds."

Erik took a deep breath and stared at Liv. "You are coming with me today."

Liv stopped chewing her food. "To do what?"

"To stay by my side." His face was firm, and his eyes lit up with a strength she had never seen in him before.

"I cannot stay, you know this. You continue to forget we have a curse, conveniently."

"I care not for this curse. I care for you. I need you to stay with me." He belted out, his voice demanding as if he expected her to bend.

Halfdan leaned back into the chair and explored Erik's mannerisms. He held his breath, watching Erik react to Liv. He had to get to the library as soon as possible.

Liv gazed into his eyes and then explored his face. Erik was serious, like the face she had seen men have on the battlefield before killing their enemies. "You cannot make me stay, Erik." She whispered calmly.

Erik's face was hard as he stared at her, his eyes firm. "You are staying," he stood to go. "I will come for you at midday. I have important business with the King until then." Then Erik lunged down to Liv's face, gripped the side of her neck in his palm, and bent to her lips, "You stay with me." He whispered, kissed her lips gently, and left.

Halfdan watched Erik go, studying his body language, then he turned to Liv with wide eyes. "What did you both do last night?"

She swallowed the food, shaking her head. "Nothing. We did nothing. Just kiss."

Halfdan blinked his eyes, thinking. "Is that typical of a Viking male, then? To give orders to their women and take..."

Liv gulped. "This is not the Erik I once knew in the village. He wanted me free from bondage or oppression. He wanted me to travel and live."

"He is not going to let you leave, Liv." Halfdan sighed. "It is getting worse. I must find what we are looking for today, then by dawn we leave. We have relics to find."

Liv sat there listening to Halfdan, but her heart shook her chest to death. She gripped the parchment she had shoved down her front between her breasts and sighed inside. Erik just gave her no choice but to go this alone and go as soon as possible.

After they had eaten, she waited til Halfdan left for the library to go and pack her satchel. As she pressed back down the stairs to walk outside to her horse, three of Erik's men met her at the door. The innkeeper cleared his throat, and Liv froze.

"Let me pass." She told them, her face stern.

The men blocked the door, their metal-plated armor squeaking, their sheaths holding long swords, their axes strut on their backs over their heads. Their long beards made them look older than they were, and Liv assumed they were in their mid-twenties. Nonetheless, they were bulky, mighty men. A fire shot up her spine, and she bit her tongue.

Liv held her breath. "Where is Erik?"

The middle warrior smiled. "He is busy, so we are commanded to keep you here, lady."

"Until he comes for you." The one on the right blurted out, smiling. "And he does come for you." They all laughed.

"Erik gets what he wants." Another one laughed.

They mocked her. Liv turned her gaze to the innkeeper, who whistled, ignoring her, mocking her too. She stepped toward them, and the middle warrior leaned back as if blocking the door. She lunged forward, yanked his dagger up out of his boot sheath, and stuffed the bone hilt straight up into his crotch.

He lunged backward, bent over in pain, gasping, his mouth wide open. As he fell, she raised back up and blasted the blunt end of it atop the bridge of the man's nose on the right. Her sudden speed shocked him, and he fell backwards over the table, knocking it over. He rolled to get off the table and collided with the chairs.

The man on the left stood there gasping at what she had just done, his arm reaching in to grab his sword. As he pulled on the hilt, she pushed the dagger through the top of his leg above the knee, plunging the blade through. He hollered in pain and leaned in to grab her. Liv plunged the hilt under his chin and he fell back against his comrades, who were slowly getting up.

She bludgeoned the men atop their heads once, and they fell back and stopped moving. Then she lunged her arm around to face the innkeeper and slung the dagger straight at his head, where it lodged a hair next to his temple into the wooden beam. He raised to feel a slither of blood dripping on his temple, the dagger still jiggling in delight. She had slit him open.

"The next time a woman wants to leave, you help her leave, you coward!" She seethed at them. "You are all cowardly men!"

The bartender was frozen, shaking all over. All he could do was watch her barge out of the inn, pull herself up on her horse, and ride away. The men moaned and rolled out on the floor in pain, blood flowing from their faces and heads.

"She is going to kill that boy again. I know it." The innkeeper gulped.

H alfdan had spent the whole day at the library. He sat with his hot tea and platter of bread and butter with a slice of honeycomb, pulling out parchment after parchment from the royal library that Erik had gotten him approval to explore. The wooden pillars rose around him to the arched ceilings, the windowless room lit by hanging oil lanterns. As shadows cast upon his clean-shaven face, his eyes stopped upon a parchment dated five hundred years ago.

It was a short story, but Halfdan knew it was real. The story was titled *The Immortali Curse of the Broken Heart*. He read the parchment, his mouth filled with bread he could no longer chew, his insides turning hard as stone. One passage in the story hit him as if a stone wall had fallen upon him, but a page was missing. A sudden nervous chill rushed up his arms. He sat there reading the passage over and over until a nervous twitch formed up his spine. He had to get to Liv.

Once Halfdan read the curse, he grabbed the parchment and raced out of the library into a torch-lit street. He ran down the road past the church and slid down the hill to the inn. Liv's horse was gone. He heard a commotion inside the inn and pushed himself inside. Three men sat, telling the other warriors what happened to them, their injuries evident on their faces. They had taken a beating, and one of them had been stabbed in the leg. Liv had beaten them.

The innkeeper gazed upon Halfdan as he entered, his face flushed and bleeding. "They tried to keep her here under Erik's orders, did not go well for them. I give it to her, that woman is strong! She nearly killed me, too."

"Where was Erik during this!" Halfdan cried.

"With the king, that is why he had his men watch her."

"Where did she go!" Halfdan pleaded.

"South."

Halfdan rushed to his room, grabbed his things and the leather curse book. He raced back downstairs and saddled his horse. The innkeeper met him outside. "Erik was informed, he left also! Just thought you would like to know, but he is behind her a ways."

"He goes after her?! Not good!" Halfdan pulled himself up, his face flushed, his eyes wide and bright.

The innkeeper stepped back, watching Halfdan race his horse up the road headed south, the sand and dirt flying high behind them as his head pressed down into the horse's mane. He raced miles south until he hit the coast, and the shoreline kissed his head and face with a salty taste. The moon was high over listless clouds blowing in a summer storm. He heard thunder overhead, and the ground shook. It was so thick, he felt it in his bones.

He stopped when he felt like he had reached the end of the world, and the road seemed to come to an end. The sea spilled before him like cascading diamonds bleeding in the night, and he froze at the sight of Erik sitting horseback looking out. He had Liv's horse, but she was not with it. His face was twisted in a hot anger, seared with an emotional hurt he could not describe.

"Where is she!" Halfdan pleaded.

Erik gazed at the sea and a dark dot of a ship that slowly disappeared on the horizon. "She bested three of my men. The curse makes us both stronger, no matter which one dies."

"She was not strong like this before?" Halfdan questioned as Erik nodded.

"No, not before."

"I found this on the curse." He handed the parchment to Erik, and he pulled it up and read the passage under the moonlight. His face changed into something stiff and beaten.

Erik handed it back, a weight suddenly pressed upon his heart. "The next ship does not come for weeks."

Halfdan sat there next to Erik, gazing at vast ocean, their heads bursting. But it was nothing compared to the burning pain Erik started to feel in his heart the further she sailed away from him. He would not rest. He would not stop. He would have to exhaust himself to get her again.

Halfdan watched Erik's face change, like a sickness fell upon him, as if he had been ripped apart from the inside out. "And so, it begins," Erik told himself.

Halfdan huffed at him. "It began the moment you and Liv touched that infernal relic! This curse will only get stronger. You must make a choice, Erik. You must let her find the relics."

Erik sighed. "Next time I find her, the bond will be sealed between us, so I always know where she goes, and we break this curse together."

"You mean to be intimate with her?" Halfdan scoffed. "That is but one part of it. That alone will not keep her with you, Erik! It leads you to hunt her, and she is led to break it." He warned. "She is led by the curse same as you. The curse leads you both to something, to a time we cannot see or understand yet."

There was a moment of silence, and then Halfdan huffed. "You will always hunt her! It will only get stronger. These last years you have been obsessed with finding her. I see it more now than before, even at the village the signs were there. The curse has chosen you as the hunter."

Erik clenched his teeth. "I know! Damn this curse." He sighed, his heart beating as if strings were breaking, but he could do nothing to tie them back together. "I need her, but I know to let her go. I do not know what is wrong with me."

Halfdan gasped, gazing at the empty sea. "That is the curse talking. Who knows when we will find her again? My heart aches for you. It truly does. But it aches more for her."

"Why for her?"

Halfdan sneered at him. "Because she is the one who must find the relics in desperation because you hunt her! She loves you. It kills her every time. It breaks her heart, Erik. Do you not see it?"

Erik sat beside Halfdan, a part of him dying inside as if something got ripped out of him, and he had to find it again to be whole.

Halfdan sighed, closing his eyes. "The three of us will fight this curse in different ways, and it will always be a step ahead of us. She must find the relics, Erik."

Erik swallowed. He was at a breaking point. They needed the relics to break the curse and be whole again. Only, he would never be truly whole. He would never be whole until he had her in his grasp again. He could not help himself.

L iv stood on the port bow of the ship. Its pristine white sails rose above her as if she was floating among the clouds. The seafaring men and women behind her were excited to leave the country, the whole world they had always known. Liv had been lucky to meet these villagers under King Alfred before she danced with Erik last night, and she had taken them up on their offer, bribing them with jewels.

She stood there and watched the shoreline disappear more and more until she noticed a rider. His head was low on his stallion, and his cloak blasted behind him. The full moon cast shadows over his tall, muscular body, his blonde hair whipping his braids behind him.

He stopped at the edge, pulled her horse to his, and watched her in the dark. Her heart jumped when she saw him. She could not see his blue eyes, but felt them upon her, as if some thick veil was hoisted on her bones. He watched her with those piercing eyes, his jaws clenched, his knuckles turned white, gripping the reigns. He could not keep her, so he would hunt her. He had made that clear.

She was only a means to the end of the curse for him, and in the end, she would still be broken. So, she would sail across the sea to a different land and break the curse herself. She pulled out the parchment she had stolen from the library and clutched it in her palm. And then she glared over the sea again toward Erik, her lips trembling.

This was the only way they could ever be free. The other written part of this curse was never mentioned in her grandmother's curse book, nor did she ever see it, even after her grandmother died. She still had to find five relics. She had to destroy them on the cylinder Halfdan kept.

She had maps that led her to only three relics, but she had been obsessed with finding the dagger first. Erik failed to do that, so now she had no choice but to get the relics and find the dagger last. During this time, as she searched for the relics, Erik's hunger to find her would grow worse. He would become a shroud of the man she knew, which could end them all. She had no choice but to do this alone and could not allow them to follow her anyway.

She needed a head start on them both because even she knew Erik was voracious and strong. She would take the wealth she had brought with her from the years of hoarding her people's precious stones and would figure everything out on her own.

She would keep going until she broke the curse, death took her somehow, or the curse cast her out. She would oversee her destiny and life. She would break the curse whether it wanted her to or not.

On the shoreline, Halfdan grew more nervous. Now, he and Erik had read the parchment. They continued sitting atop their steeds, gawking into the night of the sea.

Erik turned to him. "I know she conversed with the villagers before we danced. They told me what she was doing. She needs to find relics and has maps of where to find some of them." Erik sighed. "She will need pirates to help her."

Halfdan swallowed, his eyes wide. "What? Are we sailing now, then?"

Erik huffed. "No. We wait for her to come back."

"Why? I thought you needed to get her."

"I need to gather Vikings loyal to me to help me fight the pirates to get to her."

Erik pulled out parchments from his satchel that copied the maps Liv had on her. "I had them copied while she was contained. My men had orders to take her belongings if anything happened to me. We wait until she comes back looking for the gem."

Halfdan's heart beat wildly. "You will ambush her?"

Erik turned to go, sighing deeply. "Yes."

Halfdan took a deep breath, blinking his eyes, his lips straight on an unamused face. "Why did you have to dump the relic in my lap?"

They stared out at empty waters, the ship gone now. Halfdan kept reciting in his head over and over what the story said, even as chills raced up his arms.

Immortality comes at a price for the heart. When the curse has spent ages hunting love and is forsaken, it renders upon itself, and death's malicious grip flees them. To die with a broken heart is the most painful death of all, as the one stricken with grief never rests, and the one last to fall never forgets.

7

The Seas of Iniquities

L iv slept sitting up in the hull of the Longboat with the other women. They had children with them, too, and their whole life of material things and wealth alongside them on this long journey. A big part of her knew why: they had been embroiled in wars for a long time and suffered loss of life. She let her dreams recant the last hundred and fifty years of her life since her seer grandmother passed.

She replayed in her mind those sea blue eyes of Erik and then saw him fall to death with her sword. She breathed heavily, remembering gazing up at him from the prison floor and the look he gave her. There was contempt in his eyes but with an edge of pity.

"I have you now." He said, his lips firm, his jawline clenched.

But he no longer had her, and she had escaped him, just as he had done to her. The boat rocked and hollers of strange voices echoed, and Liv's eyes flew open suddenly. The ship had stopped and was being boarded, the boots echoed and shouts of a strange dialect hit her. The women and children began to cry, and whimper in fear. But Liv pressed herself up past them and climbed the stairs.

As she bopped her head on the deck, she saw twelve men wrapped in furs. They had scruffy faces and wore leather tunics. They pressed into the men and lined them up against the starboard, their long swords and axes pressed into them. There were only five men aboard, and the rest were women and children. As they noticed her emerge, their faces lit up, they whistled and cawed. She, too, was wrapped in fur about her shoulders and had leather bands around her arms. Her long tunic dress danced to her boots. She gazed out and saw where they had pressed their longboat against theirs and tied them together. There was nothing but open sea, a perfect place to attack.

They were pirates, and they were hijacking them. Liv continued to walk toward them on the starboard, her eyes watching their mannerisms, their eyes wavering at her. She stopped a yard from them, her hand hanging over the hilt of her long sword. Liv's battle axe was still strapped to her back in her sheath.

The pirates froze, gazing upon her. "Release them. There are enough treasures in the whole world for us all to partake." She warned.

The leader of the pirate crew raked his dirty fingers through his long gray beard and smiled at her, missing his front tooth. His wrinkles had aged him so that Liv realized these men had spent decades on the seas robbing people, and killing them too. She would not allow them to kill these innocent people. He laughed at her and then motioned for his men to take her.

"Where are you from." She demanded.

The leader scoffed. "The place where women like you get taken."

She huffed. "Oh, I am not so easily taken."

Two scruffy-faced pirates slid their swords back into their side sheaths and rushed her. She pulled her long sword and swished completely around, cutting them straight across their midsections. They hurled back in pain, shouting at her.

"Come for me and you will die." She warned them.

The pirates gawked at her, grabbing their sliced bellies. As they leaned into the side of the starboard to bleed out, she raised a long leg to their chests and kicked them both overboard. As the bodies fell, she faced the pirates and pulled her axe. The old pirate growled at her.

"You will pay for that! Kill the winch!"

Liv flew into them as if a flock of birds of prey had kissed her. Five of them, including the leader, stood back to guard over her crew. They pointed their swords at them, their eyes shifting back and forth, watching as Liv cut them down. She belted her axe around her head, twisting it in midair at her face and it chopped two heads off. The headless bodies fell as they stood, and the deck became a river of blood.

When she finished, she marched to face the pirates left and the pirate leader, her face sprayed with blood. "I said release them." She rolled her eyes. "Men never listen."

They dropped their swords, and the crew stood up. Liv sighed at the crew. "You men must do better. What did you do at Alfred's kingdom?" She pointed her axe in their direction, blood dripping off it.

One of the crew swallowed, speaking up. "Farmers."

Liv laughed at them. "Where I come from, farmers' fight! I can train you to fight and protect your families. This will ensure your survival." And then she turned to the six pirates left standing, pressing her axe and sword into them.

"You, fool, you will take me to your king."

One of the farmer crews hollered. "No, they will kill us! They are pirates."

Liv pressed her axe blade harder into the pirate leaders throat, and he gasped, his eyes wide. "What are your people called." She commanded.

"Curonians, we come from the Baltic."

The farmer crew gasped. "Curonian pirates!" They began mumbling amongst themselves.

Liv turned to the farmer crew. "You may go wherever you wish. You are not obligated to carry me. You would not last a day there with your cowardness."

She smiled; the blood spray smeared across her cheek as she pressed harder into the pirates. "You fools will take me to your people. I need t find relics, and the pirates will help me until I find them."

The pirates swallowed, their faces pale, their bodies shivering. The pirate leader scoffed at her, his lips shaking. "What. Why?!" Liv watched the color drain from his tanned face as quickly as the winds picked up to carry them further to sea.

"Because I need help in finding relics." Her eyes were bright as she clenched her jaws at him.

Hours later, Liv waved the families off as they sailed away from her. She stood along the bow as the older pirate joined her, and watched them sail further out. The surviving crew manned the Longship as best they could, but it would be a longer journey without help. Liv did not care; she was going back with them to meet their tribal leader. She had a plan.

"They did not take you up on your offer." The old pirate mentioned, his accent echoing.

She looked at him; he towered over her by inches, and her eyes fell on the ship, disappearing. "They did not. They will die if they do not learn to fight."

He huffed. "They will all die."

He rubbed the salty spray from his face, his brown eyes withered. "What do your people call you?" He asked.

Liv swallowed. "Liv Andora. What are you called?"

He gazed upon her, squinting through the spray. "Oka, mighty eagle. Oka." And he walked off to help his survivors man the jig lines.

Liv watched him, although her hand was not as itchy to handle her sword, or pull her axe. She wondered how he knew what her name meant. After all, it was the middle name her grandmother had given her. Liv sailed with them into unknown waters, her heart still busting inside. The memory of Erik's blue eyes gazing upon made it seem like the whole world had been pulled from her soul.

She pulled out the parchment and unrolled it, and read it again. And then she raised her palm up and compared the runes. They were an exact match, she shivered inside. It was strange that Baltic pirates had come to her. It was strange because the Baltic Sea is where the map on the parchment led her. The Baltic Sea is where Erik's tribe was from. She was so desperate to get away from Erik that it did not matter if the ship was going in the wrong direction.

She pressed her face into the wind, pulled her fur cloak tighter around her shoulders, and gripped an impossible reality before her. It was one in which she should not be alive. Yet there she was, standing on a Baltic pirate Longship, her long blonde hair blowing in the wind behind her, her axe strut over her head on her back, and an uncertain curse hunting her through the man she loved.

While the ship Liv had originally taken was headed south, she traveled due East over the North Sea until they reached the Baltic Sea. Oka had warned her the tribe was brutal. He warned her their leader, Bartolomeus, was vicious. That he would want vengeance since she slew a majority of the crew, even to protect her own people. She stood on the bow as the men coasted into an inlet, rising caves kissing the shoreline and waterfalls cascading down through an immense forest of evergreens.

Thatched roofs rose up from a rocky plan and the ship coasted into a straw grass inlet, stone platforms had been carved from the mountain so the ships could coast against them, and seafarers could step out on flat ground. She was impressed, gawking about her as the rising cliff walls became alive with the lives of villagers gawking back at her.

Oka and his men moored the ship and she followed them over the platform to a grassy road, where a rising thatched roof and stone tower hung over the field. Women and children gawked at her, some rushed into their homes. Some stood there, their faces pale with horror, gossiping upon themselves. Liv noticed the men behind them tossing nets into the streams brimming in from the sea, they too had stopped working.

She was not one of them. Oka nodded at them all, it was his way to let them know she was not their enemy. However, the leader thought otherwise as she entered the tower room. It sprawled out in to a wide expanse of sandy floor, and pirates and their women alike sat or stood aside long tables, feasting together. The room silenced as she entered, and Liv froze at the sight of a dark-skinned man with pitch black hair and eyes as dark as obsidian.

He was not just tanned from piracy or life at the sea, his skin was beautifully brown to her. She gazed upon him, and she stopped just short of the throne he had erected, and let him wonder upon her too. He had a purple cloth around his head, and his garments were not shrouded in holes or age. He wore leather cuffs, and his boots matched them. His tunic was tucked into his trousers, where a leather belt as thick as his broad sword kissed it. His black hair was loose and silky and spilled over his muscular shoulders and he had golden facial rings on his nose and eyebrows.

He immediately lunged straight up from his chair, gawking at her. He bolted up and faced her, his eyes gazing over her body, lingering on her weapons. He picked up her long blonde hair and smelled it. Then he flung it down and stood before her, his eyes fomented in a mysterious wonder.

"What is this." He demanded. "What are you doing Oka?!" He commanded, but Oka stepped back.

"She came to meet you. She overcame us, my king."

Bortolomeus scoffed in her face, his muscular physique bursting out of his tunic. "This woman forced you." He laughed. "This woman here." He pointed at her.

Oka cleared his throat. "She is skilled with the blade and moved fast. She has favor with the gods."

Bartolomeus paused when he said that, huffing. "She is nothing but a fool to come here." He turned to her, his eyes exploring her facial features.

"What are your people?" He asked, his breath on her face. "Vikings of Scotland."

He paced before her as the room fell to an eerie quiet. "We are Vikings also, but more deadly. Vikings of your lands fear us."

Liv met his stare. "I have no doubt of your prowess. This is why I have come."

He gazed at Oka. "Where are the rest of the crew."

"I killed them." Liv said flatly.

Oka nodded in agreeance. "She slaughtered them like cattle. Tossed the bodies in the sea."

Bartolomeus gasped. "Take her weapons." He stepped back and the room became a mass hysteria as they seized her and stripped off her fur cloak and weapons, and parchment. Liv let them.

Oka laughed at her, the survivors of his crew joining him behind their king. She dismissed them and sighed.

"I need your help to find relics. You may keep any other treasures we find. I have maps to find three of them."

They laughed at her. Bartolomeus scoffed. "You must be very skilled with the blade to have bested half of Oka's crew; I will give you that. You are a fool to think we would allow you the privilege of pirating with us. Your sentence is still death, Viking, for killing my people."

Liv sighed. "Death is nothing. I am giving you one chance to help me."

The room roared in laughter. But Bartolomeus was not laughing, he eyed her with great suspicion.

"You will not like it when I come back." She warned him.

"The dead do not come back." Bartolomeus pulled his broad sword and Liv held her breath.

He plunged it through her chest and she felt it go out her back. Her mouth filled with blood, and she convulsed in pain. Her head spun, her heart raced and then it stopped. She closed her eyes and they let her fall, her blood pooling on the sand.

L iv did not remember them carrying her lifeless body out, but remembered hearing voices. Something burst inside her, as if she was floating in a sea looking down upon her soul. The light was blue, filling the void around her. It changed to a brilliant white and she was blinded by it. She remembered the light whispering her name, telling her to get up. It was a strong voice, filled with masculine authority, but carried with it a weary caution edged with pity.

"Get up."

She twitched.

"Get up."

She took a deep breath.

"Get up!"

Her eyes flew open.

Liv sat straight up as if a hand had pushed her, even as rock pushed into her backside, and her legs twisted behind her. She leaned into her arms and stretched her legs out. She grabbed her aching chest that had healed over, and glared up from the cavern they had tossed her body down into. Her tunic was still wet with her blood.

All around there were bones of the pirates' other victims. The bones stretched from one wall where she lied to the end of this field like death cavern and had been there a long while. She took another deep breath, gazing up at the moonlight cascading hope on her. Her eyes caught a rocky path to her left. They must have walked down part ways with her body and then tossed her into the death pit. She stood up and marched up the path back to the village, her face clenched.

O ka sat at the table with his survivors, their plates piled high of fish, berries, and breads. The ladies passed around the wine vats; their cups stayed full. The room was filled with pirates of higher stature and their women, their laughter thundered around them.

Bartolomeus held his goblet but did not drink it. He gazed around his room full of his people, the food filling the tables, the wine vats never going empty. The golden treasures and fine furniture were piled high aside him as if his rewards were just those empty things. He gazed into the wine at his expression, his handsome dark face and defined features. But he did not smile, even as his earrings and necklace filled the reflection with prosperity.

He sighed to himself just as screams filled the room at the entrance. He jerked his head up to see Liv barge in through the double doors, her tunic still dripping in blood at her chest. Her face firm, her eyes like a seared fire. He froze at the sight of her, even as chills numbed his spine into his heart, pressed into the back of his chair as if to disappear.

Oka froze, spitting out his wine, the woman sitting on his lap sliding off, and many other women pressing behind their men. He gazed around the room, but everyone else had the same expression. The terror on their faces was felt, even as Bartolomeus lunged up from his throne to face her, tossing his goblet aside.

He held his arms out, hollering "Stop!" Just as the tip end of blades began touching Liv's neck.

She glared at the pirates, huffing in their faces. They stepped back, and Bartolomeus approached her with caution, his face stern, his eyes lustful upon her strength. He eyed her up and down, his eyes wavering at her, his jaws clenched.

"What are you?" He whispered, standing away from her, cautious, even as a half-smile crossed his handsome face with superiority.

Liv took a deep breath, her blonde hair disheveled around her shoulders, her blue eyes meeting his like a fire had lit her face up. "Something that does not die." Her voice was loud and echoed.

Bartolomeus sighed. He took a deep breath looking at her, his eyes as wide as the gold bullion he had in his chests behind the tables.

"I need your help." Liv commanded.

The room fell as silent as the dead. Bartolomeus leaned away from her for a moment, his mouth open, his dark eyes wide at her. He held his arms out either side of his finely tuned body, bowing to her, smiling at her ear to ear.

"Whatever you need, my love. I am yours."

The pirates stepped away from her and lowered their swords, their faces ashen as if a horror had come upon them. Liv smiled at him, a dimple showing up the side of her cheeks that had been long gone, her blue eyes sparkling at his face.

She allowed him to gaze upon her, his face lit up with a passion she had not seen in ages. She would take his passion and others who came after him to use it to bend her will, even as one relic she desperately needed would allude her for many years yet.

8

The Heart-Rending Curse

Bartolomeus had a bath drawn for Liv and had given her new clothing. As she soaked in the bath with views of the ocean before her, the pristine turquoise waters roared and flowed like her heart. She wondered how long it would take Erik and Halfdan to find her. She had little time to find the relics, but was confident the pirates would know where to begin looking, especially since she had taken a parchment to show what they were, and she had kept the maps from her grandmother's curse book.

She slid into the brown trousers, her long blue tunic hanging to her knees and buckled around her waist for a long sword. He had women of his village come and braid her long blonde hair atop her head and down her back. Bartolomeus spared no expense to make her happy and give her what she wanted.

That afternoon, he led her out a trail behind his tower through the woods to his seer. The trees twisted over her to form a canopy and moved like fingers interlocking as the sea blasted in a breeze at them. He held her hand leading her, and Liv let him. They walked barefoot and the cool sand refreshed her feet. He was quite the gentleman to her, which was surprising as she had heard horror stories her whole life about the brutal Curonians.

They stopped under the canopy before the woods opened to a rolling plain and rising mountains. "We must find what affliction you have. I cannot help you if I do not know what we war against."

It had bothered Bartolomeus that she was immortal. The only one who could find out why was his village seer. Bartolomeus was a vicious protector when it came to his people, but he was also suspicious and believed if things happened he could not explain, it was an omen.

Liv followed him inside a stone house brimming with windows and views and she gasped at its splendor. It looked as if a breath of fresh air filled this inviting space with hope. She gawked at the wide breadth of this round house that seemed to have eyes all over the plains and forests before she felt eyes upon her.

An elderly woman slithered out from a side room by the table and froze. Liv held her breath. The woman was very short, but her hair was white as snow and filtered down to her waist. Parts of her hair was braided and she had golden beads sewn in the braids. Her eyes were grey and hard like a storm, but her face was soft and her laugh lines evident on sun kissed skin. She wiped her hands on her apron over her long tunic and approached Liv.

"Look at you." She gasped. "Ohhh, look at you."

Liv met her stare. "I do not know what I am."

Bartolomeus took a deep breath and smiled. "My seer, Aldonia, very wise. Whatever afflicts you she will find."

Aldonia pulled up Liv's hands and noticed the runes. She held very still and raked her fingers across them. Her face lost its color and her eyes grew wide as lemons. "I have not seen these in ages, since my grandmother told me the stories from her books."

Liv watched her inspect them and then the old woman sighed. "These are deep. Soul deep."

"What do you see?" Bartolomeus asked, perplexed.

Aldonia sighed. "She has a curse of the heart." She stared at Liv. "Where is your mate?"

Liv pulled back, gasping. "I do not have a mate."

Aldonia huffed. "You do. Or this curse would not have taken you."

Liv watched her walk to the table in the middle of the room and begin pressing herbs. The home smelled of wild honey and citrus and Liv loved it. She felt a warm coziness inside.

"I do not understand." Liv swallowed.

"In order to find a cure, you must tell me your story. What happened to you." Aldonia asked. "I will put on a pot of tea. Please sit."

Bartolomeus pulled out a chair and they sat around the table drinking tea until three pots had been emptied. Liv told them everything about how the curse came and what year it came, and what had happened to them all since. Rain had come and so they were content sitting in the beautiful stone house listening to the comfort of the solitude and pinging sounds hitting the roof.

When Liv finished, she set her ceramic flowery cup and saucer down and waited for their response. The silence became too much to bear at first, until Bartolomeus leaned back in the chair, his face on edge.

"I like older women but, this..." He smiled suddenly; his eyes lit up.

Aldonia lunged her arm over and slugged him in the forearm. "You always play. Do not play with this one, her heart has endured enough."

Bartolomeus sighed, his face flat, blinking his dark eyes. "Damnit."

Liv gazed across the table at Aldonia, but she smiled back, her eyes understanding. "I will tell you the stories I was told my whole childhood."

"Centuries ago, a young seer fell in love and was promised to a warrior. The warrior did not love her and found another. That seer beget this curse in her grief, with her broken heart, and in so doing, cursed the world with the chaos that followed her love, the hunter..."

The room became still and the only sound was the rain falling.

Bartolomeus rolled his eyes. "Surely there were other men at that time."

"You see, she also put a curse on the man she loved. He began to hunt her, but not in a good way. Her curse turned against her, and made him possessive, instead of loving. Us seers know of the story because it has been passed down for generations, but there is a lesson there too."

Liv grew rigid listening, her heart beating to death.

"The curse makes love come at a price. Even with immortality, as powerful as it is, this curse renders the heart broken over and over...."

"It was my great ancestor..." Liv mumbled. "My great ancestor made this curse."

Bartolomeus gawked. "Your ancestor was evil." He widened his enticing eyes. "I must respect her."

Liv gawked at him as Aldonia continued.

"My darling Viking, this heart curse is a cruel one. If you do love Erik, and he loves you, it does not matter. The curse is possessive, so it will not let true love remain. For you, Erik and Halfdan to stop being immortal, you must find the relics and destroy them all."

Liv swallowed, her eyes staring into the cup.

"If you do not find the relics, then the curse renders upon itself, and feeds on Erik as the hunter. It will make him the same evil that beget it, because it is a living thing. It wants to come back and cause chaos. It wants to breathe again..."

A tear fell down Liv's face. "It is anguish that does not die."

Aldonia continued. "If Erik finds you again before you can destroy them, he will take you and imprison you. Just like your ancestor. She died a horrible fate, all because she was not willing to let the man she loved go to love another. You will die together, but miserable in your grief."

Liv dropped her shoulders, leaning into her elbows on the table, listening.

"The immortality will stop if Erik is successful in keeping you. In the end, it will kill you both in your misery for one another, and Erik will be the cause of great sorrow for our world in the chaos he leaves behind."

"Your ancestors warrior came to hunt her, and left much chaos behind. In his grief, he destroyed the whole village and killed nearly everyone. The only reason we have this story is because the youngest sister of that seer escaped."

"There is no worse death than that." Bartolomeus whispered, gawking at what he had just learned. "No worse death than a broken heart."

"Chaos follows him, and the world suffers." Liv sighed.

"When the curse is broken then you will stop being immortal, that is when you begin living." Aldonia added.

Bartolomeus leaned over and wiped the tear from Liv's cheek. And then he met her eyes and smiled into them. "Do not fear, we will help you find the relics."

"Where is the cylinder relic?" Aldonia asked. "The relics must be broken upon the missing runes with the dagger."

Liv lunged her head back and sighed, huffing.

Bartolomeus sneered. "Is it with that Erik who continues to break your heart?! I will kill him." He paused, narrowing his brows. "Never mind. He will not die." He sneered; his eyes wide.

Aldonia sighed at him, turning to Liv. "You will need it. You may have to encounter Erik again after all. Bartolomeus is right, you will have to kill him to make this work."

Bartolomeus blurted out. "I hope you are strong."

Liv gazed out the window to the pitter patter of rain and a fog raised to the windows. "I will kill him again and then take it from Halfdan. I just need to ensure I have all the relics first this time."

Bartolomeus slammed his hand on the table and everyone jumped, their eyes wide. The loud slap echoed and the table jarred and the tea cups fell over. "It is decided! We begin the hunt for the relics at dawn." He shouted.

Aldonia slugged him in the arm again. "Stop doing that! You will break my favorite ceramics and give me a heart death one day."

Bartolomeus grabbed his forearm and gawked at her. "You are strong for an old woman. You scare me."

Liv laughed at them, the most she had laughed in a long time, and then froze when Bartolomeus glared at her too.

"And you. You beautiful Viking woman." He paused, eying her up and down, and Liv held her breath. "You scare me more," He smiled, "much, much more." He laughed with them.

The three of them sat around the table drinking another pot of tea and laughing among one another, and Liv grew wings inside because she was where she belonged for now.

9

The Amber Road of Uncertainty

Liv stood on the bow, her fur wrapped around her shoulders, her axe on her back. Her braids flew behind her as a wild wind pelted them. They led six long boats up the Vistula River from the Baltic Sea. The boats were low-lying and wide, and the dragon heads gaped open with wide mouths at the bow. The pirates rowed in silence behind her, the colorful round shield adornments kissing the sides.

Bartolomeus slithered up behind to join her, his black trousers and tunics adorned with daggers and swords, an axe in his sheath over his head, and a round shield strapped on his back over his axe. He turned to gaze at her, his black cloak trimmed in fur blowing behind him. His face was tanned beautifully, dark, and mischievous, and Liv liked him more and more.

Liv took a second glance at him. He looked dreadful, as did all his Curonians. His black hair blended in with his horrific attire. Even his weapons were engraved and powerful. He stood taller than her, but not by much. He met her stare, his eyes lingering on her face.

"We trade Amber with the Lechitic tribe. The Vistulanians are brave and vicious as we are and will help me protect you until we find the relics."

Liv sighed. "Thank you."

Bartolomeus huffed at her. "Do not thank me yet." He turned to go and then paused.

"What do you want from me then?" She asked him. "In return for you helping me find the relics."

Bartolomeus took a deep breath, staring into her eyes. "I do not want the world to burn in your mate's chaos following you. It is my duty to protect my people, and this is the way I will do it."

She held her breath, and he glared at her, his face hard. "As he hunts you, I will divert him with all my power." He swallowed, looking at her, his eyes bright at her face. He clenched his jaws, turned to the stern, and marched away from her.

Liv turned to face the wind again, tears filling her eyes. She closed her eyes thinking of Erik, missing him. She pressed her hand to her heart and gulped. Her chest ached. Her loins burned for him, still. She swallowed her pain and fears and gazed into a burning sunset on this open plain river system, her guts toiling inside her backbone.

H ours later, they had sailed up the Vistula River and took a left on a tributary to Wiślica. It was the Nida River valley, and Liv held her breath at the city's magnificence as they coasted to shore. A stone church rose at the end of roads. A rising tower seemed to watch the river and its inhabitants. Liv stared at the city and fisherman, the market traders, and the families filling it.

The valley spilled before her and rose in emerald fields of peace, towering evergreen trees shadowing the lands like distant shadows playing with the city. As far as she could see, longboats and fisherman and their families were working along the shores of this river. They toiled on the waters, teaching their kids. The street system was elaborate and well-maintained, and the people living or working dressed like her.

She felt a firm hand on her shoulder and turned to see Bartolomeus smiling at her. "Ready?" He asked.

"I am ready."

She followed him off the ship, and they walked up the wide street, their shadows dancing behind them and their weapons accentuating their already intimidating stances. Everyone in the city was armed, even the women. Liv found them nodding at Bartolomeus, their eyes shifting in curiosity to Liv. Other than that, they paid her no mind.

"Do not fear them. We go to see their king. He is called Henryk. He is very wise but superstitious, and his people are knowledgeable about ancient curses."

He led Liv up the street, turned right, and walked past the massive church. She craned her neck to gaze upon its splendid tower and construction. "I never knew a civilization existed this far across the sea. This is wonderful."

Bartolomeus paused and let her catch up to him. He smiled at her and then pulled her along by her hand. "You can look later, come Viking." He laughed at her.

They walked down a slight hill that ended in a bend of the road in the valley. Stone houses dotted the plains before her under a sprawling forest and streams. A peace overcame her like she was home again in her village, and her heart skipped a beat.

She followed him into this house, which seemed as long as the church. Men in royal cloaks sat in a line as if waiting for them. On either side, tables lined the walls full of fish, bread, and cheeses. Wine vats filled the tables, too, and Liv smelled the pungent aroma of the finery.

But all along the walls stretched behind them were armed men dressed in dark cloaks and tunics. They were fully armed, with axes stuck over their heads and long swords at their sides. Their round shields danced on their muscular backs. The men were rugged and full-bearded, their dark eyes glimmering and vengeful. Liv liked it.

Bartolomeus paused before them, bowing. The man he bowed to perked up at Liv's presence. He had a long white beard and blue eyes.

"Henryk, high king." Bartolomeus adored him.

Liv froze at the sight of him, bowing her head herself. He lunged up from his seat and eyed the men sitting beside him, their faces frozen. Liv held her breath as he approached her. Before Bartolomeus could speak, the king loomed over Liv, grabbed her hand, and stared at the runes.

"You can see them," Liv whispered.

He met her stare, huffing. "Sadly, yes." Then he turned to Bartolomeus and sighed. "Do you have my amber, pirate king?"

"I do. Six ships full."

Henryk paced before them, clasping his hands behind his back and staring at Liv, his blue robes cascading the intricate stone floor. "We call it our gold of the north, this amber. We do much trading with Bartolomeus, and it has made us rich beyond measure. It has given us power and resources to do as we wish."

Then he eyed Bartolomeus. "She has a curse upon her. Am I to assume you come to discuss this? Else you would not have brought a Viking warrior here from the Isle."

Bartolomeus agreed. "I do. She is searching for relics, and I humbly ask for your people's protection until she finds them and lifts this curse."

The men sitting behind Henryk gasped and began talking among one another. Henryk sighed and gazed at Liv, his hands still behind his back.

"What is the name of this curse, dear Viking." He commanded.

Liv swallowed. "The immortali..."

Henryk twisted his face and closed his eyes. "...Curse of the broken heart." He interrupted her.

He turned to his high council and then back to face her. "Chaos follows you with this hunter mate chosen for you. We have no choice but to protect you."

"Hunter mate." Liv swallowed, her eyes wide.

The king let out a raspy, throated laugh, his face gleaming at her, sneering. "Yes, Viking. Yes. Your mate comes for you. He comes for you. He comes for us all."

"He is not my mate." Liv disagreed.

The king froze. "Oh, he is your mate. Else, this curse would not have taken you."

"My ancestor made this curse, and he did not love her. He killed her and destroyed villages to get to her..."

Henryk sighed at her face. "Yes, we have heard the tales. It matters not what the tales say. It matters that you and this man are now warring with an ancient dark power that can kill us all."

Liv closed her eyes as Bartolomeus nodded. "Indeed. The first relic we seek is a gemstone. A king of precious stones, blood red, and magic. We have searched the maps, and it shows Scotland."

"Do you have the map?" Henryk asked.

Liv pulled the map to the first relic out of her tunic, and Henryk took it. He walked back to his chair and studied it, his eyes narrowing and his face wrinkled in frustration. Then he walked back to her and gazed at her runes again, huffing.

"How fitting you have a curse of the heart, and you must find a stone that enhances the unconditional love you must flee..."

Liv froze.

"The blood-red stone is a stone of passions. It controls the heart. Yes, you must find this one first." Then he froze, stared at her sternly, and walked over and laid the parchment map on a table. He gazed at the men, and they immediately got up.

"There are countless caves on the coast of that isle. We have not been successful in its exact location." Bartolomeus warned.

The seven men joined Henryk, gazing at the map. The map showed Scotland, where Liv's village was. It showed the Baltic Sea region with no direction or placement ofcities. Liv never understood the map entirely. All she knew was that one of the relics was in Scotland, and she needed help deciphering exactly where. She needed help this whole time, and Halfdan could not do it.

One of the men standing around the table demanded. "This is incomplete. Are there other maps or parchments?"

Liv jerked them all out and handed them over, and the men got to work placing them. They pointed and talked among themselves, and Henryk stood back and let them, watching Liv. She had a slight headache thinking about the difficult tasks ahead. She closed her eyes briefly, the men's voices echoing through her head and her heart fluttering wildly. She thought she needed to sit down until Bartolomeus pressed a firm grip upon her shoulder and met her eyes.

She opened her eyes and faced him. "How do I find one stone among a vast ocean of them, hidden in caves I know nothing about? It will take a wealth of men to find it."

Henryk turned his head and smiled at her, huffing. "You do not find it. It has already found you, Viking."

He moved out of the way, and she approached the table with Bartolomeus, her face drained of color. Her knees gave out for a moment, and chills darted up her arms looking at the placement of all the maps on the table. It made a picture, and told a story.

She held her breath, gripping her heart and gawking at it. Henryk smiled at her. "You are not so lost after all, Viking."

The three maps she had taken from her grandmother formed a map of Scotland when placed together on the runes. Each map had a rune marking to match one of the ones on hers and Erik's palms, although two were missing. The runes flittered over the pages, and as the Norse words came together, she recognized the word *heartstone*.

She huffed, gazed at it again, and sighed. "That is where Erik left the first time. There are cliffs there. My people never ventured in there due to the dangerous tides."

Henryk laughed a raspy throated hum at her, his old face smiling into hers. "You will need protection in that cave from this man who hunts you. He will have men hunting you by now if he is wise. We will help Bartolomeus protect you."

Liv smiled and bowed her head. "Thank you."

Then the king breathed in through his nose, shaking his head. "You understand we have no choice. As chaos follows you, I expect you to be strong as we find the relics, dear Viking. We have worked hard for our way of life. Would be a pity it falls because of a woman."

Liv nodded, agreeing with him. Her eyes teared up, and her throat formed a knot, but her heart beat as if it were going to kill her.

Bartolomeus smiled at her as the men continued to gaze upon the maps. "Ah yes, the woman. The demise of all mankind."

Liv met his stare, but she was not smiling.

T hat evening Liv soaked in a bath with views of the flowing streams and valley out her window. She soaked until her body felt wrinkly, but her bones were no longer aching. She creaked her neck and stretched her shoulders, then stood up and stepped out of the stone basin, closing her eyes, and stretching her back and shoulders.

When she opened her eyes again, Bartolomeus stood gawking at her naked body, his eyes roving her up and down, his mouth wide open. His black frocks and axe were still on his back, and his black hair spilling down his back in a tail. His dark eyes shimmered at her, his sculpted cheekbones high and clenched.

"Holy goddess of women." He gasped and fell against the door frame as if his knees were weak.

Liv froze as he walked toward her, gazing around to find her cloak, but realized she had put it on the bed. So, she stood there facing him butt naked, her privates and breasts exposed to his hungry eyes. He stood before her and took a deep breath as if smelling her very essence. His face clenched, but his eyes were soft, and he enjoyed the view. Then, he met her eyes and stared.

Liv waited. "Yes, pirate king," Her chest heaving, too late to cover up now.

Bartolomeus grimaced, his eyes wide, pursing his lips. "I am forbidden here." He moaned at her face. "If I touch you, I will surely die, and I do not want to die." He complained.

Then he sighed and moaned, lingering his eyes over her body. "It would be worth it."

He leaned into her lips. As Liv opened her mouth to meet his, he bent back. "But I will die, and that frightens me more than your perfect breasts and curvy hips."

Then he turned away and marched to the door, peering back at her. He grabbed his hard groin and closed his eyes. "Why do you have to be cursed!"

As he slammed the door shut, he belted out, "Do not let me find you naked here again!" He closed his eyes and moaned. "It is not fair." He shook his head, his face twisted in pain.

Liv stood there naked, still, her eyes wide at this spectacle. Then she rolled her eyes. "I cannot even lie with a man. This curse has taken everything from me." She grabbed her cloak to cover up, even as her loins ached.

10

The High Tide of Reckoning

Four months later, the Vistulanian king Henryk had kept his word and given an armed escort for Liv. She stood on the bow alongside Bartolomeus, coasting inland toward a rising cliff. They had their furs on and draped in black clothing and capes, as dark and mysterious as the cavern. Its shadow loomed over the five long boats, thirty-five warriors in each one. They sliced through the waters and headed toward the mouth of a massive opening next to a beach.

She was home again, and her heart soared, but an uneasy quake shook her bones. The one hundred seventy-five warriors lingered behind her as her eyes pressed upon the darkness of the cave ahead them. The cold bit at them as Fall had come, the choppy waters pecking at their ships as the spray washed their faces with bitter salt. They were bitter because they had heard rumors about this cursed woman, and they must protect her until she finds relics to break the curse. If they did not help her, chaos would follow and kill them all.

Liv had not seen true chaos yet, but it had followed Erik. She did not want anything to happen to these people she had come to love in such a short time. They were ferocious and brave, and she felt a kindred spirit with them. Her sorrow increased daily as she also knew she would outlive them all unless she broke the curse soon. She wanted to live and not linger throughout the ages.

They beached the ships, with two lingering offshore, waiting. Bartolomeus led the party with Liv, and when they hiked through the sand to the cave, the men lit torches and readied their bows. It would be a day's journey to explore the cave. The sea roared within it to form a river, and on either side, the rock carvings created by water formed a smooth platform to walk upon.

"We look for a wall of red gems and then dig," Bartolomeus warned.

So, they split up in half on either side, with Liv and Bartolomeus on the same side together, their torch lights filling the space of blackness with a warm orange glow. The thirty men veered to the right of them across the water and disappeared into a side cave. Liv watched them go, her heart beating steady as she gazed around and crept deeper in.

"What lies above this?" Bartolomeus wondered, eying the cavern pillars hanging down upon them.

"There was a village east of here atop the cliff when I grew up. I do not know if settlements still live there. There are forests and springs and endless open rolling plains. A beautiful place." Liv admired.

Bartolomeus turned and stared at her. "Indeed." He turned to lead the men again and paused at an opening by the raging waters flowing aside them. "We could have brought a ship here; this canal is wide enough." He mentioned.

He turned back and nodded, and two of his men turned to leave. "They will do just that in case the worst should happen." He eyed Liv from the side as she followed him, the brisk cold biting her face.

They walked through the cavern opening and found a wall ending the cave. Liv stood and raised her eyes to the ceiling, holding her breath as red gems in the wall gleamed across her face. "This is it. I know the gem is here."

Bartolomeus nodded at his men, and they pulled their axes and began chipping the wall until red chunks of gems spilled at their feet, and an echo filled the cavern behind them. He lunged his head back and walked to the path, peering over the waters with Liv. They watched as wooden shields floated past them and then helmets.

Bartolomeus pushed Liv back inside. "He is here!" He pulled his long sword and stood guard at the opening as the men continued to axe.

Liv's heart raged, and she met the men at the wall, peering at the rock they chipped to help them find the stone. "I know you are here. Show yourself!" She demanded.

"Augh, he has killed them all!" Bartolomeus raged, his face clenched, watching the bodies wash by him from the other side as his men joined him to face Erik.

Liv craned her neck to see shadows looming from the paths and pressed her palm into the rock, and her hand burned. She turned to see Erik standing across the water on the path, glaring at her and the men cutting the rock, his eyes on her. Around him came more Vikings, over forty of them. They crept up on the side where Bartolomeus stood, too. Their eyes were dark; they were burly and fully armed, too, and Liv began to panic inside.

Erik did not pull an axe or a sword but stood still across the water, staring at Bartolomeus and his Curonians, who stood beside him, ready. Bartolomeus nodded at his ten Curonians, and they lunged into the Vikings who had crept up on them. The path became a sword-in-fested blood bath, and both sides were taking losses. The Curonians flew into them and cut them down on the path, pivoting off the rock walls and using the stone as leverage to lunge into them midair.

They pushed the bodies into the water, and Erik took a deep breath and huffed at him. The water was too wide to cross without being swept further into the cavern. He would have to cut them off some other way. The Curonians were proving to be mighty warriors after all.

"You keep someone who does not belong to you, pirate king." Erik scowled, his Vikings glaring at him. "Bring her to me."

Bartolomeus sighed, gripping his long sword and pressing it into the stone at his boots. "Let me think about this." He raised his eyes to stare at the cave ceiling and then dropped them back to Erik's face. "No." His face was flat and firm.

Erik scowled at him. "You will bring her to me, or you all die."

Bartolomeus huffed, his face twisted into a slight smile. "I do not think we will, Viking."

"She does not belong to you, pirate." Erik seethed at him.

Bartolomeus did not smile. "Come and take her. You will meet a swift end."

Erik laughed at him, scoffing.

Bartolomeus smiled. "Ah, yes. The immortal Viking. Erik, is it?" He pointed the tip of his blade at Erik. "You can die though! You will continue dying until we have what we seek."

Erik pulled his long sword, and Bartolomeus watched beside his pirates as the back of Erik's men began walking back the way they came to cut them off at the entrance.

Bartolomeus smiled at Erik's face across the water. "See you on the other side, Viking." His eyes shimmered in malice.

Liv saw a stone sticking out, and the runes on her hand pulled her into it. "Here! Cut it out!" She pointed as a Curonian plunged into the wall with his axe.

As a chunk of the wall fell, Liv pulled at the stone to free it, her palm burning. She had to secure it and get out of there before Erik got her. She was lucky Erik was on the other side of the water, or else they would all be dead, and she knew it.

The Curonian cut it, and Liv pulled the chunk of red gem into her palm. She held it atop her rune hand, saw the shimmering runes inside it, and then the cave shook. She fell back, landing on her butt, her heart chasing in her chest. "What is happening to me." She closed her eyes and shook it off, pushing the rock into the pouch hanging around her neck.

Bartolomeus and his men eyed the cave as it shook and rocks slipped into the water. "Been a joy to meet you, Viking, but we must go now."

As they turned to go and Liv chased out with them, Erik watched her from across the water and gave chase with his Vikings to head them off. Liv met his eyes, and Erik clenched his face. "Liv! No!" He bellowed, following them. "Liv, do not run from me!" He commanded.

Liv stared at him, her heart racing, her stomach fluttering at the sight of him. His Viking clan were intimidating, mighty men like him, and Liv's knees weakened at their presence. The pillars in the ceiling slithered off and fell into the water. They were now dodging them to keep from getting gored alive or smashed.

They raced each other on both sides across the water. Liv began to fret about the encounter because Erik had more men, and they were just as fast as the pirates. They also had more weapons. Liv breathed deeply, lunging around the rocks hitting their paths. Bartolomeus pulled her behind him, yanking her to the opening to beat the Vikings.

A shadow loomed in on them from outside as they all neared the opening together, and a longship catapulted between them, bridging the gap between Erik and Liv. The water would have been shallow enough for them to cross. Erik and his Vikings lunged into the longship from their path. The screeching echoes of blades pinging off one another filled the cavern's opening to the surrounding beaches. The thirty-five Vistulanians met Erik's Vikings in midair on the ship's deck, the Vikings aiming to use it to pivot across the other side to get to Liv.

Liv hollered as Bartolomeus pulled her away from the ship and lunged into the sand up the beach for another ship of theirs to get them. Erik lunged over the Port Bow and jumped into the sand, and Bartolomeus turned to face him. He pressed his long sword at Erik, but Erik just calmly pressed his sword out and pulled his axe. He eyed him with a precision glare, making Liv weak at the knees.

All around her, the Vikings jumped down from the ship's deck, and the Curonians and Vistulanians followed them. The beach became a battlefield as Liv stood amid it, going nowhere suddenly. Her eyes craned to Bartolomeus, who lunged against Erik's blows, sand flying around them as they pivoted around one another. Bartolomeus deflected Erik's blows with stealth precision, pulling a short sword to counter Erik's axe.

Her eyes craned to the Vikings Erik had gathered to help find her. They were such mighty, brave warriors. Then she stared at the Curonians and the Vistulanians, her eyes filled with tears. They were all strong men and a tear fell down her face to her neck as some fell. She pulled out the leather satchel on her neck and gripped the stone against her rune palm. Above them, the cavern shook, the ground quaked beneath them, and the wall caved into the waters atop the ship.

The rocks filled the cave opening, and the ship splintered, sending shards of wood planks darting through the air like arrows. Ten pirates and five Vikings got hit with the slivers, and boulders landed atop them as they fell. Many others were impaled through their arms or shoulders and let out screams of frustration at the inconvenience. Liv opened her mouth to scream, and it was then she saw arrows fill the space in the air over her head aimed at Erik.

Erik had dropped his axe and pulled his round shield as the arrows plunked into it, with one lodging through his leg. He hollered in pain and lunged at Bartolomeus, pushing his sword off his blade. He knocked him off his feet past Liv, his strength pressed into the pirate. Bartolomeus slid into the sand past Liv. Erik gazed at Liv with a clenched face and wide eyes, then tossed the shield off his arm. Liv backed away from him, her eyes wide.

As Bartolomeus pushed himself back up to face him, Erik lunged into Liv at her midsection. He pulled her over his shoulder and ran back to the cave opening. He jumped into the water, dragging her into the deep waters with him at the end of the decimated ship.

Bartolomeus jumped up and watched Liv struggle against Erik as he pulled her into the raging tide. They got swept past the rocks and then disappeared as the beach ended there. There were other beaches, so he whistled for his ship to get him and the survivors and get Liv.

Erik yanked her under by her waist, and they swam with the current past the beach together, even as the air rumbled around them like a quake was hitting the cave again. Liv lunged up for air, her eyes folding to the cliff, and a village was now caving in at sea to the east of the cave. She screamed, watching it, then turned her neck to see Erik rise before her in the sea.

He rose at her face from the water, his eyes marking her like she was prey he had just found. The sea cascaded off his long beard, his furs sticking up like daggers around his neck. He lunged through the water and reached a long arm under it to grab her.

She turned to paddle, but he pulled her with him by her waist, and twisted her around. He wrapped his arm around her neck in the water and swam with her, lingering behind to another beach around the cave-in. She coughed and sputtered salt water out her nose, gripping his strong arm around her neck, helpless. "Erik!" She cried, her legs kicking to stay afloat with him, but she stopped fighting and conserved her energy. She was going to need it to kill him again.

"No." He spat, his voice deep and his grip firm, his breathing intense.

They swam with the tide away from the cave. Erik pulled her onto a beach with him, her heart roaring, her head pounding, their bodies freezing. She pulled herself onto the sand and laid over on her back, gulping air as Erik leaned over her. He stretched her arms out either side of her and held her down, his whole body shaking from the cold.

He loomed over her, and stared at her face, the salt water dripping off his long beard onto her neck. He closed his eyes and then met her stare again, his chest heaving. He raised his head and hollered, moaning in frustration.

"Whyyyy!" He yelled into the heavens. "Why do you run from me?" He bellowed in her face.

Liv met his quivering mouth, and her eyes softened. "I..."

She lunged up and kissed him. He met her kisses, shivering and inhaling her breaths within his own. She tasted salt water from his mustache, his kisses hot and hard against her lips. He raised over her and melted into her open-mouthed kisses, his body stiff and eager, his face pressed hard into hers. He gripped her backside with a strong arm and yanked her harder against him, and if they were naked, they would have given in to one another on the beach.

Then he stopped kissing her to breathe and pressed his mouth against her neck to catch his breath. He lingered his lips on her skin and closed his eyes to suck her neck. Liv did not stop him from kissing her or fighting her anymore. She wanted him to stay atop her forever. So, she lay there with her head back as he sucked the life out of her neck, and his warm breath warmed her skin.

They lay there, gulping in air, wet as the sea lapped at them on the shore. They laid there with Erik atop her holding her down, her arms stretched out as he clasped his strong arms around her wet body, their long hair caked with sand. Liv closed her eyes and found herself leaning her head into his, and their breathing slowed as if they were dancing again. She felt his heartbeat through his leathers and let the sound of him charge her soul.

Liv gulped, her lips dry. "You cannot just let me find the damn relics."

Erik raised back up, his arms clasped around her bottom and waist, his chest pressed atop hers. "I found you. That is all I know." He stared at her face, leaning in to kiss her again. "I only need you."

"Erik..." She gulped.

Liv jerked her head as Halfdan emerged from the end of the beach, gawking at them. He shook his head at them, his eyes wide, his hand clasped to a bow and arrows in the sheath hanging off his arm. He was coming to meet Erik as they had planned.

"Halfdan!" Liv hollered.

Halfdan cleared his throat. "You both could have died. Did you not feel the quake? Chaos has happened."

Liv tried to get up but Erik pressed her still. "Let me up." She blurted out, still coughing in his face from the salt water inhalation.

Erik pulled her up with him. She collided against his chest, and he stared at her, but was not happy. "Give the relic to Halfdan," He told her, still breathless from pulling her through the tides to shore.

Liv gripped it against her chest and sighed, eying Halfdan. "Fine then." She paused as she headed toward him, gazing back at the roaring ocean they had just survived.

She admired it, and they took notice she gazed at the waters. "It is beautiful." She smiled, backing up to Halfdan.

And then she lunged into Halfdan, pulled the bow from his weak grasp, and yanked an arrow from the sheath hanging off his arm. She twisted around in midair as she pressed the arrow atop the nocking point, pulled the string back, and fired into Erik's chest. Erik convulsed and fell, the arrow protruding out the other side, and Liv fell, too. She pulled another one and shot him again through the heart so he had two protruding out his back.

As Erik eyed her and his face twisted in pain, she dropped the bow in the sand, leaned atop her knees, and belted out a scream. "Aughhhh!" She cried, her heart breaking again.

She gripped the gem at her heart and cried into the sky. She had killed him again. She belted out her rage, her body shaking all over. She leaned her head into the sand and moaned in her agony. She clenched her teeth and bit her tongue. And then she raised and cried into the heavens, the frigid coldness shaking her to the bone.

"Whyyyyyy!" She cried, her face tormented in pain.

Halfdan gasped, falling to his knees, too, as Erik died. Liv crawled over to touch Erik, but Halfdan screamed at her. "Do not touch him! Do not," He pressed his long arm out to warn her.

He leaned back and closed his eyes, the sand pooling around his cloak. "Do not touch him, Liv. Just go." He whispered. "You must go."

Liv cried, watching Erik lifeless in the sand. "I love him." She whispered, tears running down her neck.

Halfdan opened his eyes at her, and a tear fell. "I know." He took a deep breath and gripped his heart like he was in great pain. "I know, Liv." He closed his eyes again as he said that.

They sat there broken on their knees together as Erik lay dead between them. Halfdan gazed upon her, a pain bridging between her and Erik. His eyes fell back to the sea, and he saw two longships rowing in at them. Bartolomeus sliced onto the beach in his longboat. He jumped out, his face hard and stricken. It lit up as he noticed Liv had killed Erik, but he also knew Erik would be back. They had little time.

"Go, Liv. Find the other relics." Halfdan warned her.

"I only have maps for two more, and one map is incomplete! I am missing two Halfdan." She worried.

"I know," Halfdan whispered to himself but did not respond to her. He watched Bartolomeus yank her up by her forearms and press her into the ship.

Liv called back to him. "I am sorry." She cried.

Halfdan watched them pull her on board, craned his neck skyward, and sighed. "I am sorry, too."

When he opened his eyes again, he glared at Liv. "I am sorry." He mumbled again, watching her leave.

The pirates had successfully rowed out deep again and were slowly disappearing. Only now they were depleted of men. Halfdan sighed, walked over, and plopped down in the sand beside Erik. He would wait for him to come back to life. He eyed him with great suspicion, thinking. Then he lunged over, yanked out the arrows, and tossed them in the sand.

"Why would you have me meet you here with a bow and arrows? I think you like her killing you, great Viking." Halfdan shook his head.

Halfdan gripped his heart again and sighed. "Everything hurts about you two. It gets worse from here."

He sat beside Erik's body with a knee propped up, watching the sea ebb and flow. His strong face pressed into the sun, letting the waves calm his heart.

L iv sat with her back into the Starboard Bow, shaking from the cold and hurting deep inside. She gazed around. Many of their men died. She had no idea how many Vikings survived. Bartolomeus tossed her a wool blanket, his eyes ever watchful at sea. He gripped his long sword in his sheath, his eyes roaming the world around them. He survived Erik, but Liv was taken in the process. It was too close.

Bartolomeus stared down at her. "You were right to tell me I would not like it when you came back to life."

Liv met his stare, shivering. Her face was pale and caked with sand and loathing.

"I hate it." He added, turning his neck again to stare out. He pressed a long leg against the trim and leaned atop his knee. "We will need more men next time."

Liv would have cried, but she was too cold. She stared at him, closed her eyes, and breathed deeply. She gripped the gem hanging at her heart as they sailed back to the Baltic Sea. In her mind, she wanted to lay on that beach again and let Erik kiss her. In her mind, she dreamed of a time when they could be free to be together. She grasped a lingering hope for a time when Erik would not be compelled to hunt her, and she would not be compelled to run.

Whatever time that was, it seemed far away.

H ours later, Erik sat horseback, watching the sunset alongside Halfdan. The sea glittered like diamonds had burst from the depths but bled out. Dolphins rose up and down in the waters. The sun warmed their faces despite the bitter wind belting in at them. Erik's blue eyes shone almost clear as the sun hit them. He breathed easy and sunk in the serenity of the moment.

"I did not tell her." Halfdan sighed. "I did not tell her everything I found at the library."

Erik did not look at him. "She does not need to know. Not til the end."

Halfdan closed his eyes and dropped his head. "So be it."

"We still have a long way to go, Halfdan. Come, let us bury the dead and eat. Then we must rest. We must be ready. She still has relics to hunt."

Halfdan nodded as a deep, gut-wrenching sigh came out of him. "And you continue to hunt her."

Erik sighed with him, crossing his hands over the saddle, and leaned back into it. "I know, Halfdan. I know." He swallowed, his eyes tearing up. "I need you to help watch me, ensure I do not enslave her."

Halfdan closed his eyes and shook his head. "I hate this curse."

Behind them, the surviving Vikings had started the fires to burn the bodies they could find, not crushed under stone. Behind them laid endless waste of a cliffside village tossed into the sea. The chaos filtered behind them for miles.

Halfdan's mind kept replaying what he had found with the third relic, as the parchment showed the number DCCXCV. The third relic is from the year they raided the abbey, and his mind hurt thinking about it. If he was right, when Liv's ancestor made the curse, she created it so the relics would not have been made yet. So, the curse would linger on regardless, bringing chaos, hence why it was so cruel.

To Halfdan, it was not the fact the third relic may not exist yet. What bothered him the most was what he was destined to do to break it.

11

The Heart of Great Compromise

L iv sat with her back to the door, her long dress spilling to her ankles. She sat with her knees up and barefoot, gazing upon the rolling plains of the house Bartolomeus had given her. She sat with her arms crossed over her knees, and her long hair spilled down her back, the humidity of the beach curling her hair to her waist. She heard footsteps behind her and knew it was Bartolomeus, but she did not acknowledge him.

He brought her a pot of tea and food on a tray and set it down on the bed, and then he joined her at the window, sighing. "You have eaten very little since we got back. You need your strength, immortal or not."

Liv sighed at him. "I am sorry for the losses."

He stood looming in at her, his face calm and resolute. "We lost many," He paused, sighing, "the Vistulanians have now made demands because of you."

Liv eyed him, waiting.

"This puts me in a predicament I was not expecting." He warned.

Liv thought she was going to be sick. "What?"

"With the king and his court knowing what you are, they need a legal proclamation you remain invested in us and our future until the curse breaks."

"What does that mean?" She fretted.

He pursed his lips and stood gazing out the window. "You will be my wife. It is the only way I can protect you and secure men for our mission. It would be a legal order through our kingdoms."

Liv swallowed.

"I know you are immortal and that I will die one day." He turned to stare at her. "A contract. It will help unite our people so they can continue helping you. It will combine all our vast wealth and resources together to break this curse."

Liv pressed her face into her elbows and sighed. "This is the type of marriage I have been avoiding," She closed her eyes, "I die all over again."

He sighed. "If you do not break this curse and outlive us, moving forward, our laws will be written that you choose your husband. Contract only. To continue securing our allegiance, you must choose a husband of our people only."

He sat down next to her. She leaned her head into his and sighed, tears falling. He leaned in and kissed her head and then stared at her. "I saw your pain on the beach when you killed him."

It was then that Liv leaned up to look at him. Bartolomeus pressed his hand to her face and wiped her tears. He then grabbed her face and stared into her eyes. "I cannot imagine killing someone I love." He whispered. "I can only imagine your pain."

Liv closed her eyes and cried. Her tears fell upon his fingers as he held her face in firm palms. He pressed his forehead into hers and closed his eyes. "I am not the husband you seek." He whispered, his face clenched as if he was in pain.

She met his eyes as he leaned back and stared at her. "But I will give you the world and pleasure you until my dying breath. There will never be a moment within my power I will not fail to bring you joy."

Liv cried at his face as he continued. "Until I die, as you linger on, I am here for you." He kissed her forehead again and wiped her tears.

Then he sighed at her face again and stood up, pointing to the teapot. "I have cakes and fruit for you. Eat something. You grow weaker by the day, and I need you strong. We still have relics to hunt, and your mate still hunts you."

Liv wiped her face again, and her eyes followed him to the door. Then, he turned again to face her. "He loves you, you know."

"How..."

"Ohhh, we men know when another man loves a woman." He looked around as if thinking. "A powerful aura follows them, and we can see and smell it. Like magic. His aura for you is so powerful there is nothing that will break it, not even this damn curse."

His tanned face glowed at her. "I saw it in his eyes."

She pressed her fingers to her neck and closed her eyes. It was black, blue, and sore. She was not so sure next time that she could resist Erik. It was getting harder to fight the urge not to stay with him, but she was becoming close to Bartolomeus as the days passed. He let her be the free version of herself she had always wanted to be, and he made her laugh.

"I crave your happiness until the curse breaks and my are people safe." He whispered. "Our success together depends on this."

Bartolomeus took a deep breath and stared at her. "He will destroy everyone and everything to get you. That makes him the most dangerous power in the world." He turned and left her all alone.

Liv glared outside. "I am forbidden to love. I am forbidden to lie with a man. I am forbidden to live. I cannot even die to get some peace."

She clenched her fists so her knuckles turned white and gritted her face into the horizon. "So be it." Her eyes were lit on fire as a torrent of pain burned through her insides and lingered somewhere in her heart. She craned her neck back to stare where Bartolomeus had gone and sighed.

I n the following weeks, Liv watched as the city became a bustling reprieve of lush exoticness and elaborate decoration as the leaders and kings prepared for the wedding and the feast afterwards. Liv took a deep breath, gazing upon the beauty of the Viper's bugloss and Scotch heather flower arrangements lining the path. The purple and pink blossoms filled the air with sweetness and hope. But Liv knew there was no hope.

She was marrying, in contract only. It was something she never wanted and would have rather died. But she could not die either, so she took a deep breath and watched the busyness around her as if time stood still anyway. King Henryk and his leaders and warriors had accompanied him to Bartolomeu's city, and they had spent the better part of the week drawing up the contract.

For Liv to continue securing pirate forces and protection, she must commit herself to a husband of their kingdoms. She had a choice not to be intimate with them or consummate the marriage, but she also knew that would be hard. She craved intimacy and needed it, as it was carved into her backbone.

As the night before the wedding to Bartolomeus drew closer, Liv sat on the private beach below the harbor and watched the sun set like raging diamonds. The water gently lapped at her toes, and the sand was cold and soft. She breathed in the beauty and let it sing to her soul, her heart swimming in hopes she dreamed of. She leaned back in her loose nightgown tunic and let the sunset kiss her body, her blonde hair flowing to the sand at her bottom.

Bartolomeus lingered up to her and plopped down aside her, gazing out. He stretched his legs out and leaned into his naked arms, his chest heaving. She eyed his handsome face, high cheekbones, and long black hair. She admired his brazen nakedness around her as he was only wearing loose trousers. Their feet met in the sand, and she noticed she was getting a sun kissed tan like him. He met her eyes with his own, sparkling as if some devious humor lingered inside him.

"It is beautiful here. I love it."

He sighed and gazed back out. "Yes, this beauty invigorates me."

"You gave this to me." She whispered.

He gawked. "You came to me. This beauty is free. Fate has brought you here. You will have some peace here til the curse is broken."

They sat there in silence, enjoying the view, lingering into one another as if the world had blessed them with a subtle moment of comradery.

"Will you forgive me for killing you? When you first came?" He wondered.

Liv smiled. "I knew you would. I needed your help, so my coming back was the only way to get it."

He laughed at her, shaking his head. "I see."

"I cannot marry you by contract only," Liv mumbled. "That does nothing for me."

Bartolomeus clenched his teeth. "Is that so?"

"You are not the man to sit on something and not enjoy the fruits of your labors. I am not that woman either."

He smiled. "Also, true."

"We are at an impasse." She wondered.

Bartolomeus smiled and huffed, thinking. He pursed his lips. "We marry in the morning. You ready, Viking?"

She half smiled. "Are you?"

He stared at her. "That is not what I asked." His face lit up, and then he turned his body to face her, his naked chest heaving.

She swallowed, sighing into the sunset. "No."

He laughed at her. "Good. You will always be on your guard if you are never ready." Then he lunged into her waist and pulled himself on top of her, pushing her into the sand. "But not right now." He smiled, his long black hair looming around her, his pecs and biceps flexing against her.

Liv gasped. He kissed her, and she met him back, her heart beating wild. Then he raised over her and rushed to her lips again, kissing her with an ambitious, open mouth. Liv met him there as he sunk between her legs, roaring into him with her kisses. She breathed wild, her eyes wide as he gripped her with strong hands.

"You said you were forbidden to touch me..."

He breathed on her lips. "I said I was forbidden to touch you there. Took everything in me to walk away from you. That was a long, hard night."

"I would rather die than take a husband I am forbidden to enjoy." Liv smiled at his face.

"I can walk away from you no longer. Cursed or not." His eyes met hers, his face lit up and clenched. "I will ravish you til my dying breath." He moaned against her neck, his strong hands grasping her thighs as if she was a slippery rope.

Liv moaned as a surge of desire lingered within her that would not go out, and her excitement grew. She let Bartolomeus ravish her on the beach. As the sun fell, the crimson sun doused their bodies in shimmers of blood. Bartolomeus breathed in deeply of a woman he was destined never to keep. A gem he had taken.

The hard truth about Bartolomeus is that he knew it. After the battle at the caves, he was willing to die for it. He would enjoy his life with Liv regardless of her destiny to another. As the sun disappeared on the horizon, they lingered into one another on the sand.

Their moans filled the gap between the ocean waves, lapping in at their naked hips like a gentle breeze had touched them.

T hat following morning, as the sun rose, Bartolomeus led Liv hand to hand to the isle on a different beach. He pulled her gently with him, his face lit up in passion, his eyes upon her as if he had found a priceless ruby. He pulled her hand to his lips and kissed it as she walked with him.

She followed him, her face smiling into his eyes, her future led by a pirate king. They walked under a canopy of twisty trees to the pristine beach together.

He had filled her fingers with dainty golden rings to match his, he had adorned her with a golden necklace and earrings. They walked barefoot together, he in his royal robes and she in a long draping gown of brilliant whites and teal blues. It hung off her tanned shoulders, accentuating her curves. Her hair was loose down her back and kissed with golden clasps, and his hair was long down his back and kissed in silver beads.

Adonia stood and recited the vows as King Henryk, his warriors, and his people gathered all up and down the beach. They were holding bouquets of the purple and pink flowers, and purple petals lined the path where they walked. As they stood there, Bartolomeus was handed a golden crown, a sliver of a lacey adornment. He smiled at Liv, and nodded, and she bowed and let him lay it on her head.

Then she took a silver crown and laid it on his head as he bowed to her. His eyes never left hers. Then King Henryk stood before them and they signed the proclamation into law before the people. When they finished signing, Bartolomeus pulled Liv into him by her waist and kissed her ferociously as the world around them cheered.

As they stood there, Bartolomeus took her face gently in his fingers and gazed into her eyes as she melted against him. They melted together and swung into a gentle dance as if a wind controlled them. He kissed her lips again and whispered, "Hello, my wife. My strong, beautiful wife. Even if for a moment in time. I gladly take it..."

Liv let his gaze linger on her, the sun warming their faces as the ocean kissed the sand. "Even if for a moment..." She replied and kissed him back, a part of her breaking inside.

The people celebrated. They gathered on the beach and lingered in the city, dancing. They feasted the week away with their rye bread, wild game, smoked fish, and platters of berries, mushrooms, and nuts. The wine vats stayed full. Their bellies were as full as their hearts and the celebration of hope for their people.

Their joy filled the horizon, and for a moment, Liv lived. She breathed. She loved. She danced. She let this pirate king love her and fill her with passion and peace she had never experienced before. For twenty years, Bartolomeus doted upon her and loved her with all that he was.

But this curse was a cruel one of the heart and would not let love rest.

12

A Feast of the Rune Stone, 20 years later

Erik stood on the Starboard Bow with his knee up, his bulky frame leaning into it, peering out at the Baltic Sea. It was full on Winter now, and his fur cloak hung on him as if he had been born of a beast. He narrowed his blonde brows as the bitter wind ate at his braided hair, the black liner under his eyes shadowing his face to show a sinister maliciousness.

His thick hair rose on his head braided in rows down his back. He had shaved the sides of his head, and his beard was longer. His beard was braided down his chest, too, adorned with golden rings.

Erik was plenty warm enough in his wool trousers and leather boots. His embroidered knee-length tunic hugged his magnificent warrior frame. Behind him, thirty-five Vikings rowed. Behind them, twenty-two long ships followed through an endless fog as they sailed through the cold directly into Svealand, his family's home. This is where he came from.

Halfdan popped his head up from the galley, his eyes peering around at the men and the cold. Erik turned to him, his hand on the hilt of his long sword, his broad axe on his back under his shield. "Come, Halfdan. The cold will not kill you."

Halfdan huffed. "That is what you said last time. Let me know when we get to the Varangian Guard." Halfdan was wearing a fur cloak and dressed like the Vikings, but he did not like it. He preferred his long wool tunic of the monks and a simple wool cloak. He had no choice anymore since he had to follow Erik, and they did not know where Liv was. It had been twenty years already.

Erik smiled at him, his face older, and his body bulk and muscle mass the most defined he had ever been. He clenched his high jawline and his fist atop his knee, his Yggdrasil tree tattoo kissing the top of his palm. The tattoo rolled up his arm and twisted around like branches sewn into his skin. He took a deep breath and peered out, leading his Vikings toward an end goal.

He had been meticulous the last twenty years, training and picking Vikings for his missions. He had thousands. Erik's heartbeat was steady and strong sailing to Mälaren Valley, where the dense forests kissed the region and the lake spilled into the Baltic Sea. He was meeting the brutal Varangian Guard to annihilate the Curonian pirates and take Liv. No matter what happened, he would get her. He would keep her this time, and the Curonians would all die.

L iv stood on the Port Bow with her pirate crew of thirty-five, rowing silently behind her. Her eyes were shrouded in black up to her brows, and her long locks had been braided atop her head and hung down to her buttocks like a whip. She wore a leather tunic over chain mail hanging down her muscular arms, a short spear and axe crossed on her back over a thick fur pelt. She gripped her long sword hanging from a wide leather belt at her side and pressed her daggers into her boots.

She stood and peered at the lake filling the Mälaren Valley, its tributaries spread out like fingers and glowing in diamonds in the night. The sun would be up in a few hours, so they pressed forward in their lone ship, ever watchful, with Liv's presence drawing the Varangians. She knew they were followed, and as her senses pricked up her spine, her mind wandered to Erik. She still needed to get as close to the relic as possible.

She needed a rune stone, and the maps King Henryk's leaders had interpreted showed it would be on an island in the valley along the river. The cylinder Halfdan had kept all these years, which was the source of their curse, had missing runes, with one being a rounded object. The rune stone would be smooth and have the missing rune for the cylinder relic.

She pressed a knee on the railing and stretched her leg, her split wool gown showing her form-fitting trousers underneath to her fur lined boots. She found it odd that this valley was where Erik's people had come from and that the rune stone she needed would be here. She pressed her tanned face into the bitter Winter wind and squinted her eyes in the darkness, waiting.

Moments later, the skies lit up with flaming arrows.

Liv ducked by the ship's side, and her pirates raised their shields, the flaming arrows plunked into them and burned, flickering flames lighting their faces up. It sent the darkness into the light as they coasted closer to an island off the tributary they had sailed into. Across the lake from another tributary emerged a horizon full of long boats and Vikings, their arrows aimed at them.

Behind them came a bellowing horn call into the morning, and the tributary they had sailed in filled up with Varangians. Their fur pelts and black eyes were as dark as Liv's, and more sinister. Liv perked her head up from the bow and peered out to see Erik leading his Vikings across the lake at her. She widened her eyes at the sight of him, her heart fluttering.

He had matured also. He was broader and more muscular. While Liv's men were protecting themselves from taking hits with their shields, Liv stood up to face the Vikings. They paused shooting arrows as Erik noticed her, his face clenched, his eyes recognizing her. She saw him lean into the bow, his eyes wide at her, and he clenched his fists. Liv glared at him for a moment and then ran to the back of the ship, and jumped up on the Starboard Quarter, and dove into the icy water.

Liv hit the freezing waters and held her breath, emerging and shaking. Then, she swam to the island as her ship pivoted in front of her. Behind the Varangians shouts echoed into the dawn as arrows filled the gap between them and the Curonians coming up behind them. They slithered up behind Erik, too, and began firing upon the Vikings, and the morning dawn became as black as night with darting arrows as the Curonians drew their attention away from Liv.

Liv took a deep breath and when she felt the rocky ground beneath her, she walked out of the water and pressed into the island's foliage. Her heart beat steady, but her emotions were desperate. She had to find the relic and get back out of there in one piece. She lunged through the forest canopy and over shrubs, following the memory in her head of what the map had shown.

In the middle of the island was a cavern. A waterfall crested back into the lake with a hidden cavern. She shook from the cold, her attire heavy and soaked, but she slung herself to the middle of the island. As she neared the middle, a boulder rose surrounded by Evergreen trees, and a light dusting of snow crept up on her. She paused, glaring at it, her teeth chattering, and walked around the boulder to a cavern opening and steps leading down.

The sun was up now and another horn bellowed behind her on the water. Shouts and screams of death echoed, and she closed her eyes and sighed. This was a bloody curse and she hated it. She peered into the darkness, her eyes catching a glimpse of light at the bottom where the falls opened, and she plunged down the steps carefully.

The wind pelted in at her, and her head ached from the cold. She would prefer to be on her warm beach half naked, soaking up the sun sea views than this. She blamed Erik for his hunting her. She blamed this stupid curse for her having to chase all over the world to find relics, with many of the leads being dead-end ones. She leaned into the cave wall and breathed deeply, her lips burning from the cold.

As she lingered longer down the steps, the roaring sounds of waterfalls rushed through her ears and vibrated her spine. She stopped at the end of the steps and gazed back up to the black hole which she had just come from. She pressed forward on a path where the falls lunged before her, and paused. She stared at the beauty and danger, drawn to it. She melted against the wall, still shaking from the cold, and met a dead-end wall of runes.

The falls kissed the wall that towered over her, and in the middle at her face lied a smooth round stone with the missing runes the cylinder relic needed. She pulled her dagger from her boot, pried it out of the wall, and stared at it, her insides shaking. The ground shook beneath her as she gripped it in her rune palm. She widened her eyes and pressed it into the leather pouch hanging around her neck, and then turned to face Erik, pressing his blade against her chest.

She froze at the sight of him.

He was soaked, and his eyes were upon Liv as if a Winter storm had come inside him. His mighty fist clenched around his hilt and the veins in his hand popped up. He clenched his jaws at her face and loomed over her. He was Viking through and through, only this time, worse. She backed away from him against the wall, her chest heaving.

"Give it to me." He demanded, pressing the blade into the soggy furs at her chest.

"No," Liv whispered in his face, her lips chattering.

"You think I will not kill you, Liv?"

Liv leaned her head into the wall, her eyes following his lips. "You have killed me over and over, Erik."

Erik pulled away from her, his eyes wide. "The feeling is mutual." His voice deep and echoing. He pressed his free palm out to her. "The relic. Now."

Liv took a deep breath and sighed. "You will have to kill me."

Erik sighed, shaking his head. "You are the one running in this curse."

"You are the one chasing me! You know the curse is forcing you to hunt me more and more. To keep me from finding the relics to rid us of this." She moaned, her lips chattering to the cold. "I want us to live, Erik. Just let me go so I can get the remainder and free us of this."

"Do you have any idea how tormented I am because of you?" His voice cracked. "The years linger on, and my heart dies, over and over. I cannot rest."

Liv gazed at him. He was still handsome and strong. She stared into his eyes, those beckoning blue eyes that always drew her to his defined face.

"You do not know the torment I have. I cannot forget." She warned him, her face hard. "You will not take this relic unless it is over my dead body."

Erik closed his eyes and pursed his lips. "You do not understand, Liv. You are not the one who breaks the curse. Halfdan is. The curse leads you to find them, but Halfdan needs the relics, and once you find the third relic, there are two more which are not..." He paused, his head turning to see Curonians rush down the steps, followed by Vikings.

Liv gasped as Bartolomeus split them wide open, his pirates pressing into Erik to drive her away from Liv. The Vikings pressed down the path at them, and Liv found herself pulling her long sword to defend her husband as Erik pressed into him. Erik lunged into Bartolomeus and growled while behind, them the path filled with Viking and Curonians fighting one another.

"You again?!" Erik sneered.

Bartolomeus huffed, blocking Erik's strike. "Ah! The immortal Viking!" He laughed in his face. "You have aged very little! Still terrifying to look at!"

Erik faced him off, smiling. "You have aged pirate king. Still ugly."

Bartolomeus sighed, pressing his blade out. "I have aged happy. You are in torment. I see it in your eyes, Viking!"

Erik glared at him. "I am not tormented."

Bartolomeus scoffed, rolling his eyes. "Tell me, Viking, does your immortality feed you joy? I do not think you are joyous. You are missing out..." He smarted off.

Erik growled and lunged in at him, and Liv pressed her blade atop Eriks and pinged it away from Bartolomeus. As Erik scowled at Liv, she pushed into him and he blocked her strikes, his face clenching at her. Bartolomeus jumped in to join her, and a Viking lunged a blade through his back. Liv heard him gasp for breath before turning and shoving his blade through that Viking's shoulder. The Viking hollered, and Bartolomeus kicked him back with his boot.

As Erik turned to face them both and block their strikes, Bartolomeus lunged between him and Liv and pulled her through the falls by her waist. Erik hollered as they disappeared over the falls.

"No!"

Erik turned to follow them as a wall of Curonians flanked his Vikings. He had no choice but to engage them and fight.

Liv held her breath again as they slid down the falls together and hit the bitter waters. She lunged up in the water to face her husband, and they let the flowing rapids pull them downstream toward a shore on the lagoon. They swam to the shore, the ice lapping against them, and lay there, freezing. Bartolomeus gripped his stomach and took a deep breath, shivering all over, sighing at her face.

Liv lunged up when she noticed his deep wound. "No. No!"

"I am getting too old for this, my love." His voice shook, his lips chattered. "When we get home, I want to retire and ravish you on the beach til I die. Does that sound good to you?" He turned his face to her, his eyes full of laugh lines, his black hair with strips of gray. But his face was stricken with pain, and his voice weak.

Liv gasped, gripping his stomach in her palm, trying to stop the bleeding, desperate inside. "Time to go, pirate king." She pulled him up, their bodies shivering, and marched him to a tiny sliver of a forest away from the island to a tributary where their long boat awaited them. They would sail back out of the lake into the Baltic and go home.

Behind them for miles, the Curonians who survived to escape made their way back to the Baltic, and the ones who met their bitter end filled the waters with dead, frozen bodies. But they were not the only dead in the waters. The Vikings had taken losses, and the Varangians, too. And the losses were greater than they had all anticipated. The Curonians had proven once again that numbers do not defeat them.

Hours later, the pirates saailed them home. The cold Baltic ate their pride. Bartolomeus lay against her lap, and she leaned her head over his. The pirates had given them dried furs to ward off the cold, but

Liv did not care if she froze to death anymore. Bartolomeus's blood pooled around her on the deck, and she gripped his now weak, bloody grasp within her own and held him in her arms, shivering in pain.

"You have been a good husband to me." She cried, her lips quivering.

"I lived happy with you, my love." A tear fell down his cheek, his eyes smiled in hers, and then he grew silent.

His hand went limp in her palm, and she watched his eyes die inside. Liv pressed her face against his. Her eyes roared in frozen tears upon his cheek. She leaned into his lips and kissed him one last time.

"I lived too." Her voice cracked. A cry she never knew could exist burst out of her as she whispered against his face. "I lived because of you."

She went weak against him and cried against his head. Her shoulders slumped in defeat as her body convulsed in anguish. A fog rose around them as her breath froze in midair, her moaning cries filling the ship.

13

The Cursed Hearts

Erik watched from the shoreline as warriors pulled bodies from the water. Long boats were sinking, still alight with flames from burning arrows plunked into them. He had changed into dry clothing as campfires burned behind him so the Vikings and the Varangian Guard could bury their dead and do last rites. Halfdan had sailed in to join him to make camp for the night, even as snow fell upon them.

Erik was restless. The Curonians had dealt them harsh blows and had increased their numbers to help Liv, which was why she got away. Erik saw the blood all over the pirate king, and wondered if he survived. He thought about the way Liv looked at the pirate too, and began questioning if she loved that man. He stood there over the bloody waters, crossing his arms and glaring at the devastation. His heart beat steady, but his knees were weak.

"I cannot rest. I love her." He swallowed. "I love her so much it grieves me."

Halfdan sighed. "I take it she got away with yet another relic? This will not end well if she does what I fear she will do."

Erik shook his head. "I keep failing with her, over and over. No matter how much I want to take her or the relics, I cannot win this curse. Something holds me back."

Halfdan shook his head and glared up at Erik, his face hard. "That is because you truly love her, Erik! The warrior of this original curse did not love the seer. There may be hope yet."

Erik watched Halfdan march away from him to join their survivors around the fire. A fire lingered within him, itching to get out. He clamped his fist over the hilt of his sword hanging by his side, his eyes folding over the lake and the warriors still in their ships patrolling the waters for bodies. The lamps lit up the waters and their reflections.

He closed his eyes and remembered gazing upon Liv when he found her at the rune wall. His eyes had lingered upon her backside and magnificent weapons, her hands working diligently with the dagger to dig out the stone. Her hands shook from the cold, and water had drenched where she stood, dripping wet. When she turned to see him, her eyes filled his soul with a resonate pain he could not describe.

Erik opened his eyes and breathed her in deep, letting his tears fall down his face, his heart busting inside.

The part of the curse he hated most was the fact he could never rest.

L iv stood on the beach as the sun set upon Bartolomeus. The village had gathered around him to mourn their king. They all lined up along the beach and stepped knee-deep into the sea. They held their lanterns and placed them upon the gentle waters, and the sea breathed alive with flickering light. Liv bent down and kissed his lips again, and whispered. "Thank you for letting me live."

She stood back as two pirates pushed his body out, and a gentle ripple followed him. She watched him leave her in the crimson sunset, and a part of her died inside. The lanterns followed him, dimly lit and kissing the waters around his flower-laden body, his royal blue and white robes wrapped around him.

Behind her, a row of pirates let their flaming arrows go once Bartolomeus had reached afar out. Liv watched his body burn in the sunset, the flames engulfing him as the sun dropped beyond the horizon. Liv stood there and crossed her arms over her body, her heart racing to her knees. She just lost a husband. She did not mean ever to marry, but it happened. The union had gotten her two relics so far.

The union had given her a moment of peace. Bartolomeus had brought her joy and passion she had never experienced before. She had been free because he made sure she had that choice.

Then her mind went to Erik, and she felt him upon her as if his memory had seared into her soul. She closed her eyes and remembered how he gazed at her at the rune wall under the falls. His eyes screamed, filled with a resonate pain. Even though he was indeed powerful, he did not force her. She dropped her head to her chest and cried, her moans echoing over the beach. She cried for the husband she just lost and cried for the true love she could never keep.

The part of the curse she hated the most was being the last to forget.

14

The Place of Tuscan Shadows

A valley kissed a rolling plain under puffy clouds, and Liv took a deep breath of its beauty. She meandered down a cobblestone street between stone houses with clay-tiled roofs. She rested at the end of a lane against the hillside where a townhome rested within it. She smiled.

"This is perfect. This will work until the curse breaks."

She met hundreds of pirates in the Tuscan village, her eyes rolling over the farms, the lake at the bottom, the endless expanse of freedom from the rising mountains above them. The street spilled down the hill and rested in the valley, giving her a bird's eye view. She also owned it. She and Bartolomeus had bought it, and he deeded it to her.

Her people were busy in the streets behind her settling in, and she would make this a second home for many of them. It would work great because it was safe. Erik would never find it, and she could safely hide the relics she had found so far. Once she had them, she would break them upon the cylinder relic as soon as she took it from Halfdan.

She turned around and stared at the pirates busy in the streets cleaning, hauling in supplies, and preparing for the evening feasting. Liv sighed. Bartolomeus would have enjoyed feasting with her and then making ravishing love to her through the night. Liv sighed, thinking about him. She would never forget him or what he had taught her about living life to the fullest. She walked into the townhome, shut and locked the door, breathing in the stale air. It needed to be cleaned and furniture, but she would make it a home nonetheless.

She marched upstairs to her room and bent in front of the picture window overlooking the town. The room was simple and painted in earthen hues and tons of light, and she loved it. The bed was cozy, and there was a painted art piece of the beach Bartolomeus had given her one year for their anniversary.

She pulled her dagger and began cutting at the plaster in the wall to hide the relics. So far, she had gotten the ruby gemstone and the smooth rune stone. She still needed a key, as the maps showed a golden box with a key in it. The cylinder relic Halfdan had on him was missing runes that matched the relics she had taken, but she still needed the dagger to break them upon the cylinder.

She had no idea where it was, and now Bartolomeus was dead. Erik had failed from the beginning to find it. Finding the relics was taking a long time it seemed, even with skilled pirates all over the world searching maps and treasures. She pulled out a chunk of wall, placed the two relics between the beams, and then pushed the plaster back.

She sat there on her knees and peered out over the emerald rolling plains, her people busy in the streets. Her heart lingered, worried about Erik and Halfdan. It had been another year, but since Bartolomeus had died, it seemed to linger longer than usual. Liv questioned if it was because she did love that pirate king in a way.

Next month, she was sailing back to the Lechitic tribe. The Vistulanian's new king ensured Liv would continue honoring the agreement and take another husband from them. They had given her a year to mourn. Liv took a deep breath, wondering which man they would have chosen for her. He would need to be strong and brave because he would eventually die, like Bartolomeus did. She nodded her head and closed her eyes in annoyance at her circumstances.

"How many husbands must I endure before I die in this curse or break it?" She pondered, dropping her head to her chest and folding her hands across her lap at her knees.

"What would happen if I just go to Erik," She questioned. "What would happen if I find this other relic and break them all on the cylinder..."

She talked to herself, the sun beating in on her and warming her face. The more she talked, the more her heart hurt. The more her knees felt old and creaky like her soul. She plopped over and sat on her hip, her eyes lighting up from the sun hitting her face, her head hurting. She had no choice but to see Erik again. She needed him to find the dagger still. She needed Halfdan to get to the cylinder relic.

She would see them again in time. But a big part of her missed them both, and as time lingered on, she wondered how much longer she could go without Erik in her life for good. Halfdan had become like a brother to her, and the longer she sat there, a pang gnawed her deep inside.

Next year would be the year 900 A.D. The world had changed so much already since she and Erik raided the Abbey. She wished she had never grabbed that relic or fallen in love with Erik. She wished she was back on the beach with Bartolomeus. Her mind played over and over the memories, the moments, the pain. She could not forget and it was driving her mad.

She sat there, with the sun making her face sweat, until she lay over on her side on the cold, hard floor and fell asleep. Her mind played memories over and over in her dreams. Then, something broke like a dam deep within her, and flooded her soul.

It pried itself into her heart, burst through a door in her mind, and watched her. Not only did it watch her, but it wanted her. She opened her eyes for a moment and saw Erik's eyes looming upon her. A fear reverberated off her spine and then settled into a desire to kiss him. Liv lay in a deep sleep on the floor, her soul lit afire of this unending, powerful force stalking her from the deep vats of her mind.

I n the evening, Liv awoke to a face looming over her and a voice she recognized as her general. "Liv, are you ill?!" Alo questioned, his long black beard dancing above her and his dark eyes as wide as his sunburnt forehead.

Alo pulled on her shoulder to get her to move, and Liv opened her eyes. "I cannot believe I fell asleep like this." She gasped and let Alo help her up.

He laughed at her. "If I did that, my back would kill me. I came to fetch you for the feasting tonight."

Liv stretched her back and widened her eyes. "Oh, okay. See you and your family there."

"Are you feeling well?" He worried, eying her. "You have endured much sorrow."

Liv rubbed her eyes. "I slept. That is all I know."

Alo smiled at her, turning to go. "After you stuff your face, I recommend sleeping in the bed tonight, okay?" He laughed as he walked down the stairs, and Liv laughed.

But then he turned and mentioned, "I will have the carpenter fix your front door right away. It was swinging wide open. Looks like the hinges were pried loose, probably from the storm we had last night."

Liv stopped laughing and nodded as he disappeared down the stairs. "I know I locked it." She mumbled to herself as a sudden chill danced up her arms.

Liv washed up and changed into a long, flowing gown with short sleeves, and left her hair long and flowing. Spring was in the air, and the cool breezes blasting through the plains were a welcome reprieve to the harsh winter her pirates had endured there. They planned a grand feast to celebrate Liv taking another husband tonight, symbolizing them staying united and putting Bartolomeus to rest for good.

She hoped her pirate scouts had found maps to help her find the dagger since Erik was unsuccessful. She had lingered in this Tuscan village for weeks, hoping to get news, but nothing so far. Liv knew Erik would still be using his Vikings to hunt her Curonians, and by now, word had spread that Bartolomeus had died. She knew Erik would be questioning her purpose with the pirates and her role exactly, and one day, both he and Halfdan would know what she had to do to find the relics.

She walked downstairs and paused at her door as the carpenter approached her from the street. He bowed and smiled and spoke Italian, which she did not. However, she knew very little. She gazed upon the metal hinges and held her breath. They had been pried apart, and the door left swinging wide open. She remembered shutting and locking it to secure the relics. She would never leave her door open.

She stepped away from the carpenter and swallowed, a sudden nervousness rising within her. She gazed around at the setting sun spreading shadows up the road at her from the forests on the hills.

"The curse follows me." She whispered to herself. "It is getting stronger to get me." She backed away from the door, her shadow blending into the shadows of the sunset as if a dark shroud had been pulled over her. "I am safe no more to find the relics."

The darkness engulfed her shadow and consumed it as she rushed up the road to join her people for feasting.

15

The Cornerstone of Where Death Lies

H alfdan did not like it. He stood on the Bow with Erik, their fur cloaks tight around them, gazing at the Iceland terror of uncertainty before them. The shoreline rose up and down in pillars of rolling plateaus, and sharp mountains piercing the heavens in the distance carved in obsidian. They sailed into an inlet, and Halfdan noticed the rock outcropping looming over the waters with a door carved into it.

There, he would go with Erik to find a relic Liv had neglected. It was something Halfdan had known about before he left Iona Abbey by the elder monk, and one he had kept hidden for ages. But he could no longer hide the truth of what it meant and had to secure it before Liv did something drastic. Erik had already informed Halfdan he was losing control more and more, and that a part of him deep inside wanted to just love Liv and let her be free.

The darkness of the curse also lingered there, pulling him into a spiral obsessive hunt to get her, even though, at times it had been years apart. As the Vikings rowed them ashore and Erik and Halfdan jumped out, they nodded to their king, waiting. Halfdan led Erik up the rising ravine to the rock outcropping where the Papar would be. The Papar were old Irish monks who had settled in these lands.

The map the elder monk had given him had proved useful, as Erik had it interpreted by the Viking seers, who were serving him and his cause to break the curse. Many years had passed already, but the curse was a cruel one and very slow. Everywhere Erik went, where Liv was, death followed him. The last battle cost the Vikings and Varangian Guard, along with the Curonian pirates, four thousand twenty.

And Liv had the rune stone. She still got the ruby gemstone. The curse was alive and well within Liv, too, pulling her to take the relics when Halfdan needed them. Liv was meticulous in fleeing them at King Alfred's kingdom and then getting the pirates to take her and use them to find relics and interpret maps she had taken. Though Liv was running, it was the curse pulling her to do so. Halfdan was now at an impasse with her and had no choice but to implement his stage in the curse.

They reached the top of the rising knoll and the rock outcropping, and a red-headed bearded monk met them, his green eyes sparkling at them. His long tunic robes and cloak spilled onto the ground at his boots, his hood down upon his shoulders. He nodded at Halfdan, recognizing the monk tunic, and huffed.

"An ancient monk comes to us. Finally." His Irish accent echoed in their faces, and he turned and motioned for them both to walk into the darkness where their fortress lay built into the rock overlooking the sea.

"I am Beccan, welcome." He stood behind them, shut the door, and led them down carved stone steps as wide as the breadth of the plain. The cavern opened to pillars of magnificent rock formations that loomed over them, and the warmth from torch lights danced along the walls all around them.

Halfdan lowered his fur hood, gazed around, and then pulled out the parchment the elder monk had given him. Beccan took it, gazing upon its contents and shaking his head. He handed it back to Halfdan and sighed. "Follow me this way."

He turned to gaze upon Erik. "I see you brought the cursed one with you to retrieve the relic. Good. He is the only one who can get it."

Erik swallowed, his eyes wide. "How so."

"Only the cursed to hunt may touch this particular relic."

"You knew we were coming." Halfdan stared around, feeling a cold blast from the ocean spray begin to hit them from somewhere.

Beccan nodded as they passed a multitude of other monks, but all they did was continue their chores and nod at him back. Many of them were making leather, and there was a cavern section where a blast of heat hit them. Erik smiled, watching them make swords. The steam from the fires pressed into them as they passed by.

Beccan continued. "Curses spawned open a door for people with foresight to see its devastation. Then, we create defenses to kill it. To protect the world."

"This curse is slow and cruel." Halfdan sighed.

Beccan agreed. "Indeed." He stopped walking and turned to stare at them both. "You have been alive a long time already, and the curse is not near its end."

Erik huffed, and Beccan acknowledged it. "Do not fear Viking. You have a pivotal role in this to help break it, even though you are the hunter."

"Really?" Erik feared.

They rounded a corner on a bend in the cavern, which opened to a vast labyrinth where the wall was open to the sea. The spray hit them, but the views drew them closer to gawk at it. They stood on a ledge under the mountain, and the waves roared and ebbed and flowed. The white caps battered the stone wall beneath them. As they gawked at the splendid power of the open sea cavern room before them, Beccan motioned them to a wall of ice to their right.

Embedded in the ice was a knife with a ruby handle, and runes were carved into the silver blade, kissing the metal. It was smaller than a dagger. Beccan pointed to it, his bearded face firm.

"The Viking must retrieve it. You may use your axe to cut it out." As Erik pulled his axe and they stood back to let him cut the ice wall, Beccan then warned him.

"Once your love successfully retrieves the three relics, you must kill her with it. Until then, she will stay weakened in your presence."

Erik froze mid-swing and lingered to the wall alongside Halfdan, his face drained of color.

"I must do what?" Erik gasped.

He lowered his axe as a whisper came from the ice, filling his head with murmurs he could not understand. As Erik approached closer to it, the ice cracked at his face, and the runes shimmered in blue within the ice. The room lit up as if that pristine blue had doused it with flames. Erik's eyes glowed with that blue as if something had come alive within him. His face clenched, gazing upon it.

The wall cracked to the end where the roaring waves splashed upon the stone at their feet. The ice began chipping off at Erik's boots, and cracks spread from one end of the cavern to the other. Erik lunged his axe up and hit the ice once, and it shattered around them like it had snowed a torrent of pain. The wall caved in around them in billows of white.

As the ice settled, Erik picked the knife up at his feet, the runes on his palm glowing like the fire in his eyes.

Halfdan swallowed. "I hate this part of the curse. I hate it with all I am."

Beccan sighed at them. "Now the curse begins its abject cruelty on the heart." He turned to Halfdan, nodding his head. "And within you also, ancient monk. You know what you must do."

Halfdan swallowed, his face lighting up as he watched Erik hold the knife, his eyes burning inside, too. He did not see his eyes like he had witnessed Erik's, but Beccan did. Halfdan's eyes shimmered crimson. The glow from his eyes lit up the sudden darkness of the cavern room against the ice like hell's lair had come to life at their feet and bled out beneath them.

16

An Ambush of the Heart

L iv pulled her layered tunics higher on her thinning shoulders and huffed. She missed her sandals and walking on the beach, and she hoped she would be going home. Since her Tuscan house had been invaded by the curse watching her, she felt drawn to the third relic.

She walked the streets, her crimson and cream embroidered tunic dragging the ground at her feet. She left her hair long down her back, braided around her ears to keep it off her face. She pulled a wool cloak over her shoulders, pressing into a side pocket where her dagger lay.

The co-prince of Salerno was ruling Italy now. Liv had to be cautious because the Saracents were still lingering in the countryside, harassing the villagers and residents of the city. Prince Guaimar had employed mercenaries to help him hunt the Saracent barbarians, and with Liv still having a pirate presence in the vicinity, she knew she would be well protected.

Until her general Alo came for her, Liv decided to venture into Italia and adore the markets and artisans. She would then venture into the countryside with the pirates she had scouting the city for the third relic. Liv lingered on a cobblestone street that veered under an arched tunnel with steps leading to houses above it, and admired the beauty.

A violet Clematis vine hugged the railing and danced up the stone wall before her, and she closed her eyes for a moment to smell it. Along the wall where the street turned right, a blue morning glory vine lingered, filling the stone wall to the roofs of the homes. In big ceramic pots around the steps to the homes were blue Passion Flowers splayed in a glorious tribute to her senses.

She walked under the tunnel, exited a street, and followed it to the Pantheon. She walked out from the street into a bustling center and eyed the inhabitants. The Pantheon was a church, and people lingered under the pillars, their shadows stretching over the cobblestone. She turned to see her general Alo come up behind her in the street from out of nowhere, his eyes on her back.

She froze at first but then relaxed at his presence. He had been her general for a year, and his family had become her protectors. He sighed and gazed at the Pantheon. "We have found the map that shows an area in Estonia where the dagger lies."

Liv gasped. "But no hope of the third relic yet."

Alo grimaced. "Not yet, but it is here just as you have warned us. We will find it."

Liv sighed. "I will retrieve the dagger and then hunt the relic. I have no choice." She stared at him. "Where is the map?"

Alo turned to go back the way she had come. "Come this way." He lured her. As she followed him, he gazed back at her. "We had to employ the services of others to get to it, you understand."

And then he stopped in the middle of a three-way street, and Saracents surrounded Liv. They froze from the shadows of the houses and emerged to cut her off, and Alo backed away from her. Liv gazed upon the barbarians, their intentions evident upon their scruffy faces, their strong fists clasping long swords at their sides. They wore body armor over their long robes, and their dark eyes were as sinister as their faces.

"What are you doing, Alo," Liv whispered to him as she counted twenty-one men surrounding her.

"My people should not have to serve you since Bartolomeus died. You bring great pain upon us all with this mate who hunts you. I will not let my family suffer because of you."

Liv huffed. "We have a law signed. It is binding until I break the curse."

Alo smiled at her and backed away, disappearing behind the wall of men lingering closer to her. "You are in their hands now, cursed one. Perhaps you can entice them with your beauty to serve you as you did Bartolomeus." And then he laughed. "The pirate king had a soft spot for you, too soft. It was his demise."

"Are you saying your people are no longer honoring it?" She belted out.

Liv watched Alo disappear and she faced the barbarians. "Are you going to kill me?" She wondered, craning her neck to watch them move in on her.

The men laughed, and one who led them approached, his dark face lit up at her. "It would do no good to kill you, would it, pirate queen?"

Liv sighed. "No. It would not."

"And your escort is not with you." He warned.

Liv swallowed as they slithered closer to her. "You know that Prince Guaimar does have mercenaries in the city?"

The men paused, and Liv saw them recognize that in their eyes, but it was too late. She felt a ripping pain lunge through her back, and the arrow plunged through her heart. She gasped in pain and fell to her knees. All she remembered was two men lifting her in their arms and dragging her through the street away from the city. She closed her eyes as they lay her in the back of a wagon, the barbarian voices echoing over the countryside as they took her away.

When Liv woke up, she had been bound by her hands and feet, and her eyes raised to see the clouds moving. She was in a wagon still, the bumpy road aching her back. A mountain rose around her and evergreen trees lingered over the road. She turned her head to see the barbarians ride alongside her horseback and one laughed as she woke up.

"It has awoken!" He pestered her.

Liv grimaced, pulling against the ropes and grunting in frustration at them.

"You will not get out of those, cursed one. You may be strong, but not strong enough against us."

Liv huffed. "What do you want with me?" She asked, leaning on her hip to stare out.

"You will see, immortal one. You will see." He smiled.

"How long was I dead?" She was curious.

The barbarian sighed, shaking his head. "Not long enough! When we stop to make camp, I will shove another arrow through your cursed heart to keep you down."

Liv lay back down, flaring her nostrils. "Damnit." She huffed.

She looked around her and guessed it was midday, but she was not sure what day it was or how long she had been dead. She guessed it was the very next day, and they were taking her deep into the mountains, where she assumed they had an encampment. She laid her head down in the wagon, her mind going to Alo and what he said. She still needed the pirates to help her and would not have found the two relics she had if not for their skills.

She was at an impasse now in this curse and helpless. By nightfall, they had reached the mouth of a mountain she did not recognize, and more voices echoed, solidifying her gut concern that she was now in their stronghold. They would just continue killing her over and over until they did what they wanted to with her, and for the first time in a long time, she shivered inside.

She was drug out of the wagon by her feet and landed in the dirt with a thud. She held her breath to their cruelness. They dragged her to an open fire, tied her hands with more rope against a tree, and left her there guarded by a slew of them. They had their backs to her as if watching for something they could not say, and Liv suddenly got a shiver up her spine.

Just as she began perking her ears to strange whistles from the mountain, the leader lunged at her. He pressed the tip end of his blade under her chin, raised her face up, and explored her. Liv gazed at his face, his dark beautiful skin, his dark sparkling eyes. His looks reminded her of Bartolomeus, only this man was malicious and cruel.

He eyed her up and down and then huffed. "Do you know who I am, immortal?"

Liv held her breath. "I do not care. You will die eventually."

He sneered in her face. "I am your redemption, you know. As this curse Alo speaks of follows you, my people will use the chaos following you to take the world."

Liv widened her eyes. "You hunt me also? The brutal Vikings hunt me, or did you not know?" She swallowed as he pressed the blade firmer under her chin, and a sliver of blood drizzled down her neck.

"Is that so?" He stood up and removed the blade. "No matter. We will kill them also, for the power in your eyes, I see, will bring us great fortune and strength."

Liv breathed deeply and closed her eyes, leaning her head against the tree. "What I bring you is death." She warned him.

But he did not care. He smiled at Liv, his eyes full of greed. When she opened her eyes again, she gazed around and took inventory of the barbarians lingering around. Her ear perked again to a whistle coming from the forest behind her. Her spine tingled, and she fidgeted the rope around her wrists.

The barbarian leader paused, his back going stiff. "Go." He ordered his men, and Liv watched them suddenly disperse into the darkness away from the fires.

Liv sat there aching and watched as the air became consumed with flaming arrows. She thought she was back at the falls, fighting Erik again. She pressed into the tree and bit down, struggling to get free of her bonds. The men guarding her fell one by one, and one hit her lap, bleeding out his mouth. Liv pulled his midsection into her atop her legs and stretched him up to her face to get his sword at his side.

She grunted with the weight of him on her lap and broke open the skin at her wrists, pulling the blade out. She let him roll off her knees and propped the sword up, shoving it through the rope on her wrists to cut through the layers binding her. All around her, shouts echoed, and in the darkness, mercenaries on horseback lunged into the barbarians with spears.

The mercenaries wore silver helmets and chain mail tunics to their knees. They burst through the darkness into the barbarians and chased them from the mountain, killing them where they stood. As Liv cut herself free, she gripped the hilt and sliced it through the bonds at her feet. She was finally free.

She lunged up and rushed around the fire, cutting a barbarian down through his midsection, helping the mercenaries. She became enraged at fighting them on her way out until she found the road and was knocked off her feet by the barbarian leader. The sword flung out of her grasp as he struck her. Liv gasped as the breath got knocked out of her.

He gripped the back of her dress and jerked her up, pressing a dagger against her throat as they faced dozens of mercenaries on horseback. "I will kill her! Let me go." He demanded, and Liv let out a gasp as blood began trickling down her neck again. He was going to kill her again, and for some reason, she was not empowered to fight back. A weakness overcame her as her breath labored. Her knees grew weak as a presence she had not felt in a long while overcame her.

From behind her, A firm grasp lunged around her throat and pulled the blade off her neck. As she fell away from the barbarian, Erik lunged his sword through his back. Erik ripped the blade from his lower back to his shoulder. His face was clenched hard, his eyes stone cold. Liv fell on her butt, her head hitting the stone ground. As the weakness overcame her, she tried to crawl away from Erik on her elbows.

Erik pushed the body off the road, and his face lighted upon Liv. He shoved his blade into his sheath and catapulted to her, yanking her up in his arms. Liv met his intense eyes with her weak ones, and Erik caught her as she fell.

He moaned at her face as if a sweet reprieve had bitten him. "I have you, Liv." He pulled her over his shoulder as she fell limp in his arms, turning to his men. "Kill them all," Erik commanded.

As the mercenaries filled the mountain with the hunt, Erik marched up the road to his horse. He climbed on it with Liv over his shoulder and let her fall into his lap. Her head fell limp, and he gazed at her neck and chin wounds. He pressed a desperate grasp on her cheek with his palm. He rolled his fingers down her neck and leaned against her forehead. He kissed the side of her temple and closed his eyes, his lips shivering against her.

"I have you now." He whispered.

17

Passion in Peace

L iv did not know what day it was. She turned her head and saw Erik sitting with his elbows on his knees, his hands clasped together, watching her. Beside him was an arched window, and they were in a small stone house with just a bed and a rustic table leaning against the wall. There was a fireplace, too, but not lit. She heard birds chirping outside, and a gentle breeze blew in and moved her hair off her face.

Her eyes widened as she leaned up, and Erik leaned into the wall. "I will not harm you, Liv."

He handed her a vat of water. "Here. You need this."

She took it, gulped it down, and sat upright to face him. "Where are we?"

"A village outside Italia. You are safe here." Erik stared at her, his breathing intense.

Liv stared at him back, his simple tunic accentuating his naked arms, his trousers fitted on his long legs. A trimmed beard accentuated his face, and his hair was in a pony tail down his back. She caught herself lingering her gaze on him longer than usual, and something opened from the pits of her gut and grew there.

"How did you find me?" She whispered.

Erik sighed, staring at her. "I will always find you, Liv." His jaws clenched at her face. "Time means nothing."

"You always have, haven't you?" She whispered in his face. "How long have you watched me sleep?"

Erik leaned his back against the wall again when she said that. "Two days."

Liv went to stand up and then fell back down, her legs weak. "Two days?! What is happening to me?"

Erik lingered at her and swallowed. "You are weak in my presence now." He stood up and loomed over her. "Rest. Eat. Looks like you need it." He sighed. "You have lost weight."

Liv forced herself to stand anyway and found herself pressed against his chest for support as he loomed over her. She melted her gaze up at him and held it there. He did not move, but she felt his heart beat against her breasts. His face softened at her, and he swallowed. Liv closed her eyes and hugged him, wrapping her arms around him as tears filled her eyes.

Erik was caught off guard at first, but then he wrapped his arms around her and pressed his chin atop her head. "You are still my people, Liv." He told her, closing his eyes.

"I will always be your people." She cried in his arms, her tears filling her face like a spout had broken open a dam of pain.

Erik felt her body shivering through her tears, and he clung to her as if their world was ending. Erik's heart busted inside, feeling her grief, and he found himself pulling her tighter against him, tears filling his eyes on her hair.

"I am tired. I am tired of this curse." Liv cried. "It hurts."

Erik moaned, taking a deep breath, his palms open wide and pressed into her back. He swayed her back and forth as if they were dancing, and he let her cry into his arms. "I know." He whispered into her hair. "I am sorry."

Liv cried until her sobs became gasping moans against him. She buried her face into his chest, and all Erik could do was let her cry while tears filled his eyes and his heart ached.

"I am sorry for hurting you." She bit her lips.

They stood there for endless moments, holding one another, their tears falling on each other, their breathlessness digging into their souls. "I am sorry, too," He whispered.

When Liv was ready to stop hugging him, she leaned back, and Erik caressed her long hair with his fingers. He grazed her chin with his fingers, pressed his head against her forehead, and sighed. He wanted to get lost in her kisses.

"Get some rest. Eat. I will send you clothing, and you can wash up." He kissed her forehead, and she closed her eyes.

Liv watched him go, her eyes craning to the table by the window full of grapes, cheese, and bread. She held her breath, walked over and sat in the chair, and shoveling food into her mouth. She gazed at her wrists that were now bruised, but healing. She felt her chin and neck cleaned up of blood and wondered if Erik cleaned her. Her eyes melted to the window as a stream of light burst in, warming the cozy house in hope.

She grabbed the pitcher of water on the table and guzzled it, the water flowing down her chin into her bosom. She did not care. Her body screamed for water and food. Her body screamed for rest, too, and her head ached, but it was the warning of her heart that panged her worst of all.

Erik had a woman from the village bring her new clothing, and she washed up and changed. Her hair was still damp, but she did not care. Liv opened the door and walked outside to a forest of trees, flower gardens, and pillars of stone houses on a rolling plain. She held her breath as the sun began to dip below the plain, and the village beamed in tangerine. Her face lit up, and she watched the sunset as peace overcame her.

She stared around for Erik but not see him or Halfdan. She followed people through the street to an open meadow at the end of the lane, where there was feasting and people dancing and laughing among one another. She stared at them for a moment and then sighed, turning to go. She ran into Erik's chest. He had followed her. She stepped away from him.

"Erik." She breathed.

Erik took a deep breath. "Liv."

Liv gasped. "Where is Halfdan?"

"He is at the monastery on top of the hill." Erik held out his hand to her. "Dance with me. You look rested."

Liv stared at his hand with the runes and gave in. She took his hand, and he pulled her into the dancing circle by her waist. Liv stared at his face, her eyes not wavering, her heart beating wild against his chest. She swallowed, gazing at him as he met her eyes.

"I cannot escape you." She whispered in his face.

Erik pulled her hand to his heart. "I won't let you."

"I do not want to." She mumbled. "I am tired, Erik."

Erik held his breath, his eyes roaming her beautiful, strong face.

Liv closed her eyes and leaned her head back, and Erik gazed at her naked skin to her bosom. She danced with her whole heart with him. She let him pull her tighter into him, his heart throbbing against hers. His hand grasped over her waist tight. She let him pull her around the dancing meadow, her long skirt billowing around them, and his bulky strength leaned into her.

She was free. She did not think of relics. She did not fear the curse. There was only her and Erik in this moment, and she let it eat her from the inside out and ravish her deep inside.

"You saved me. You always save me." She leaned back up to face him.

Erik froze when she said that, and before he could reply, Liv lunged up and pillaged his lips with her forceful kisses. Erik met her kisses with an open mouth, and they stopped moving. He wrapped both arms around her and held her there, his strong hands moving up her back. Their faces melted into one another as their breaths were hot on each other's lips. He pulled her up to his face, his arms gripped under her bottom and stood there with her and pelted her with kisses.

Liv did not care anymore. She wanted him. She had endured losing a husband, and the pirates turned against her. What did she have to lose? She wanted Erik. She always wanted him. The curse would never take that from her.

They walked back to the house like the ground beneath them was lit on fire. Erik slammed the door shut and pressed Liv against it, ripping her gown off her shoulders. His mouth lunged against her lips, and she moaned as he pulled her dress off. He leaned back, roving his eyes up and down her curves. He jerked his tunic off as Liv pulled at his trousers, pulling them down. He was stiff and throbbing, and his chest was breathing heavily.

They tore their clothes off each other and pressed against the door, their mouths open in fiery kisses. Their fingers lingered on each other, caressing the places where desperate passions lived. Liv raked her hands down his sculpted chest to his groin and stroked him. Erik melted against her face and closed his eyes at her touch. She melted her palms over his hips and raked them up his back, pulling him closer to her.

Erik roved his palms to her breasts as he lunged against her lips, rolling his tongue down her neck and sucking her. He stroked her sides and hips, gripping her with strong hands as his heart beat wildly. Her touch lit him on fire, and his body clenched, touching her. As Erik sucked her breasts, Liv gripped his head in her palms. She held her breath as Erik wrapped his arms around her buttocks and picked her up, twisting her around toward the bed. He met her eyes as he carried her over, his face impassioned.

He fell with her, pushing his knees between her legs as he dove in between them. Erik pressed atop her on the bed, their mouths hot in each other's breaths. He raised over her, his arms flexed. Liv spread wide to accept him, and Erik plunged inside her, shifting her body with his forceful thrusts. Liv let out a roaring moan as he took her, and Erik breathed wide open against her lips.

He moaned into her breaths, lunging in and out of her with forceful thrusts. Liv gripped his back, sinking her fingers into him. Her mouth breathed into his moans as his body flexed over her, thrusting slowly and deep like a river flowing from raging falls. Erik gripped her sides in his palms, and Liv met his thrusts, writhing with him as if they were dancing. Erik gripped the back of her neck, moaning with an open mouth against her cheek as he thrust in and out of her.

Liv reared her head back, holding onto his shoulders as she swayed under him. Erik held himself up by his free arm, and she gripped his forearm in her palm, his muscles hard and flexed. He held his breath and clenched his face against her neck as he exploded inside her like agony had taken him, but it was sweet and desperate.

They took each other through the night until rising dawn kissed their ravished bodies, and their tears filled the pillows in sweet agony. The sweet agony woke Erik shortly after sunrise to find Liv had gone.

He lay there alone, still naked, and turned his face to see the sun coming up through the window. He propped his head up on his long muscular arm and stared into the sunrise. His breathing was steady, but his heart was broken. He would see her again, he just did not know when. Until then, his soul would sing their passion they had with each other until they could finally be together again-for good.

He closed his eyes, gripping his heart as grief would not let him rest. Then he got dressed and armed himself with every weapon he could carry to go get Liv back, whether she had found the relics or not.

18

Mountains of Sweet Sorrows

L iv had awoken before dawn when it was still dark out, as a whisper pried into her mind.

You are weak with him. Run. Runnnnnn.

Her eyes flew open in the bed, her heart racing.

He will hunt you. He will always hunt you. Run runnnnn.

She was still exhausted from her and Erik's all-night ravishing one another, but the whispers tugged at her mind and pulled her out of bed. She slipped into her tunic, crept out barefoot, and stole a horse.

She lunged into the rising dawn away from the mountain to return to her Tuscan village. The dawn warmed her face and dried her tears, her thoughts on Erik. She would never forget, but she still had to find the dagger and one more relic. There were still two missing relics she had not been able to find, and she clenched her jaws thinking about the frustration of this damned curse.

If she had stayed with Erik, they would have stayed in the bed all day and night again. They would have continued to ravish one another until they died anyway. The curse would never break, and they would war against one another deep inside. Erik was stronger than her and would eventually kill her as the curse took hold of him to hold her prisoner, their immortality spent.

Liv pressed her face into the horse's mane, her long tunic racing behind her in the wind along her hair, her bare feet gripped into the stirrups as if she was climbing a rock wall. Her mind recanted what Erik told her: *You are weak in my presence.*

She lunged up the mountain road to her village, the anguish of this curse eating her from the inside out, the anger from her general Alo's betrayal filling her with rage. The horse's hooves sounded throughout the silence and echoed over the plain as she neared her house at the end.

She lunged up the stairs, pulled out the wall by her bed under the window, and stared at the ruby gemstone and runestone. She picked them both up in her rune palm and listened to the whispers, her eyes lighting up to a blazing silver.

Find all of us. Hurry. The hunter comes for you.

As she turned to put them up, movement outside caught her eye in the street. A few of her pirates lingered around the horse, which clearly belonged to a mercenary. They whispered to one another, and Liv perked her ear, listening, her messy hair stuck to her neck and face from her sweat.

"Do you think they are hunting her also?"

"Alo was successful? That is surprising."

"Surely not."

She gazed out the picture window, her eyes lighting up inside her as a lingering fire burned. A sudden urge to kill came over her like a fire lit inside her. It made her pause as she blinked her eyes.

"What is happening to me." She blinked her eyes again, and they returned to normal, but her heart raced.

She leaned forward on her knees, pressing her palm into her chest as it ached. Something was wrong. "What are you doing now, you damn curse?!" She whispered to herself, closing her eyes. "What are you doing to me."

As the runes on her palm burned, the whisper came again. *Empowering you.*

Her eyes flew open, raging into a flaming silver as if her insides were burning. She melted downstairs and kicked the door open to face them all, a surge rushing from somewhere deep inside a vast pit of her soul. All she knew was that these traitors and Alo must die, and then she would need to find the relics and the dagger and kill Erik again.

The pirates would bend to her will, or she would be their downfall. There would be no more negotiation or husbands. As she burst through the door, the pirate men and women standing by the horse gasped and dropped to their knees. They raised their hands and begged.

"Please, queen, do not harm us! Alo has not returned, and we have only found out what he plotted against you." The old man cried as the street filled with pirates behind him.

Liv took a deep breath, her eyes returning to normal, her knees weak suddenly. "You are not plotting against me?" She shook, looking around and noticing the pirates shaking their heads no. "Was he plotting with anyone else here?"

The old man pulled his cloth hat from his sunburned head, his brown eyes quivering. "No, my queen! We love you. Alo's wife turned against him, and she came and told us just yesterday what he plotted. He has not returned yet."

The woman spoke up. "Our people returned from Italia worried for you! They said you were taken, and when they were to give chase, the mercenaries assembled to get you! They outnumbered them in great numbers and power!"

Liv widened her eyes. "They were hunting me also. Erik!"

"Yes, they were hunting you as well as the barbarians. This is not good." She worried. "The curse beckons the hunters, my queen." She whispered.

The old man sighed. "You are our family and have given us a home here. We serve you, my queen, and honor the memory of Bartholomeus. Anything you need, you will have!"

Liv sighed. "Thank you because I need you all!" She leaned against her doorframe and closed her eyes, raising her head into the sun. "I am taking a long bath. Let me know if Alo comes." And then she turned again to warn them.

"Alo is working with the barbarians. I must assume he may have given them directions to find us. Prepare the men. I need to prepare to sail back to Estonia. When I am away, secure this village with all our resources."

"My queen, if they come for you..." The old man worried.

Liv swallowed. "Be prepared in case."

She turned to go, and they swallowed, nodded to her, and then left back down the street. Liv closed the door and locked it, pressing her head against the door. "I have killed enough people for a thousand lifetimes. I need a rest."

She walked to the back of her house through her kitchen to take a bath in the pool running down the hill in her backyard. After a long soak, and she had washed her hair and body with soap and lavender oil. Then, she dressed in her warrior pirate attire and armed every inch of her body. She braided her hair around her head, and the tail swung down her back like a rope. Her face clenched as she locked her door and marched down the street to the stables.

Bartolomeus ensured every man under him was trained in seafaring ways and brutal tactics, so she was not surprised to see the warrior pirates gathered in the stables working. They had spent the day sparring with one another in the fields too and secured their defenses on the hillsides before entering the town.

In the stables, she stood at the entranceway and gazed upon the naked-chested Estonians shooing horses and cleaning the stables. She stopped at a stable and gazed in on Rait. He was perfectly tanned, slender, and muscular and renowned for his sailing and swordsmanship skills. She smiled at him before he froze and craned his neck at her, his brown eyes wide.

"My queen?" He wondered, standing up to face her.

She eyed him up and down. "You are very strong. You are my new general. We leave for Estonia by nightfall." She marched away.

Rait froze as the other men gathered around him in the stables, their faces wide but not with smiles. One of them patted him on the shoulder and shook his head.

Rait sighed. "Damnit." He went back to shooing the horse.

B y nightfall, they rode through the night to Torre Mozza, where the pristine teal waters kissed the glorious sandy beaches. They had longboats there and a slew of pirates inhabiting Piombino. It was a small, quaint village but nonetheless powerful, with the fortress looming over the sea. There was also a port perfect for their long boats and getting in and out of the Ligurian Sea and Tyrrhenian Seas.

By dawn, Liv's party of ten with her new general Rait paused on the sloping hill overlooking the sea. The rising sun kissed their tanned faces, the sea sprayed them with hope. The tops of orange clay tiled roofs popped up over the woods, and the stone monastery loomed over the shore, its towers stretching shadows on the beach.

They were all fully armed, and their heads covered with black or purple cloths to ward off the sun. Their loose tunics and trousers were light and comfortable. Throughout the years, Liv had ensured her pirates also wore engraved leather breastplates and bracers for their arms, the bracers crafted to hold daggers. She could not escape her Viking heritage, for even her pirates wore meticulous armor.

Liv closed her eyes, sighed, and leaned back in the sun. Rait stared at her and shook his head. "Alright, sun queen, we need to go." His voice was deep and powerful.

"I am in charge." Liv gawked at him, smiling.

Rait laughed, his mouth wide. "Sure." He pressed away from her, and they lunged over the incline and into the village.

Liv and her pirates laughed with him, too, the echo from their voices carrying to the beach in the early dawn. They rode under a canopy of tall pines, admiring the Etruscan villas. Rait led them under the canopy into the streets until they neared the rising walls of the fortress, and it was there they paused and admired its majesty. It rose over the waters, lingering into the shore, with views of the rolling hills and the Island of Elba.

Two pirates met them along the wall as they slid from their horses, and Liv froze at the vast expanse of sea sparkling before her. She flung her long braid over her shoulder and sighed. She was sailing back to Estonia to sign another document securing a husband. She still had relics to find, and she far from finding the next one, a golden rune box with a key inside.

The key to your heart. Liv kept hearing a voice whisper to her over and over. The map she had taken from her grandmother showed it somewhere in Italia, but even her pirates had yet to locate it. They had, however, noted it was there, so Liv had stayed close to her Tuscan village in the mountains since Bartolomeus died.

Liv watched her pirates pull the horses away back up the street and begin following Rait down the stone steps to the harbor. Their dragon snouts bobbed gently up and down along the sea wall. A rocky platform over the water had ten long boats on each side. They were only taking one today, as she left the extra boats there in case her village needed to escape back to Estonia.

As she neared the last step, Rait lunged into her and pulled her off atop him onto the platform. Liv heard the swishing of arrows filling the skies over their heads, and she jerked his head over Rait to see barbarians lunge down the street from the top of the hill at them.

"They come for you!" Rait yelled, yanking Liv up and pulling her to a long boat at the end of the platform.

The barbarians hollered and readied their arrows again in their bows, their horses beating the horizon around the village in vibrating echoes. Liv turned to see arrows hit her pirates coming with her, three of them falling in the street. She became enraged, her pupils dilating to a flaming silver. Rait pushed her into the longboat, and Liv fell to her side.

She raised to see Rait had jerked up and raised it to his face before her. Three arrows hit it at his face, and Rait clenched his jaws.

The other pirates, not hit, jumped into the boat alongside him and readied the ship to push off. Liv peered over the edge to see the barbarians pause the attack on the hill. Their bodies fell suddenly, and Liv held her breath as Erik plunged into them from behind. His mercenaries and warriors filled the woods through the village atop the hill.

"Shit!" Rait hollered. "The immortal Viking from hell has found you also!"

The pirates readied the long boat to push off and get out to sea. Liv found herself staring at Erik in his full-body armor, his face clenched, and his arrows finding their marks in the barbarians. When he was done firing, he slid his bow across his chest and pulled his long sword. The mercenaries outnumbered them easily ten to one, and Erik was not playing around. Liv's heart skipped a beat watching him, her loins aching.

"Handsome Viking." She whispered, finding her thoughts drift back to their passionate lovemaking.

Erik pummeled through them as the first line of barbarians reached the platform. They lunged into the longboat to attack Rait and his crew of seven who were left. Liv's pirates living there had emerged to join her in attacking them, shooting their arrows from the fortress towers and the high wall rising over them. That meant Erik may die again, but she had no choice.

Rait pulled his long sword with his pirates as the barbarians lunged into the boat, his back to Liv, fighting them off. He was strong and an expert swordsman like her crew. The barbarians were gored and stabbed endless times, but they were not giving up. Their eyes were on Liv, their prize. They held an obsessive air about them as they noticed her.

Liv stood to help and pulled her sword, and it was then she felt the longboat jerk back to the platform and hit the rock wall. As she turned to face what happened, she met Erik at the wall. He pulled her in with a rope and had hooked the bow, the muscles under his tunic bulging. His face clenched at her, and his eyes shimmered like a fountain of desperation swimming in him.

When the ship hit the rocks, Liv flew back against the mast. Behind her, Rait and the pirates were still fighting the remaining barbarians. One of them went overboard when it hit. Erik let go of the rope and jumped on the bow, his eyes on her and her alone.

Liv froze, staring at him, her eyes wide, her lips quivering, her knees weak. She raised her face to meet him as he rushed across the deck and lunged against her lips. She kissed him back, their mouths open and moaning. He pressed her against the mast, oblivious to the warring behind them. He stopped kissing her and stared into her eyes, his chest heaving.

"I love you."

He stepped back to grab her, and she raised to meet his lips again. A brisk wind hit them. Erik glared at his forearms and chest, jerking his head back to the wall. Four pirates lunged into him with whips and ropes at his forearms. They wrapped around his bulky arms like slithering snakes, and the pirates jerked him away from Liv. Erik atapulted backwards away from her and went flying midair over the wall.

Her pirates pulled him off her from the wall. Erik flew over their heads into the woods on the hill. A normal human would not survive that, but Liv knew Erik would. He would probably have injuries. She found herself collapsing to her knees and hollering for him.

"Erik!"

Rait threw the last barbarian body off the long boat, and the pirates pushed off again to sail out. He glared at where Erik had gone. Liv sat there, her eyes staring, meeting Rait's face as he loomed upon her. Rait breathed heavily, splattered with blood, his dark eyes wide. He put his free hand on his hip and shook his head down at her, pointing his blade at her face.

"You want him dead. You want to kiss him. What do you want?!" He shrugged his shoulders, then pointed his sword to where Erik had flown. "He is dead again." He pointed his blade toward his pirates as they coasted toward the open sea. "Let's go!" His eyes were on the horizon.

Liv leaned her head against the mast and shook her head, gripping her heart. "I love him."

Rait turned to her again, sliding his sword in his sheath as they crested the wall and hit the open waters. Behind them in the street, the mercenaries cut down the barbarians, and the pirates left in the village lurked in the shadows to avoid them. Their main goal was getting Liv away from Erik, and they had done that. Now, the mercenaries Erik led could finish off the others.

Rait sighed. "You know, If I die because of you and this curse, I will come back from the dead and haunt you and your great-great-great-great-grandchildren!"

Liv widened her eyes at him and swallowed. She believed him.

Rait huffed, narrowing his brows, and turned his face into the wind. "This has got to be the worst love story ever." He rolled his eyes.

Liv believed that, too. If their love were meant to be, the curse would break so they could be together. She stood up slowly and sheathed her sword. She watched the shoreline at the fortress wall continue to erupt in battles between the mercenaries and the barbarians, though the mercenaries were winning. She craned her eyes over the trees on the hill but did not see Erik come back out.

19

A Marriage of Ill-Repute

Six months later, Liv and Rait stood before the new king of the Lechitic tribe. This new king was younger than Henryk and held a cruelty to him that made Liv pause. Henryk had passed away suddenly due to illness, although Liv questioned it. Behind this new king, Andres, stood a wall of seers fully armed, just like Liv's pirates. They peered over his head at her with dark eyes, a mixture of them being women this time.

Liv gripped the hilt to her sword by her side and held her breath. She was tired of this-all of this-and of running. King Andres pulled his long robes up and stood from his throne, eying her with disdain as a new parchment was brought in. Behind the council bringing that in came three men, who stood by the king.

Liv eyed the men, who were taller than her. They were dark-skinned with dark eyes, long beards, and long dark hair. She wondered if this king was trying to mimic Bartolomeus. But no one could mimic the pirate king who gave his life for her, ever. Andres held the parchment up and sighed, his beady dark eyes rolling over her fully armed body covered in armor.

"Since the demise of Bartolomeus, thanks to you, the pickings for a husband are slim. Your cursed mate hunts us with his Vikings, even to the farthest reaches of the world." His voice echoed. "He hunts you as if he knows where you are."

"I understand. He also ambushed us." Liv sighed.

Andres rolled open the parchment. "We have had to increase our forces to keep him from coming upon us with his warriors. You continue to draw him like a plague. It is no secret this curse has changed for the worse."

"Am I signing that or not." Liv belted out.

Rait glanced at her, his face lit up at her remark.

Andres slithered to her, his long black beard braided down his chin and golden beads sewn in it. "We have altered it." He handed it to her and then pointed to the three men. "We need you and your general to retrieve maps we had drawn up over the years to keep your cursed mate from finding us."

"What?" Liv gasped.

Andres then pointed to the men. "You have three to choose from. Since their lives are now on the line for you, they will be allowed to lie with you."

Liv froze.

"After all, they must get something out of this arrangement." He added. "I am certain that since you are immortal, you cannot bear children now, but you can pleasure your husband."

Rait widened his eyes and cleared his throat but Liv huffed and rolled the parchment back up. "I do not approve of any of them. They are not muscular. They look as if you just pulled them from the farming fields. They look malnourished."

Andres lunged at her face, scowling. "These are three warriors I have not sent to battle because of you."

Liv stared at him. "I prefer warriors to bed, not farmers already broken by your harsh policies since Henryk has died. However, I am happy to have them join me in Estonia, where I will feed them and their families."

Rait bit his lip, and a sliver of laughter came out.

Andres sighed. The tower room bustled with noise as it filled with his armed warriors. They surrounded her on each side of the room. She stared at them but knew where this was going.

She sighed. "You are not honoring our agreement. I am to pick a husband of my choosing, and I still have a relic to find, four of them."

"We lost Bartolomeus, and that was only two of these cursed relics!" Andres yelled. "We will lose no other great warriors because of you."

"So, you give me farmers, and by the look of fear in their eyes as they look at me, they would die the first night in bed with me anyway." She laughed.

The three men gulped, and one nodded, agreeing with her. Rait watched them and shook his head, his eyes wide.

"You will sign this agreement." Andres threatened her.

Liv stared into his eyes. "Or what."

He smiled. "We all know you do not fear death. The only way to truly stop you is to imprison you. If you do not sign, of course."

Rait eyed the king suspiciously, clenching his face, but stayed silent. He was cautious with this new king, and they knew Liv had chosen a new general.

Liv laughed. "Erik follows me. If you imprison me, he will come upon your tribe. I do not think you want his Viking warriors here upon you. He has already secured mercenaries because of me under Prince Guaimar. He has proven to be a mighty war leader who can navigate the perils of any place, time and people."

As Liv said that, her heart ached thinking of him. "He is the bravest warrior I know." She whispered and then froze as she said that.

Andres stared at her and nodded. "Yes, you love him. We see it more as time goes by. Regardless, he continues hunting us as he hunts you, and I expect you to find our maps to help protect us from him."

"I will not take any of these men as a husband. They have suffered enough, looks like." Liv warned him.

"The agreement was that you will take a husband of our people, Viking."

Liv stared at the three men again, and tears filled her eyes. "If I take a husband of your people again, he will die. I cannot bear to lose another husband..."

The three men stared at her wide-eyed.

"I loved Bartolomeus." She whispered, her heart aching.

Rait turned to her face; his jaws clenched. Liv closed her eyes and sighed. "I am asking you to change the proclamation. I will find your maps, but you will not expect me to take a husband. I know the one who hunts me will be my husband once this curse breaks. I will not dishonor him again."

Andres took in a deep breath. "You will find the maps of our people that are missing. And once you have done so, you will forever disappear from Estonia..."

Liv stared at him emotionless.

"You will never return because if you do, and we catch you on our shores again, we will imprison you. Or cut off your head. That should keep you dead." He warned her.

His words stung like bees in Liv's backbone. He was not kidding, and she knew it. They were brutal people who were fierce on the seas and veracious warriors. Liv still needed them. This curse was taking too long to break. She nodded her head at him and sighed.

"So be it. Where do I sign."

Andres handed the parchment to his council. "He will alter it again, and then you shall sign. Then you will leave immediately with your new general and begin searching for our lost maps."

Liv held her breath watching, the council leave with the parchment. Something in Andre's voice warned her, but she rolled it off like water on her tongue.

"Once I find the maps and bring them to you, you will no longer give me resources to continue finding relics?" She asked.

Andres scoffed at her. "No, we will not. Chaos is everywhere, and there are many curses in this world. Yours is more of the heart between you and this Viking. It matters not to us. My father was a fool to believe it."

He turned his back on her and smiled. "Let the Vikings and Curonians war with one another. My Lechitic tribe do not need to be bothered with it."

Liv shook her head at him. "You will not like it when it comes upon your people. I have seen it. I have seen whole villages collapse into the sea, and waters filled with bodies..."

"I care not!" Andres yelled at her, scoffing. "We have lost good men! We sacrificed our best warriors for Bartolomeus to help you. And then we lost Bartolomeus, the king of the Amber Road, for our people. Because of you! Because of this Viking who hunts you like you are his prey."

And then he turned to face his warriors and shook his head. "I change my mind. Take her away."

Rait glared at him. "What."

The warriors surrounded Liv, pulled her arms out, and took her weapons, pushing Rait aside. Liv froze as her traitorous general Alo marched in and stood aside the king. She fumed at him as they held her. Andres smiled at her and then turned to Alo.

"Ah! Alo, so glad you could join us."

"Traitors." Liv snarled, her eyes craning to Alo.

Andres loomed into her face. "Since we know where the third relic is, we shall find it, and keep it."

"No!" Liv begged.

"And when your cursed Viking comes looking for you, we will behead him, and you will watch. Then it will be your turn, and the world will be rid of your immortal kind." He sneered in her face.

"There are still more relics. The dagger, and then two more..." She warned him.

But Alo began laughing, and then Andres joined in. Liv widened her eyes as Andres loomed into her face, smiling. "Oh, you do not know? The monk must not have told you..."

The room fell into laughter, and Liv eyed Rait, but he glared at her from the wall wide-eyed. "Why do you think the barbarians hunted you, drawing your cursed Viking to them also..."

Liv gasped.

"While you spent your last year in Italia hiding wherever you hide, our seers traveled and researched this curse..."

Chills darted up Liv's spine.

Andres breathed in her face. "You and Erik are the last two relics, cursed one." Liv's knees gave way, and the color drained from her face.

"Once you die, or kill one another, the curse will break. After the relics are destroyed, of course."

"No! It cannot be." Liv shouted, pulling against the warriors to no avail.

Andres laughed in her face. "Once we have the third relic and secure the dagger, we will take this monk and the relic he carries..."

"You will never find the two relics I have!"

"Oh, my dear, we already have. Alo will lead us to your little village in the mountains. He must go fetch his family, after all."

Liv's eyes teared up. "No! I must break the curse myself. You do not understand!" She pleaded, even as they drug her out.

They left Rait standing against the wall, his face clenched, watching her. Then he turned his eyes upon Alo, and his cheeks burned red with a vengeance. As the chaos unfolded in the throne room, he crept out to follow where they were taking his queen.

That night Liv sat on her butt in the prison cell with her head against her knees, her arms wrapped around her legs. She closed her eyes, missing Erik. She even missed Halfdan. The curse began making more sense to her after what Andres told her. Once she had the third relics and then the dagger, she could break the relics on the cylinder Halfdan had on him.

If she and Erik were the last two, what about Halfdan? What was his purpose then?

Liv raised her head and stared at the wall as she saw the future for the first time. "He has to kill me."

She closed her eyes and sighed, realizing that was why Halfdan had told her at the beach, "I am sorry, too. I am so sorry."

She raised her eyes to the ceiling in the darkness, took a deep breath, and something lit inside her and whispered. *"Get up Viking. Get up now."*

Liv stood as if a hand lunged from an invisible sky and pulled her up. She walked to the bars, her ears perking up to muted grunts and bodies sliding down the wall. As Rait met her at the bars with the keys, he sighed at her face. He unlocked the doors, and her eyes flew open, flaming silver.

"Hello, my cursed pirate queen." His voice was sarcastic and edgy.

He did not cringe at the sight of her eyes. He pulled her out, and they lunged up the path away from the prison under the woods to the harbor in the darkness. Liv's pirates, who came with her, were waiting in the night. They sailed away from the Lechitic tribe, headed back to Estonia, and then they would sail back to Tuscany. They had little time because Alo would also be leading the tribal warriors there.

The tribe would slaughter the villagers and find the relics. Liv could not let that happen. As time moved on more and more, she could no longer work with the Lechitic tribe. She would stick with her Curonian pirates. The new king had not honored her agreement with Henryk and Bartolomeus anyway, giving her the right to choose any husband of their people. Andres picked three of his weakest farmers and tried to make her settle.

Liv did not believe in settling. Her life may be lingering on, but joy mattered more. That is why she married Bartolomeus, because he genuinely loved her, doted upon her, and encouraged her to be free. She bit her tongue, facing the wind as they sailed on through the night, craning her neck to stare at Rait. His eyes were hard, and his face clenched.

"Thank you," Liv told him. She turned to them all. "Thank you all. I am sorry. I am sorry for this damn curse."

Rait met her stare and sighed. "He is not a wise ruler, or he would have seen this coming."

Liv smiled.

Rait continued. "Andres never believed anything his father or the seers told him. We were all concerned when Henryk died, and his son took it. He is only about power and wealth. It will be their demise. You will see."

He paused, staring at her. "You are a brave woman to have endured all you have endured, and that is why we follow you. The Curonians stand with you." He smiled at her and bowed.

Liv turned and stared at the thirty-five pirates manning the ship. They, too, agreed and bowed their heads to her. She stood there on the bow aside from Rait, tears falling down her face under a dim lit moonlight, and her heart on fire.

"You are brave, too, and my heart is full because of your people."

Rait shook his head. "Our people, Liv." He had never called her that before. It caught her off guard.

He reiterated. "You are our people. We are one people. Our people stay together. We fight for one another."

He pressed a firm hand atop her shoulder and smiled at her face. "You are our people. We are your people. Okay?"

Liv smiled at him. "Okay."

Rait turned into the wind; his face clenched. "Now on to Estonia! We must gather our people and then sail to Tuscany. Alo will die."

Liv agreed. "He will die. Anyone coming for my relics will die."

Rait agreed. "Indeed!"

Liv took a deep breath and gripped her heart, tears falling. Rait gripped her shoulder again and met her stare.

"Hey, you, okay?"

Liv's lips quivered. "Bartolomeus," she took a breath and closed her eyes, "He has protected me even in death. He was a good husband to me, and," she gasped, "I will never forget the hope he gave me. Because of him, you all trust me, and I can never repay it. He is gone because of me."

Rait's sighed and pursed his lips. He did not say anything but stood aside her on the bow. They pressed their faces into the wind and let the patter of the ocean fill their souls with the peace of solitude that only comes from the sea. Liv took a deep breath, her heart busting inside, even as her soul would never let her forget.

The curse was a cruel one of the heart.

20

The Curse of
Unending Grief

Erik sat with his back against the wall in his little stone house in the village outside of Italia. He sat under the window and stared at the bed. He leaned his head against the wall and breathed in deeply of Liv. He closed his eyes and saw his hands cupping her body again and tasting her neck, roaming her skin in the delicate places. He was plunging deep inside her and moaning against her lips. He was gripping her as if it was the last day of his life.

He opened his eyes again, his chest heaving in deep breaths, his loins aching for her. And then his mind wandered to the kiss on that ship before the pirates lunged him away from her. She raised to meet his lips and meant it. He clenched his jaws, his eyes wavering, thinking. How much longer would this curse haunt them all?!

He stood and opened the door, and Halfdan met him there. "Erik, I found something..."

Halfdan followed Erik down the street, his stride wide and shoulders high. "What are you doing?" Halfdan asked.

Erik turned to him. "I will not stop hunting her. I love her."

"So, you are going to hunt her again, I presume? Even though the monk warned us a third relic must be found first." Halfdan complained.

Erik sighed. "What do you have?"

Halfdan narrowed his brows. "Does this have to do with the last time you died? You have been sulking in your house since we got back. You have not eaten, and you are losing weight."

"Yes, when the pirates slung me into the woods over the hills. Damn bastards."

Halfdan laughed. "That was ingenious on their part."

Erik glared at him. "Something Liv taught them, no doubt."

Halfdan smiled. "Cannot stop smiling. You are stronger every time you die. But you do need to eat, Erik."

Erik huffed. "What do you have to tell me, Halfdan?"

"You need to come with me to the monastery."

Erik followed him up the winding road over the hill, and Halfdan led him to a small library room with vast views of the roaming hillsides and a crisp breeze pelting in at them. Halfdan pulled a book from a pile he had made and then opened it to a parchment he found stuck in its pages.

"This is the same curse, the immortali curse of the broken heart." He opened the parchment. It showed a hand drawing of a young woman with black hair, the seer. It looked like a portrait. She was sitting on the ground, and her bare feet lingered in water that rippled around her toes.

"Do you notice anything?" Halfdan wondered.

Erik stared at the picture and then his eyes fell upon the ripples in the water that reflected her face. Within her eyes was the shape of a small key. Halfdan pulled out the cylinder relic and turned it to show missing runes shaped like a key.

"Yes, the key is the third relic." Erik agreed.

"But what else do you see?"

Erik stared at the picture again, his eyes roaming around the woman in the picture. She was clearly in the city, and a cathedral loomed in the distance behind her. Erik clenched his face, because the cathedral in the picture did not exist there yet. The one there now was crumbling with age. It seemed the seer who made this curse also saw the future. Erik shivered inside.

"This curse is killing me," Erik complained.

Halfdan sighed. "The key will be at whatever cathedral this is that will be built in Italia. Just as I feared, a time we do not see yet. There is no way to trace this relic until then."

Erik turned to glare out the windows, his face hard. "I cannot go another day without her. What will I do, Halfdan?"

Halfdan sighed, shaking his head. "What you always do. You keep going. You keep moving. You help those in power. That is what you will do. Do whatever warring you feel led to do to keep busy til then."

Erik swallowed, shaking his head. "Will we ever be free of this curse?" He pulled his rune palm up and sneered at it.

Halfdan clenched his jaws. "Once Liv finds this relic, and we get that dagger, we must return to Iona Abbey..."

Erik did not look at Halfdan. He continued to stare out the window as night came, his face filled with mourning. "What if she breaks the relics herself Halfdan? She has two of them already."

"You will have no choice but to kill her with the knife then. After that, I can break the curse in Scotland."

"What if I cannot do it?" Erik swallowed. "What if the curse has already taken me then?"

Halfdan slammed the book shut. "Shit." He sighed, "I can only assume you will be unstoppable, and Liv and I will be in for the fight of our lives."

Erik craned his neck when he said that, his brows furrowed at him. "Will I hurt her?"

Halfdan cleared his throat. "Yes, Erik. You will force yourself upon her and keep her until the immortality is gone. All that will be left is you and her dying in agony with one another. The seer was murdered by her love, Erik. After he imprisoned her, he killed her, he killed everyone in that village, and then killed himself."

Erik closed his eyes and clenched his face. "I cannot let that happen, so here is what you will do when that time comes..."

"Erik!" Halfdan shouted, his eyes wide at him.

"No, Halfdan! I will die over and over for her if it means I can save her from this treachery. I need you to trust me while I am still in my right mind about her." Erik faced him, his face hard.

Halfdan's face was pale. "What do I need to do?" He swallowed as a pit of unending grief filled him up inside.

21

The Mountain Reckoning

Liv pressed her head to the ground beside Rait on the rolling knoll. They were two miles from the village and had gotten back late last night. Rait clenched his face and narrowed his brows aside the pirates as vibrations kissed the road and a haze of dust billowed at them. Alo led the Lechitic tribe into the village, and Liv could not let that happen.

Liv had a haven with the Tuscan village for many years, and she would keep it that way. She needed a place of refuge from the curse and life in general. Her pirates, Rait included, wanted to keep it hidden from the world. They needed it as a place of rest and safety for their families.

Rait nodded his head to the pirates, and they gripped their long bows and waited til Alo reached the knoll. Liv peered to see the Lechitic tribe of twelve follow him as he led them on. The road looked like it would end in a grove of olive trees, but it just swerved inside it and met another sloping hill onward to the village.

As Alo loomed beneath them, Liv nodded, and Rait and her pirates slid down the embankment to cut them off in the grove. They lunged across the grassy path and over the dirt road, the dense trees shrouding over them to form a shaded canopy. The rolling hills kissed the horizon behind them toward the village and melted onto plains dotted with vineyards. Liv loved it here. She wished she could stay and live out the rest of her life here.

Liv stepped out in the middle of the road behind them with an arrow in the knocking joint aimed at the back of Alo's head. "You betray your people, Alo."

Alo froze, and the twelve warriors turned to face her, their shadows bridging the gap between her and the road. He huffed at her, shaking his head.

"Did you honestly believe you could live at peace, immortal Viking?!"

Liv narrowed her brows and flinched, clenching her face. "You know what I seek!"

Alo turned his horse to face her and walked it through the warriors. "You have been seeking for hundreds of years. You have not lived. You are a sad soul filled with desperation, and I grieve for you."

"If you grieve for me so badly, you would not have betrayed me and helped me break this curse!"

Alo scoffed at her. "You are years away from breaking this! Why must you torment my people?" He yelled.

Liv dropped her bow when he said that and swallowed. From the sides of the rolling knolls, arrows filled the air between the grove, and the Lechitic warriors fell from their horses. They gasped in pain and died until Alo was the only one left alive. He took a deep breath and clenched his face at her from his horse. He craned his neck to see Rait and the pirates surround him on the road and huffed.

"Unlike this immortal, I have a family." He pestered them.

Liv lowered her bow and nodded as a short woman with two young children emerged from the shadows of the grove, and Alo gasped. "No! Not my family!" He pleaded. "Please, I will do anything."

Liv nodded. "Yes, you will." She smiled at the woman, and Alo's wife approached him, her blue eyes raging.

"You betrayed us, my love. Liv will to let us live, but we must flee these lands. We can never come back, or they will kill us."

Alo's face fell to a pale white, and he closed his eyes. "So be it." He slid from his horse and helped his wife on another, and they each held a child in their laps.

Liv watched him with his family. "If you ever come back here, I will kill you, Alo." She bit. "We will no more be working with the Lechitic tribe."

Alo swallowed, pulling his wife's horse close as they moved around the bodies on the road. He nodded at Liv, his eyes wide. Liv and Rait, with the pirates, watched Alo turn around and head back where he had come before Liv called for him.

"You have something for me."

Alo froze, his backside tense. He craned his neck to her, his eyes still upon Rait and the pirates with arrows aimed at him. He pulled out a parchment and threw it on the ground. Liv watched him lunge off with his family to get away from her. She sighed and bent down to pick it up, smiling.

"Finally. I can find that damn dagger." Her eyes craned over the map as Rait joined her. "This is not the original map. Damnit. It shows me a roundabout location but not the exact location."

Rait huffed. "What does this dagger do?"

Liv smiled. "It breaks the relics."

Rait narrowed his brows. "So, you need a relic to break the relics. Will it break the curse so you can live?"

Liv held her breath. "No. But it will get me closer."

"This curse is a real son of a bitch, isn't it?" Rait rolled his eyes. He nodded and turned away from her to the bodies, yelling at the pirates. "Come on! Help me with this scum."

Liv watched him and the pirates pull the bodies off the road to bury them, but a lump rose in her throat. It filled her chest with dread. It buried hopelessness deep inside her, and from there, it sprouted like rage had burned it alive. She dropped her hand at her side, clinging loosely to the map. She turned away from them to the rolling hills, missing Erik.

At dawn, Liv lunged out of her village on horseback to the quaint village outside Italia where Erik had taken her. She did not stop. She bent her head into the horse's mane until she recognized the wide road and stone houses dotting the hillsides. She rode hard into the village and stopped at the end where the hill rose to the monastery. It was late in the day when she arrived.

Her hair was loose and disheveled down her back, her long tunic split at the knees for her trousers, and covered in dust. She pulled her horse to the hitching post and gazed at the towering monastery for endless moments, thinking. As she turned to march up the hill through the crowded street, her spine grew rigid, and chills darted up her spine. She turned to face Erik. The dawning of her arrival filled his eyes with a roaming passion Liv could not describe.

They stood there staring at one another for endless moments, their eyes roaming up and down each other's faces. Erik opened his mouth to say something, but nothing came out. Liv took a deep breath, her chest heaving at him. His shoulders were high and broad, and he had trimmed his beard to frame his seductive, strong jawline. His eyes beamed at her, and his naked forearms flexed against his sleeveless tunic.

Erik clenched his face and lunged at her. He grabbed her around the waist and dove against her lips, and she met him there. She gripped his face, wrapped her arms around his shoulders, and pulled him in tighter to her. She gripped the side of his head in her palm as he grabbed her closer. They dove into each other's lips, moaning, their bodies heated in passion and fervor.

"I love you," Liv cried. "I love you!"

Erik breathed against her lips, gripping her backside in his strong arms. "I need you! I need you, Liv."

He pulled her to his house, his loins on fire like his heart. Their desperate rage for one another screamed, filling the longing of their souls, even for a moment. She let him pull her down the road, her whole body clenched and ready. They stripped one another in a passionate rage once they reached his house.

As Erik rose above her in the bed, he met her eyes with pain and passion that he got to hold her again. Erik dove inside her, ravaging her soul. He met her passion with unbridled fervor, their moans filling the room with hope. His mouth was wide open on hers even as his rolling, thrusting lunges synched their bodies like a heated dance. He dug his fingers into her sides, her hips, her back. His fingers were as wild on her body as his heart longing for her.

Liv met his forceful plunges with desperate grips on his muscular forearms, her legs flexed around him. She raked her palms up his arms, gripping him hard down his muscular back. She gripped his buttocks and rolled her palms to his legs to push him harder inside her. She belted out moans in his mouth as he kissed her wildly, his face a raging storm in her breaths.

They raged into one another, their passion as heated as the pain filling their hearts. They roared into each other's lips, their moans writhing into their souls as hard as Erik's forceful thrusts. They bled with desperate abandon and seethed of hopeless liberation. As the day fled and night came, they let exhaustion take them.

At dawn rising, they lay intertwined together, their naked bodies breathing and inflamed. Erik closed his eyes against her forehead, his strong arms gripping her body into him as they lay on their sides facing each other. He opened his eyes and met her smile. He caressed her face with his fingers, his eyes lingering up and down her beauty.

"Will you marry me? When this curse dies, marry me." He whispered in her face.

Liv held his hand on her face. "Yes."

Erik stared into her eyes and sighed. "How much longer?" He wondered. "I am dying inside the longer we cannot be together."

Liv swallowed, her eyes tearing up. "All I know is that I love you. I love you, Erik." Her voice broke.

Erik sighed on her lips and kissed her again. "You must leave again, I know. I will wait for you, Liv. I will wait, and then we can finally be together."

A tear fell down Liv's cheek, and she rubbed his ribbed chest, sinking her fingers into his tattoos. She wanted more of him, not less. She needed him. His breathing intensified as her fingers lingered down his chest to his groin. He closed his eyes and held his breath as he grew hard at her touch again.

He took a deep breath and sighed. He raked his palm up Liv's curvy side and kissed her again. He rolled on top of her and pressed inside her before she had to leave. Erik rolled up and down on her again, moaning as he pulsed deep inside her. She breathed him in so profoundly she wanted his touch to stay with her for a long time. She wanted him inside her forever.

But this curse was a treacherous curse of the heart, and it would not let love lie.

H alfdan sighed so heavily that Liv and Erik froze in the road to stare back at him. He met their eyes and sighed again, shaking his head. "I do not like it. I hate it." He complained. "The both of you have no intimate self-control at all!"

Liv was pulling her horse as Erik walked her to the end of the village. They looked exhausted. Halfdan knew they had made love half the day yesterday, all night, and all morning. Their passion for each other was evident on their faces. His heart even ached for them. He watched them both, their shoulders slumped, defeated.

"Liv, you cannot come back here to taunt Erik's loins. And Erik, you cannot keep..." Halfdan froze.

Erik met his stare, his face tired. "What. Making love to her?"

Halfdan sighed. "Yes! The more you continue doing this, the harder it will be to leave one another. The curse will take you both. You must stay separated until the curse is broken."

Liv swallowed when he said that. "But it could be hundreds of years more. I cannot do this, Halfdan." She complained. "The final relic is not ready to be found yet."

Halfdan walked between them and pulled her horse on. "You have no choice. I will not die in this curse because if it takes you both down, I go down also. You both must be separated."

Erik's eyes met Liv's, and he followed them on. Once they reached the end of the village, Halfdan rolled his eyes at them.

"Now, say goodbye." He shook his head at them and then turned around as they kissed again. "And do not come back here again. Do not tell Erik where you are coming from, Liv!" He warned her.

Erik shook his head, grasping her face in his palm. "I love you. Never forget that, no matter what happens. Promise me."

Liv nodded, her eyes tearing up. She kissed him back, gripping his forearms. "I promise."

Then she turned to Halfdan and hugged him tight. He closed his eyes and hugged her back. "I am sorry, Liv."

She sighed in his face, and Halfdan smiled at her. She nodded at him and climbed on her horse, her eyes meeting Erik's again. His eyes roved over her, his face still impassioned with her. As she turned to go, she glared at him again.

"I love you." She turned away and raced down the road, the dirt flying behind her.

Erik's knees grew weak. "I love you, too." His eyes followed her until she disappeared behind the hills. "You will be my wife one day." He whispered, hopeful. "One day soon." He closed his eyes.

Halfdan shook his head at Erik. "That cannot happen again. We must leave this village, Erik. She cannot find you like she did. The next time, you may not let her leave."

Erik agreed. "I know. She came to me..."

There was silence, and Erik gripped his heart. "I will not deny her when she comes, Halfdan."

Halfdan huffed. "We must leave the village today."

Erik turned to go and then stopped. "She is not far away, is she?" He pondered. "Not far at all."

Halfdan met Erik's stare with wide eyes. "Erik. No."

Halfdan crossed his arms and watched Erik march back to his house, his shoulders slumping. By now, the street was busy and bustling with families shopping the markets, but the vibe was not lively as they had hoped it would stay. The village had been a great home for them to rest and live in, but it was always short lived.

By nightfall, they had packed up their belongings and traveled further north. If Liv wanted to come again, she would not find him. Halfdan had to do this because it was apparent they loved one another. Now, every time they were together, they would be harder to separate. They would fall into one another and make love until the curse rendered upon them and their immortality was spent. Then they would kill each other in their mortality, and the curse would never be broken.

Halfdan could not let that happen. He cared for them both. So, by dawn, he pulled Erik north, and they sailed to Lithuania. He had to drag Erik away from Liv while still in his right mind. Although the Viking had made love to her again, the curse still breathed within him.

He had not said anything when Erik mentioned, *"She is not far away, is she?"* *"Not far at all."* He did not tell Erik the lights of his eyes changed to fiery blue. Halfdan shivered inside. He had to get Erik as far away from Liv as possible and keep him busy until the final relic and dagger were found. The final relic was a golden key, and it existed but was not ready to be found yet.

For another four hundred and ninety-five years, Erik raged. He threw himself into the fires of war, dying over and over. Erik filled himself with warring and loathing. He was reborn stronger.

As time lingered on, his heart hardened. The curse pulled his soul from a deep vat of unending pain and sorrow, filling his mind with hunting Liv. Again. As wars and death filled the lands, Erik turned his attention back to what mattered. It was time to hunt her again.

This curse was a cruel one of the heart.

22

Teutonic Order, Malbork, 1395

The Nogat River spilled around the castle fortress Erik had called home for many years. The curtain wall rounded the interior courtyard, and its shadows melted upon the river waters. The order designed it to strengthen its control, and it sat on over fifty acres as the brotherhood kept expanding over the years.

Erik did not mind. He found it a safe solitude for him, and not to mention, Halfdan was able to build the library there. There were three separate castles behind the defensive walls, with dry moats and soaring towers hoovering over the plain. Sitting in the Vistula Delta meant they depended mostly on trading by water, and Erik felt as if a part of him from his homeland was here, too.

He marched down the lower castle halls, the courtyard kissing the breadth of the stone pillars, the crisp Fall air biting his bearded face. Erik's loose surcoat floated in behind him as he walked, the heraldry of the order embedded on the fabric. His leather-gloved hand gripped atop the hilt of his longsword, squeaking in delight. He was still tanned, but his beard was long again. His mail couf covered his head, but his hair was still long, and he kept it braided down his back.

He reached the end of the hall and a a shadow moved within the open library. He paused at the double entryway, looming in to glare at

Halfdan. Although Halfdan was still a monk in spirit, he had taken on different tasks throughout the years, becomming a wanted commodity to kings and knights. Erik knocked on the door frame, clearing his throat.

"You called?" He walked in to witness Halfdan fully cloaked in a tunic, his cloak flowing behind him as he straddled the ladder atop the library wall. A wall of books reached the ceiling, where wooden beams splayed across the arched room, windows blasting in the last of the daylight.

"It is nearing its end, finally. I can feel it! I know where the dagger relic is."

Erik clenched his jaws and held his breath. "We have been doing this for a long time. I have been a knight for many years and no closer to finding it."

Halfdan sneered. "Yes, Liv has remained steps ahead of us. She still needs to find the key that is not ready to be found yet, but we are getting closer."

"She has been masquerading as a pirate leader all this time." Erik rolled his eyes. "I do not know how I missed that. I thought after Bartolomeus died, it would end, but she has not stopped."

"Do not forget she will continue searching until she has them all. I am certain she has had them all over the world searching, and been successful at a few. She may even have them all but the key and dagger."

Halfan sighed. "Erik, we must get that dagger. We cannot let her get it. If she has the relics and then gets that dagger..."

Erik gazed out the door to the courtyard. "Yeah, I know. We are at the mercy of this damn curse. You know what to do if she does..."

Halfdan scowled. "The world will shift as she destroys the relics, and there will be chaos. You will be drawn to her, desperate to control her so she does not keep going. The curse does not want to be broken.

There was a reason my people kept it at the abbey. It is there it must be destroyed, once and for all."

Halfdan huffed and rolled his eyes. "I warned those old monks about this. I did. No one listened to me. They never listened to me."

The silence overwhelmed them for endless moments before Halfdan cleared his throat again. "If she gets the dagger relic, she will want to go it alone after, so be prepared..." Halfdan warned.

"Ah well, it has been many years since I died, so why not? Where am I going?"

"There is a port cave in Estonia that pirates frequent. The cave opens to an inlet, and their longships can sail into it. From there, a cavern lair gets you to the relic. It is a three-day hike into the wilderness."

"How did you find this?" Erik questioned, his eyes wide.

"A knight returned from scouting the area. The Grand Master also brought these copies of old maps to me. These were taken by a pirate years ago named Alo." Halfdan laughed. "I am certain she already has copies of these, but she has not found the relic yet, or we would sense it."

Erik smiled and leaned into the door frame. "Very well."

Erik turned to go but stopped as Halfdan called after him. "Erik, if this is true you must understand what this means for you and Liv. You must understand what your choice of becoming close to her may mean for you both."

Halfdan sighed. "If you do find her again, you must let her go. Or I will be forced to make you."

Erik froze, his heart beating wildly. "This curse is driving me mad. She drives me mad."

"Are you prepared for this?" Halfdan questioned. "You know what she will do once she sees the dagger relic."

Erik swallowed. "I'm more concerned I will want her when I see her," He whispered.

Erik turned to him, his face firm, his eyes on fire. "You are coming with me. It is a three-day ride. I will ready the ships, but you will await me there with the knights."

Halfdan slammed the curse book closed. "Damnit!" As he was plopping the book into his satchel, he paused.

"What?! What ships? What are you planning?"

Erik walked back down the hall, his white surcoat dancing behind him as if snakes had bent him to their will. They found her again, finally! It had been too many years again. Now, it was up to him to get to the next step in this whole plan and be rid of this curse once and for all so he could be with her forever.

23

Crusade of the Hearts, Baltic Sea

A narrow inlet of the Baltic Sea stretched for twenty miles, its small bays kissing swamps and lingering through gentle rolling plains as if emerald jewels had blessed the lands. There was betrayal, too, and the Teutonic Knights would find it. Erik led his cavalry along the inlet for miles until stopping on the outskirts of Estonia.

The small settlement stretched along the river waters, and Erik's knights saw signs of life as rumors spread the pirates still inhabited it. Albeit hidden from the prying eyes of Eriks Grand Master and the order in Prussia, Erik knew this land well. He remembered it being one of the largest ports in the Baltic Sea. It was here where his people, the Vikings, traded.

It was here his ship got pulverized by the storm, where he first died, and woke up on shore days later, and where he was from. So, it was no surprise to him that rumors were spreading on the open sea of pirates inhabiting the old dead town, and one of them was a Viking woman.

Erik knew it was Liv because, for many years, she had worked with the Curonians to find relics. Her immortality had given her great prestige, power, and wealth. As Erik hunted her again, his heart became heavy. He loved her still. Time meant nothing.

The forest covered them in a thick canopy as they crept through, their peering eyes scouting through their Helms, their white robes kissed with black crosses. They pulled their Destrier horses behind them, shrouded with full plate armor and chain mail as the knights wore under their robes.

Erik glared behind him through the forest as they crested on foot, pulling their horses along the river's edge, several hundred of his knights waiting and watching. As he neared closer to the bay town, his heart skipped a beat, and a pang hit him.

"I know you are here." He told himself, lingering closer to her.

Halfdan had been a steady source of knowledge for him these many years. Becoming a Teutonic Knight was the only way Erik could exercise his rage and continue honing his fighting skills, but she was always on his mind. He knew he would find her again. She was looking for that dagger and was close to finding it.

He stopped at the river's edge and gazed through the darkness at the lively port town. Thatched roofs rose over fields as cows and goats grazed. Wooden fences twisted through and around the town. There were no lamp oils lit, no burning torches. It was dark and quiet.

Erik held his breath and watched from the blackness of their canopy as five Longships coasted into the river, their main sails down, the river waters bursting against the limestone shoreline. The long ships curled in the water as gaping dragon mouths intimidated the crisp Fall night air around them. The oars rolled the ship's entire length, the pirates silently rowing in the dark.

They rowed two by two, with the last one lagging, more silent than usual. The rounded shields on the starboard and Port sides added a horrendous decorum to the ships, but Erik found it fascinating. These were the ships of his people, and he knew them well. The fifth ship stopped rowing as the knights moved under the canopy, filling the breadth of the riverbanks in silence, itching their way closer to the town.

They watched the four ships slide onto the shores, and men and women jumped overboard and began dumping crates and burlap satchels. Some of the items they were passing to one another were artwork and furniture. Erik questioned why they would be unloading the booty instead of sailing on to sell it. He paused as his knights ventured out from the woods to confront them.

He ordered them to attack once they had started marching into the village, but his eyes followed the fifth ship that sailed right by them in the dark. The Teutonic Knights filled the fields at the river in unison, riding on horseback into the town. Just as they reached the fences, the townspeople rose from the fields with swords and spears, and the arttack broadsided the knights.

Erik rode around the field behind his army, ignoring the fray, his eyes set on the fifth ship. He rushed through the town as other knights followed in close pursuit with him, their swords drawn. When he reached the river, he kept pushing his horse along the bank to chase the ship that had now raised its main mast.

He saw heads bopping up and down on the ship and a lone figure, slender and wearing a long cloak, watching him in the dark. He saw the long hair blowing in the breeze with their cloak as if they were one, the men rowing frantically to get to the Baltic Sea. When the river banks collided with swamp, and he could go no further, he stopped on the mushy shore and pulled his horse back to higher ground.

Several knights followed him, waiting for him along the ridge of the bank. He turned back to face the ship, seething inside. Behind him, the knights had taken the town, and the pirates would die unless given a treaty. Piracy was outlawed, and they were going to keep it that way.

He did not care what his order did with these people because, for the last hundreds of years, he had hunted her and her alone and used whatever tribe, kingdom, or order he had become part of to do it. He had been part of more wars, in more agony. He had killed people. Halfdan thought he could take Erik away, but it made Erik want her more.

Along the way, Halfdan meticulously recorded changes caused by the curse. Every time Erik died, he returned more alert, more vigorous.

Erik could not live like this anymore. If he did not find her this time, then he would die first. He knew it. He turned his horse to go back through the town and follow the river to the coast. He would ride the coast along the ridge until dawn, when he reached the cave where Liv would hide. She would be staying close to shore and avoiding the open ocean. From there, she would trek the wilderness to the cavern lair to find the ancient relic, if it was there.

L iv felt uneasy as the Teutonic Knights captured her people in the old town, but she planned it this way. She had to get the order off her back, so the four ships were bait. The knights may give them pardons, but it was uncertain. That was a risk they were willing to take for her, and she would never forget them.

She pulled her cloak tighter over her thinning shoulders, her waist-length blonde hair blowing out around the hood. Fall had come early, and she feared winter on the sea. She stayed restless deep inside. The kind of restlessness leaving her exhausted even as she slept.

She had hunted the dagger relic for four hundred and ninety-five years based on the maps Alo had given her. It was a particular relic endowed with magic from ancient Viking seers that could help undo the curse. She had studied the curse book when her grandmother passed away, memorizing the old legends and curses. The missing page from King Alfred's kingdom was what she needed to put the pieces together, but the map was elusive. Even after several hundred years, she was no closer to finding, it she feared, although Estonia pulled at her heart.

Her grandmother never told her about this relic, and she needed the dagger to bust the stone in the shaft where the original curse came. But, of course, that meant she would run into Halfdan again. She was sure the old monk had taken great care of the shaft all these years. The problem was she also needed Erik to retrieve the dagger. It was inevitable they would all have to see each other again. By dawn, she had sailed along the coastline of Estonia, nearing the port cavern where they could slide under the rocks to stay hidden.

As dawn rose, Erik tied his horse to a tree in the woods and climbed down the cliff facing from the outside wall in front of the port. The waterway spilled in from the ocean, and an open cavern jutted out from the mountain. Sandy beaches sparkled in delight around the bend. He lowered himself between the trees, following the rock crevasse to get to a specific ledge inside the cavern where the ship would rest against a platform.

Liv stood on the bow, an air of relief on her shoulders. They sailed into the cove, the Longship coasting lazily as the cavern walls closed in around them. They came to a slow stop before a stone platform, and darkness blasted them before the flickering of oil lamps dotted the dark cavern in an aura of tangerine hues.

As shadows moved along the rock paths at both sides of her ship, her eyes caught a white surcoat with a big black cross climbing down to meet her. Her heart skipped a beat, and a surging fire ignited in her guts. She yanked her Hallstatt to confront him just as the knight dropped from the cavern path to face her.

He bolted before her, pressing his longsword out to stop her blade. He pressed into her at her neck, but the blade stopped at her shoulder. She blocked him, their swords crossed with one another, and they stood there, their swords at each other's throats, facing off.

Her knees gave way as she recognized Erik, but she pulled herself back up to face him and pressed harder into the blade. Erik pushed into her harder, and his blade touched her throat. He had her. Her heart jumped a beat, and her eyes were wide at him. She clenched her thin jaws, her plush lips pursing at him in agony, her heart beating wildly.

He was stronger. He pressed into Liv with his power. The knights' hood covered Erik's head, but his strong facial features were the same. His beard had gotten longer and thinner, still blonde. His blue eyes pierced her as he held his breath, taking her in. There was an aura about him that made her quake inside. She was powerless in his presence as her chest heaved up and down while he met her at her face, their blades kissing one another.

"Hello, pirate." He taunted her, his voice hard, as he gritted his teeth at her.

"Erik." She belted out, her jaws clenched.

"Been a long time, Liv." His eyes lingered over her body.

The shadows that moved around her ship were the knights. They surrounded them and pressed their longswords into the pirates so all anyone could do was freeze where they sat. Halfdan walked to them from behind Erik atop the platform as a slew of knights explored the cavern.

"Liv!" Halfdan hollered but then stopped as a slew of Curonian Longships filled the horizon behind them in the distance for miles.

"That is not good." Halfdan's eyes were wide.

Erik kept his eyes on Liv, not flinching. Behind the Longships appeared three-masted Carracks, and suddenly, the air became engulfed in flames as the ships warred one another.

Erik stared deep into her even as her eyes melted around to see the carnage behind them for miles on the water, and his face and the cave lit up with the remnants of the explosive auras. She swallowed. The Curonian Longships split at sea as her men jumped overboard. The Teutonic Knights made a quick end to her small fleet that had followed to ensure she would make it safely to the cavern.

"All of this devastation because of a woman!" Halfdan gawked at the fires burning even as shards of Longships blew high in the air, his face as if a gaping blowhole had hit him.

Liv swallowed again as Erik's blade still pressed against her throat, eying Halfdan from the side. "Sorry." She melted, her eyes wide.

Liv watched as the knights pulled her pirates from her ship, and she was still standing facing off Erik. She relinquished her sword from Erik's throat as the knights surrounded her, and they lingered to secure the port. Liv faced Erik, speechless, her heart thumping wildly.

"How did you find me?" She pleaded, shocked. "It's been so long." She held her breath at his handsome face, but his glare was hard and cold. Erik was tired of chasing her.

He leaned into her, clenching his jaws at her face. "I am going to remove my blade from your throat. Do not run from me again." He scolded her, his voice deeper than she remembered it being.

She nodded with her eyes and sighed as he removed his blade. She stood glaring at him as he loomed over her, his eyes like the blue light she had seen when she died. His whole face was clenched at her, but his lips had a gentle slope to them of satisfaction and it unnerved her to no end. She stood there in her long chemise, her cloak blowing behind her, her long blonde hair rolled down her back in ribbons, and her dark, tanned skin accentuating her blue eyes.

Halfdan approached them from behind. "Liv, glad you are well. We have a journey to do together."

Liv stepped away from Erik, nodding her head in defiance. "No, this is not a good idea. I cannot be around him."

Erik lunged into her and pulled her over his shoulder with one arm. She was helpless to fight him. He marched with Liv over her shoulder on the platform through a series of tunnels, gripping her behind in his strong clasp.

Halfdan followed behind, smiling as Liv clung precariously over Erik's shoulder, grabbing at his robe, her hair over her face. "Good to see you, Liv!" He shouted. "We cannot let you get the dagger alone, though. It takes the three of us to retrieve it."

All Liv could do was grunt and blow her hair out of her face. Erik led them up to the forest floor, his stamina like a breath of wind, and Liv felt it.

"I warned you." Erik scoffed as she squirmed on his shoulder.

"How did you find me!" She hollered, her cheeks flushed. "You were a knight this whole time?"

"We traced you from maps we got at the Order. One of your old pirates, Alo, had made copies." Halfdan smiled. "I think the map you were given was altered."

She gasped. "Alo! I knew he lied. Should have killed him!"

As they reached a path in the woods, Erik bent over and plopped her on her feet but she pulled away from him. Erik tripped her, and she fell on her back, and he crept over her. He pressed atop her and held her down, his forearms flexing under his tunics. He pulled her arms over her head and held her there, and for a moment, they glared into one another's eyes.

Liv gasped in his face, her heart racing. "Erik." She breathed against his lips.

He sighed. "Yes, been hunting you this whole time."

Halfdan rolled his eyes. "Yes, that was a problem. I took him to Lithuania, but all he did was become a Teutonic Knight! I give up." He sighed. "The last time you two could not keep your hands off each other, I had no choice."

"We cannot stay together, Erik. I cannot control myself around you." She moaned.

"I do not care if you can or not. I have you now." Erik jerked her up to face him. "You came to me last time."

"I do not regret that." She swallowed. "But this curse is not done yet."

He pulled at her wrists and tied her fists together with rope, his face stern. He sighed, avoiding her eyes. "I cannot let you go. Not again."

She tried to kick him, but all she did was end up wrapping a leg around his backside. Erik lunged his midsection into her between her legs to keep her from hitting his groin, and she fell back again. Erik stopped her from hitting the ground on her back, his palm pressed into the middle of her back, propping her up as if they were dancing. He bent over between her legs, and Liv grabbed his tunic to keep from falling.

She could go nowhere, and he was stronger. She clenched her jaws at his face and held her breath, their eyes meeting. Halfdan sighed, watching them fight.

Erik huffed in her face. "You cannot take me. Can you? You stay weak in my presence." He bragged.

"Untie me, and we will see." She barked.

Erik smiled in her face, amused. He roved his eyes up and down her face, breathing on her lips. He wanted to kiss her badly.

"This is awkward," Halfdan paused, gawking at them.

"Seeing you two together again," he sighed, "like this," His eyes wide at them, "brings back memories," Halfdan grasped his heart.

"What are you doing, Erik?" Liv demanded.

Erik pulled her into him, grabbing her wrists he tied. "We are going to find this dagger relic together. You will give it to Halfdan. Once you find the key relic, then we can break this curse. You know what we need to do, Liv."

Liv growled.

Erik froze and stared at her. "Why did you wait so long on this dagger? You knew all along it takes all three of us to get it."

Liv held her breath. "Because I knew I had to see you again, and I," Her eyes teared up. "I know I would not leave if I saw you again. I would not want to!"

Erik stared into her eyes. "I know the feeling."

Liv froze. She held her hands up to Erik. "Untie me. I will not run."

Erik's laughter was an assault on her senses, between a sneer and a giggle. "No."

Liv grimaced at him. "Can you do something for me then?" She gazed at Erik.

He glared at her, his white robes kissing his tall frame. He waited for her response, his back as stiff as his face, not amused.

"Remove that hideous hood from your head!"

Erik pulled his long sword and pushed the blade at her. "Walk."

She turned her back on him and began walking. Halfdan lagged, watching them. Erik pushed the hood off his head, his blonde hair breathing for the first time in many years.

24

A Forest of Endless Dreams

It was not all that bad. Erik had planned this attack well, and Liv was impressed. He even had three horses saddled with supplies ready to go a half mile from the cavern. So, they began the three-day journey inland to a hidden lair where the seer dagger lay so they could break the stone in the shaft, therefore breaking the curse. They hoped.

By nightfall, they were hungry, so they found a stone outcropping, and Erik made a fire. The evergreen forest filled the breadth of the mountain before them and gently sloped on a plain. Wherever they looked, they were engulfed in trees and darkness.

Erik sat sprawled out in front of them, watching Liv and controlling the entrance. He had untied her, too, so she could relieve herself and eat and drink with them. Halfdan handed her a cup of hot tea, and she sipped it and sighed. She noticed they were both staring at her, and she froze in mid-sip.

"What? It has been a long time since I had your tea, Halfdan. I missed it."

Halfdan smiled ear to ear. "Missed you as well. To be honest, I still do not miss our time in the wilderness. I have a nice library and room now. Erik is vigorous and very fast, been hard to keep up with him."

She paused and gazed at Erik, and he met her stare as if he knew something she did not but could not say.

"I am happy to see you both alive and well." She mumbled, digging back into her food.

Erik sat silently across the ledge opening, his eyes going everywhere, watching the forest. Liv cleared her throat. "Teutonic Knight?" She looked at him, her eyes grazing up and down his white coat. "How chivalrous."

Erik craned his neck at her and then turned to watch the woods. "Pirate queen."

"I did not kill innocents. My tribe spared lives. How do you think we had so many people inhabiting the shoreline of the Baltic Sea?"

Erik stared at her, not flinching. "You have spent hundreds of years enticing them with your immortality and your husbands," he pointed at her body, "and your beauty."

"I only married once because I had to. He died." She added, popping a piece of bread in her mouth. "Only took you six hundred years to tell me I am beautiful." She rolled her eyes. "Even after sleeping together."

Erik jerked his head and glared at her. "Bartolomeus? I knew it." Erik swallowed.

"Only one husband? Oh, really?" Halfdan questioned. "That is not what we heard throughout the years."

"I married Bartolomeus, but that was before Erik and I," She whispered. "Those were just rumors to make us look stronger and instill fear. I needed the tribe to help me plunder to get to the relics. If not for them, I would not have found..."

Erik swallowed. "Found what?" He held his breath, "Found what, Liv?" He demanded, waiting.

She sighed. "They were afraid of me. They knew what I was. The stories they tell about me are still legendary."

Erik cleared his throat and took a sip of the tea. "How did you survive?"

Liv swallowed the bread. "Bortolomeus killed me after I demanded his pirates take me to their village. I knew I needed help, and the Curonians were already renowned."

Halfdan widened his eyes, but Erik stared at her.

"When I woke up, I saw the bone pit." She froze, thinking. "He did not kill me again, and the tribe was terrified of me."

"Well, it worked," Erik told her.

"I am sorry," Halfdan said. "I have been spared so far from death, but this is not easy."

Erik stared at her again. He sat his tea down, crossed his arms at his chest, and sighed at her.

The silence overwhelmed them, but Liv stared at Erik and blurted out. "Did you become a Knight to hunt me?"

Erik met her stare, his eyes falling up and down her body, until he turned away. "Yes."

"Of course you did," Liv mumbled, chills rushing down her spine.

Halfdan pursed his lips, gazing up at them from his plate of food. "I'm going to have to separate you two again, aren't I?" He got up and walked out, rolling his eyes at them. "You know, I have suffered too. I miss the abbey." He stormed off.

Erik huffed. "He is not happy I made him come. I suppose he was content to stay in the library til he died." Just as Erik went to go after him, he paused as Liv spoke.

"I am sorry for hurting you, Erik." She told him, swallowing her pride. "I did not want to leave the last time. I wanted to stay with you. Forever."

Erik met her stare. "You married that pirate king. You are supposed to marry me." He whispered. "You belong with me, Liv."

Liv swallowed. "I had no choice. He died before you and I..."

Erik sighed at her. "We have hurt one another."

She agreed. "Do you forgive me? Please forgive me."

"I do." He swallowed, a softness overcoming his face. "I still want you, Liv. You know time means nothing. You mean everything." He whispered.

She returned his stare but then folded her gaze to the rock cropping sheltering them, her eyes teary. She cleared her throat and sipped her tea, her stomach screaming that she was still hungry, but her heart ached. Just when she was ready to wipe her face, she turned to see Erik get up and walk out, too, leaving her alone against a dying fire.

B y dawn, they were saddled up again and had trekked another day, stopping only when the sun fell behind the horizon. Liv heard the gentle sounds of waterfalls, and her soul sighed inside. She loved waterfalls. It reminded her of home in Scotland, with the bubbling brooks and the flowing falls behind their village in the woods.

The day of travel was tranquil, and they did not speak to one another. Halfdan had spent the day studying more parchments on horseback while Erik followed silently behind her, watching her.

Sometimes, throughout the day, she would turn to see if Erik was still behind her, and he was. He gazed at her with precision, which made her quake inside. He watched her every move.

That evening, they sat around a fir, ate their bread, and seared game. Liv leaned back against a tree shrouded by ferns, gazed up into the sky through the canopy, and held her breath. The stars sizzled above her as if the heavens were on fire. She ignored Erik watching her and rolled over to sleep, noting that he did not eat.

25

Pools of Endless Desires

In the morning, Liv awoke by Halfdan nudging her arm, smiling down at her face. She sat up and wiped her eyes. "Forgive me, I must have slept in."

Halfdan smiled. "There is a pool of water down the path, just there. You can clean up if you wish before we leave by midday."

"Midday?"

She raised to question him. "I have reading to do, and quite frankly, I am tired of doing it on horseback."

"Erik?" She pondered.

Halfdan pointed to the pool. "He is down there. I cannot keep you both apart." He rolled his eyes.

She watched him clean up camp but then sat down to study more parchments. She was eager to clean up regardless if Erik was down there. She marched down a trodden path through knee-deep ferns until the waterfall rang in her ears. An opening under the canopy revealed a pool of water with three trickling waterfalls soaring into them and rising cliff walls. She smiled, amazed at the beauty, but did not see Erik.

She pulled her cloak off her shoulders and yanked her tunic over her head, sliding out of her boots. She marched out of the ferns and into the pool, diving in when it got waist-deep, chilling her to the bone. As she swam with her eyes opened underwater, long legs stood in the water before her. She came up for air, and Erik stood there staring at her, his naked body glowing in muscles, his privates barely covered by the water. She lunged back down into the water.

Erik sighed. "We have seen each other naked, Liv."

Liv huffed at him. "It's been a long time."

"It's been too damn long!" Erik swam away from her to the other side. "When you stood up, I saw everything." He smiled. "Damn, I missed you."

Liv opened her mouth in shock, her eyes wide, but then laughed. She ducked under the water and felt alive again, coming up to see him still in the water, watching her.

"You are beautiful." Erik sighed.

She stopped swimming, rubbing water out of her eyes. She sighed at his face, her heart racing. "You always look good."

"It's been hundreds of years again, Liv." He swallowed, clenching his face. "I am dying inside the longer this drags on."

She froze, her back to him. She turned to face him, the water covering her nakedness, and swallowed. "You still hunt me after all this time. The curse is still strong."

"You still hunt relics." He belted out. "Did you care for me at all?"

She gasped. "I remember it as it were yesterday! Time means nothing. I remember what you told me, even as my heart aches for you, still!"

"Our love does not grow cold, Liv. It never will." Erik whispered, his face clenched at her, his pecs and forearms bulging in muscles.

"I died every day since the last time we were together wondering about you!" She yelled at him, her lips quivering. "I knew Halfdan would make you leave. I had to see you again."

Erik's eyes fell on her breasts in the water, and he held his breath at her. He flexed his pecs and arms, his heart beating wildly at her beauty that beckoned him.

She lingered closer to him in the water, even as he hunched waist-deep at her face, and they floated there together. "I died every damn day hungering to find these relics to break this curse so we can be free, Erik. I had to do this alone."

He took a deep breath as she sighed at him. His eyes were hard and roamed all over her as if he were hungry. He opened his mouth, but nothing came out.

Erik clenched his teeth. His long blonde hair cascaded down his back like hers, his blue eyes piercing her tanned skin. "I followed you until the curse got stronger. I followed you through wars and famine. We had to split up after the last time we made love, and I died inside then, all over again."

Liv paused, her face drained of color. "We did." Her knees trembled. "I died too."

Erik floated into her face. "I had nowhere else I felt drawn to go, so I became a knight, fought more wars, and killed. I became a monster, Liv."

She swallowed at his face, her eyes wide. "You saved me and pulled me out of a dark place the last time." It dawned on her. "You came and loved me. You are not a monster."

"You found me over and over, Liv." His eyes were wide at her face, his lips loose as if he wanted to scream but could not.

"You had to leave me after that last time in the village, and we made love." She shivered. "I felt you being ripped from me when you left."

"I never left you! I will never leave you." His cry was deep, and he was breathing like his heaving chest. He came inches from her, tears in his eyes. "I love you deeper than the forests I have tracked our enemies through,"

Liv shook in the water, her mouth aghast as tears filled her eyes.

Erik lingered closer to her. "I love you stronger than this drive we both have to keep going, even when you run away from me." He lunged forward and pulled her face into his palms as he raised over her in the water. She cried in his hands, her arms shaking as she gazed at him.

He leaned into her face and breathed on her lips. "I love you harder than the pain of dying." He cried. "And I will die again and again if it brings me to you!" He pressed into her face, his lips quivering to touch hers.

She moaned as her lips trembled at his face. She grabbed his hands on her face, their fingers intertwining, their eyes not wavering into one another.

"I love you more than the time passed between us," Liv whispered into his lips.

He lunged in and met her for the kiss, their mouths wide open. Their hearts beat wild as Erik melted against her. A longing burst in Liv's chest as a fire lingered there. She closed her eyes and kissed him back, their mouths meeting in desperate passion. Her palms gripped his muscular forearms, and her hand lingered down his chest tattoos. She raked her fingers over his sculpted muscles, her loins aching for him.

Erik held his breath and moaned in her mouth as her palm lingered down his hard groin. They huddled in waist-deep water, touching and gripping one another as their tongues rolled in each other's mouths. She ran her fingers down the side of his face, felt his chin, and lingered at his neck. She pressed into his beard as their mouths breathed open to passionate kisses.

"I need this," Erik moaned, "I need you."

"I always need you!" Liv cried in his mouth.

He pulled her against his chest, her breasts pressed on him. His hands fell from her face to her lower back. He pressed his palms over her thighs and gripped her with a fierce hunger.

She shivered inside, but not because the water was cold. She reached behind his neck, pulled out his long hair, and clutched his shoulders. She spread her legs around his waist, inviting him inside her. Erik gripped her buttocks in his palms and lunged deep inside her. He raised her up and down against him as their chests writhed against one another. He sunk his open mouth to her breasts and moaned against them as he plunged deep inside her.

"Liv. Liv!" He moaned, his face hard and clenched.

Liv gripped his strong shoulders and leaned her head back to the water as Erik sucked her breasts, moaning. Their hair spread like ribbons surrounded them in a haven of gold as he plunged into her soul. His face was a sweet release into her breaths, finally. She held onto him as if the world was slipping, and they had no choice but to grip to one another as if time were no more. He pulled her in so tight it seemed nature had folded around them in a canopy of a desperate embrace.

"Erik, aughhhh..." She moaned, his thrusting filling her with aching pleasure.

They lingered in each other's loving embrace as Erik lunged hard inside her. She embraced him wholeheartedly as her fingers grazed into his back. She pulled him harder into her as their mouths remained locked in sweet surrender, their aching loins roaring into one another.

Erik closed his eyes in this surrender. Her body pulsated as he pummeled inside her, her tight inner thighs grinding against his groin. As he went off inside her, the sweet release ached through his bones. Her legs shook around him as his hands gripped her back, his fingers spreading like claws into her skin. He yelled into her open mouth, his body writing up and down as his seed exploded inside her. Liv closed her eyes and held her breath as he moaned, her heart beating hard against his chest.

"Erik." She moaned in his mouth.

Erik stared into her eyes and clenched his face as he continued spilling his seed inside her. "I love you." He gripped the back of her head with his palm as they continued to blast into their kisses, their breaths as hot as the fire burning them from the inside out.

One day, they would break this curse before it killed them all. One day, they would marry and make love without fear of the curse taking them. One day soon, they would be free.

Hours later, midday had passed, and Halfdan's head was spinning after his research of the parchments and maps he had brought.

He had the curse book splayed out in his lap, and he slumped over, sighing, rubbing his head. He got up and moseyed down the fern gully path to the pool, freezing in mid-step as two naked bodies lay entangled into one another. He smiled at them and turned to go but froze as it hit him. His back to them, his face drained of color.

They had just given themselves to one another completely again. Every time they did, it only made the curse stronger.

Halfdan closed his eyes, his back to them, and sighed heavily. "I hope you know what you are doing, Erik."

His research between the book of curses and the parchments and maps revealed the dagger would not completely break the stone in the cylinder relic. He stepped lightly back up the trail, shaking his head and sighing to himself inside. He might as well get another fire going for the night. It would be long, like the ages they had already been fighting through.

26

The Cavern Where Deceit Lies

T hat following morning, they had ridden through another endless forest and reached a hidden fall with a cavern opened behind it. Halfdan stopped at the brook shoreline and eyed the map. Liv
followed him with Erik behind her. They pushed away the flowering
vines dripping from the trees, and held their breaths at this beauty.

Liv gazed upon the pool that melted into the brook, flowing over a
rocky shore, its cavernous terrain towering over them for what seemed
like miles. As they walked over the brook toward the cave, Liv hesitat-
ed, but then turned to smile at Erik. He nodded back at her, his eyes
still wide and bright from their passion, his hood lowered and his hair
braided down his back.

He had not said much, as Halfdan had been talking the whole trip
about the curse and how the dagger would not fully break it. Liv
listened to him, her gaze falling on Erik as he spoke, and she watched
his eyes. She still needed the dagger, no matter what, but a part of her
wanted to return to the pool with Erik. She desired to return, let him
love her, and stay there. She wanted to feel him breathing and pulsing
inside her.

The cave careened behind the waterfall, unleashing its deafening
roar. They followed the wall until a cavern room opened. A rectan-

gular stone table lied in the middle, with one stream of light flowing upon it from a hole in the forest floor above them.

Liv held her breath. "It is beautiful." She whispered, admiring the swirling patterns around them in the stone walls.

She waited and watched while Erik and Halfdan pushed the table, but it did not open. Liv bent down and blew the dust off, the runes carved in the stone matching the ones on their hands.

Halfdan sighed and pulled out the silver cylinder. "To retrieve this dagger, it takes all three of us. But you two must press your rune hands on the stone."

Liv held up her palm. "The same. They all say the same." She confirmed, sudden chills filling her heart with dread. "Oh, why do they have to be the same?" She swallowed.

"The source of this madness." Erik huffed.

Erik and Liv stood opposite each other and pressed their hands on the stone, and the cylinder relic shimmered crimson. The stone cracked, and Erik pushed it onto the floor. They glared at the dagger with the ruby stone in the hilt. Liv widened her eyes at it at first but then reached in and grabbed it. She slid the blade from the sheath, admiring its intricate carvings.

"Liv, you will press the blade against the stone on this cylinder. Liv..." Halfdan paused, his face firm. "You are the one who must try to break it because you are seeking the relics. This relic is attached to you."

This relic is attached to you. Liv played it over and over in her mind. She stared at him, but something edged her into caution, and she held her breath at them.

"This begins the demise but will not break it completely. You and Erik will continue to be drawn together by fate until we reach the time you have found the last relic. Once they are all destroyed, I can..."

"This whole time?" She interrupted him and sighed. "Attached to ancient seer relics of our people. Our people have been our demise."

"It is not our demise, Liv. We can break this together." Erik told her, his face still inflamed with their passion.

Halfdan sighed. "We need to prepare. We three may live for a long while yet."

She gulped, turned to Erik, and bent up to kiss him. He kissed her back, his eyes upon her face, smiling into her. "I love you," Liv told him. "I love you with all I am." She whispered into his mouth and ran her fingers on the side of his face into his long beard.

He stopped kissing her and breathed in her motives. "I love you." Erik bit his tongue and leaned away from her as if something had bit him, and he swallowed in her face. Erik leaned away from her to stand to her right and Halfdan to her left. She glared at the burgundy stone and the runes and felt a whisper eat her from the inside out. *The hunter will come now.*

"Are you ready, Liv?" Halfdan asked again, waiting.

She gripped the blade in her palm and readied herself. As her eyes shimmered in blazing silver, she plunged the blade against the stone on the shaft. It cracked, she pulled the blade back, and they stood there in the silence of the cave, waiting.

Hafldan sighed, his eyes going around to see if something, some force, would awaken. As the silence pestered them, Liv twisted her arm and plunged the blade through Erik's heart. It sunk through his chain mail, and she pulled it back out again. He fell back, his face drained of color, gasping at her as if a wall had hit him. Halfdan stepped back, his eyes wide.

And then the ground shook beneath them.

Liv cried, turning to Halfdan. "You know Erik will stop me, no matter how many times we lay together. Eventually, the curse will take him. I only need the final relic, the key. I can deny him no longer when he is around me, so I must do this now."

"The final relic is not ready to be found yet!" Halfdan gasped at her.

"That does not matter." Liv nodded her head. "Erik must hunt me. He will keep hunting me until the curse renders itself upon us all, causing pain and chaos! I want to live. I want him to live and you also, Halfdan. I want to spend the rest of my life with him. I must find the relics and destroy them first before they destroys us. I needed the dagger first."

Halfdan gasped.

Liv cried. "I stayed away so long! So long, Halfdan. Because I need him, it hurts to be with him, and I can no longer deny him." She gripped her heart.

"You cannot destroy the relics, Liv! I must do that!" Halfdan warned her. "What you are doing is the curse talking through you. Look at your eyes!" He pointed at them.

But Liv did not listen. She gazed upon Erik's dead body, her head aching, her eyes flaming silver. "He will not be able to help himself because the curse is part of us, and it controls part of us now, just as I feel led to kill him and keep going. But I want to lie with him also."

"Liv!" Halfdan pleaded with her. "I see the curse in your eyes. Do not let it tell you to destroy the relics! I must do it!"

Liv sighed at him. "I must take this dagger and find the last relic until I have all the rune pieces to break it. That is why I became a pirate."

Halfdan closed his eyes, a tear falling. "Liv, if you do this, you will bring the curse to full power through Erik. Or through you! You are being stubborn." He warned. "Erik will get you next time and never let you go! It will not be the Erik you know. He will be too strong!"

"I have no choice." She cried, her arms shivering as blood dripped from the blade. "I love him."

Halfdan huffed. "I know, Liv. I know you love each other. Then you must know he senses where you go and when. He has for a long time now." Halfdan warned her. "It will be stronger next time. Not like it has been the hundreds of years. He was in wars to keep him busy and away from you, but no more."

"What?"

"You both have a powerful bond, and the curse strengthens every time you lie together. Moreso, now that you have the dagger. He can feel you where you are, sense your presence. He will find you no matter where you go!"

She shook her head as the reckoning dawned on her. "Shit."

"You do not know where the last relic is," Halfdan warned her.

"I know an area of where it will be. That is all I need." She bit and then paused, her eyes wide with terror. "What will he do to me?"

Halfdan swallowed. "He will do as the curse commands. This curse does not want the relics found. It wants to continue growing in your misery. He will not let you find the relics, Liv. It will not be his fault, but it may be his downfall."

Halfdan paused, sighing. "I will do all in my power to stall him. I have tried to stall him to give you time to find the relics, I swear it. I have pulled him far away from you but he has continued to hunt you!"

"I know. That is why I keep killing him. But I love him first..."

She twisted around to face Hardulph and plunged the blade through his heart. He fell at her feet, his face grieved. She watched him fall to his side, gulping, his eyes losing light.

"I am sorry, old friend. I cannot let you take the dagger. I know you need it, but I need it because I will destroy the relics myself." Her eyes shimmered in blazing silver.

She cleaned the blade on her cloak and pushed it back into the sheath, grabbing the silver cylinder relic. She had limited time as she truned to race out of the cave. Every time Erik died, he came back faster and stronger. Last time, she counted two and a half days. She ran over the brook and jumped on her horse, turning away from them to get a head start. Whatever that head start may be.

Halfdan failed to tell Liv what the runes said, but she knew. The written curse was nothing compared to the living curse on their palms, engraved into their soul as if it had become a part of them all these years. She memorized it in her heart as she put her head down into the horse's mane and raced faster than she had ever raced in all her lives to get away from them. Erik would need Halfdan to help control his urge to hunt her, and Halfdan would be an invaluable source for him.

Behind her, memories of her and Erik seared a pain through her like never before. It hurt because she wanted to remain in that pool with him, their bodies intertwined, their mouths open to each other's kisses, for all time. But it was too late. The curse was taking them both.

Erik was the hunter, bound to her by fate, drawn to her as they had given each other their most intimate desires. Her loins ached thinking about him, but she realized for the past five hundred years, he had been driven to find her and struggled to do so. Now that the curse had bonded them, he would find her quicker, and next time, he may not be so loving.

But he had not been so loving this time, not at first. Erik was hard and cold with her until they made love. He had been meticulous in the way he had hunted her and taken her pirates. He was firm and stronger at first. And then he melted into her with his love for her, and they had given in.

She cried into the horse's mane as she raced through Estonia, her mind reeling with the rune interpretation her grandmother had told her before she died. She left a big part of herself behind at that cavern, her heart aching a throbbing pain through her soul, her mind reeling of the curse as it echoed.

The curse has a hunter who seeks and cannot give up. As each treasure brings closure to the time, the seeker becomes more desperate to hide, and the hunter races harder to find. True love's grasp is hard to keep, as the hunter seeks by the pressures of time. When time is rendered, and the curse bleeds them again, their hearts will be kept in the palm of their hands.

B y dawn the next day Erik sat on the ledge of the waterfall cavern. His legs hung off, and he watched the sun kiss the mountains before him in tangerines and crimsons. His blue eyes peered into the woods and the wilderness all around him. His back was stiff with resolve even as dry blood splotched his coat. Behind him, Halfdan stirred and sat up slowly, rubbing his chest.

He yelled out, huffing as he stood up and arched his back. "You were right. She has a strong arm. That hurt." He rubbed his chest, eying the dried blood in contempt. "Damnit."

Erik had pulled his hood completely off his head and cut his beard. He eyed Halfdan, a calm reserve on his lips, and then turned his eyes to glare out again. His blue eyes sparkled in the rising sun as the rays caressed his face that held a firm demeanor.

Halfdan pulled his satchel from the ground and sneered. "She took the rune cylinder."

Erik sighed. "She took everything. She always takes everything."

Halfdan watched him jump up. Erik's body seemed stronger than before, and his energy was like a blast from a summer storm.

"What are you doing?" Halfdan wondered.

Erik began walking down the path to their horses. He turned to glare back at him, his fist dangling off the hilt to his longsword, his white cloak flowing in behind him. "Getting her back."

Halfdan followed him down. "You cannot stop her this time. She is endowed. I saw the curse in her eyes, just as it has been in ours."

"No matter. I will find her."

"No. The curse is clear. It will not let you help Liv! Listen to me." Halfdan pleaded. "You will hinder her, and the curse will rend itself upon us all. She must find this last relic alone, Erik."

"What am I supposed to do then? Linger on while she seeks them?" Erik stopped walking and took a deep breath. He clenched his jaws. "I will find her. You can come or stay, monk."

Halfdan moaned. "Damnit. Of course I come! I must watch over you two! Like children." He rolled his eyes.

Erik shook his head at him, but Halfdan huffed. "What will you do when you find her again, Erik? Tell me."

Erik huffed, his eyes hard.

"What will do what with her, Erik!"

Erik breathed in deeply as if wrestling a demon deep inside he could not control. "Keep her," He whispered, his eyes glowing blue.

"I know you can sense where she is going!" Halfdan worried. "Where is she going, Erik?"

Erik paused at his horse, his face firm.

"Erik." Halfdan's face was pale.

Erik clenched his jaws, sneering, his nose wrinkling up. "She heads West across the North Sea. She is going south of Scotland. I can always sense her."

Halfdan's eyes became as wide as coins. "You slept with her again and then turn around and hunt her like prey. Drawn to her motives and desires!"

"Well, no. I enjoyed it also." Erik mumbled. "I always enjoy it." He smiled.

"This is a treachery of the heart." Halfdan gasped.

Erik took a deep breath and gazed into the canopy, his heart busting in his chest. "I love her!" He gripped his chest, the dried blood on his coat wadded up in his palm. "So, no matter this curse, I will die anyway without her. Do you understand?!" His face twisted up. "I cannot go another hundred years without touching her again. I would rather die."

Halfdan swallowed, his eyes tearing up.

"I know she will get the final relic. We will be ready when she does. You can take the relics from her, and we will go back to Scotland and break this infernal curse!" Erik seethed.

Halfdan swallowed.

Erik pulled himself on the saddle. "I need her. I will go to her. Curse or no. If that means we die over and over in our misery, then I will do it to be with her."

Halfdan followed Erik horseback, his heart busting inside. The curse affected him, too. For even though he was just the monk that handled the cylinder relic after the curse had touched them, he was commanded to guard them. He was commanded to be their reasoning amongst the madness of the pain. But him reasoning with them was worn out.

Now that Liv had bested them both and he could not follow her, he had no choice but to stay with Erik. Halfdan did not get a chance to warn Erik that the things set in motion were now out of their control.

They would still need him to break the curse completely, and in the end, it may not end well after all.

It may not end well because Erik would fight him when the time comes for Halfdan to kill them both. The curse may not break after all.

27

A Cathedral of Pain, Florence 1453

You've been running away from me. Liv kept hearing it whisper in her heart. Yet she had to keep going.

She stood before the rising Cattedrale di Santa Maria del Fiore, her heart pounding as she pulled her shawl over her head. She eyed the stained-glass windows and brick dome that towered over her as if the Cathedral screamed in horrendous pain. But deep inside, it was her who was screaming.

She was here to retrieve a relic-a small golden box with runes carved on it-and she needed what was inside it. She lingered inside toward the Nave, where the high arched ceilings kissed the heaven above her by its massive columns. Her heart skipped a beat. She loved the architecture, the art, and the beauty. The vastness of the space allowed her to stretch out, her soul singing inside.

She turned away from the alter, where a row of people bent upon their knees praying. She followed the narrow staircase, dimly lit, its shadows stretching over her like prickly fingers. She paused at the frescoes on the interior; the stained glass depicted scenes from Biblical narratives.

She pressed onward, pulling her long shawl over her dress, her heart beating wildly. The beauty's exhilaration rammed a hopeful joy in her soul. As she reached the top, she moseyed onto an exterior walkway showering her with panoramic views of Florence. The Tuscan landscape made her pause and smile.

She gazed upon the red-tiled rooftops and the sparkling Arno River. It took her breath away. She found herself lost in the splendor of this glorious place and realized she had gotten lost giving herself a tour, and she was not in the right place. She turned back around to head to the alter. She needed to go to the Crypts at the baptistry.

She lingered toward the entrance, where the tomb of Brunelleschi, the Italian architect and designer of the cathedral dome, lay. She held her breath and walked in under the stone arch, her eyes lighting up to an entrance past the tomb. Liv wished she had met the renowned genius behind this lavish cathedral. She paused at his tomb, sighed, and pressed behind it through a narrow opening.

Candles lit in the crevasses of the walls and sang to her as she spread her shadow down the hall. The room opened to a vast expanse of an arched cavern, and she held her breath gazing upon it. She pulled the parchment she had stolen from her satchel, and read the diagram. The rune box was here in Roman times, and since there had been Roman houses under this cathedral, she knew it was still here, somewhere. It was the last relic, elusive, and deceitful.

She followed the pillars down a long corridor, pulling a candle from the wall and pressing into the darkness. As she neared the end of the crypt, an arched brick wall laid closed before her. She held the candle to the bricks and found one that showed a Roman inscription with the number DCCXCV.

Liv froze, widened her eyes. "That cannot be."

Then, from behind her came a voice so familiar her backbone grew shards of ice like prickly fingers freezing to her soul, and she shivered inside. She turned her head to face Erik, standing slowly as if he had sucked the breath out of her.

"Seven ninety-five, Liv. The year we raided the Abbey." His voice echoed of something profound that burst Liv alive inside.

Erik stood behind her in the corridor, his tailored top and trousers accentuating his muscular build, his mustache trimmed to show his strong jawline. His eyes sparkled at her in the dark against the candlelight. His burgundy robe kissed his broad shoulders down his back to his knees. He had cut his hair shorter, but it was in a pony tail. Her mind returned to the pool in Estonia, and her stomach twisted into knots.

"Erik." Her face lit up.

He swallowed at her and for a moment, she caught him raising a hand to his heart before it fell back down at his side again. "I know this relic you seek is from the year we raided the abbey."

She turned her head back to the brick. A small chunk was missing, so it had been pried out already. She held her hand out at him. "Hand it over. You know I must destroy it." She whispered, her voice shaking.

Erik took a deep breath and held out the small square rune box. "Come and take it." He stepped closer to her.

"I am not strong enough." She whimpered.

Erik gazed over her. "You can try to kill me again." He pestered her. "I will wake up stronger, more alive. Makes me hunt you harder. I found you faster this time." He stepped closer. "Didn't I?" He whispered.

She stepped closer to him, her long purple gown kissing her slippers, her hair knotted around the back of her head. She stopped, her eyes roaming over him. "I cannot take it from you because you have already emptied it of what I need. Haven't you?"

His face clenched, and he pressed the box in a side pocket of his shirt. Liv closed her eyes and turned her head.

Erik sighed. "I see what you are doing. You have all the relics but this one. You know Halfdan needs them." He bit. "Liv."

She stared at him. "No, I will break this."

"You cannot break this. You are stubborn." He warned.

Erik took a deep breath, his eyes hard at her. "You kill me over and over. There is no reprieve or hope for me when it comes to you."

"That is the curse talking." She stared at him.

"That is my heart!" He put his hand to his chest, his face clenched hard at her. "It grows stronger in your presence. I will not do this any longer."

She swallowed at him as he gripped his fists, his knuckles turning white. "Come with me."

She pleaded with him. "No! You will keep me from what I must do to save us!"

He stared at her, his face clenched, his eyes hard, his breathing deep. "I know the curse beckons me to hunt you. I know this, Liv. I know the curse beckons you to find the relics and that you must kill me over and over to do it. But I..."

"What Erik?"

Erik lunged at her and pulled her by her forearms so they were breathing upon one another. Liv felt his heartbeat as her fists clutched against his chest. She gazed up at him, his face tormented at her.

"I love you." He whispered into her breath. "I love you so damn hard. I cannot go on like this anymore. I need you in my life, in my bed. You live in my soul! I cannot live without you."

She swallowed, meeting his stare. "If we keep coming together, I will not stop. You will not stop," She breathed on his lips as he melted into her face, coming closer. "We will make love until we are exhausted of strength like in Estonia. We will ravish one another until the curse eats us alive."

Erik moaned as if she had taken part of his soul and kissed it into the heavens. He listened to her as she continued, "But this curse will drain us of hope. I will fight you now rather than die and not have peace. Erik,"

Erik pulled her in tighter, and she leaned into his lips and whispered, "I will kill you over and over until I get this relic. Give it to me." Her eyes shimmered silver.

Erik leaned into her lips, his eyes changing to a fiery blue storm as shadows filled them. "Do it." He enticed her, his face clenched.

"I will hunt you to the farthest reaches of this world to stop you." He whispered. "I will come after you faster. Stronger." He pursed his lips at her, his eyes grazing over her beauty. "Until you can no longer run from me."

Liv broke inside. She pulled away from him, but he would not let her go. He yanked her back through the crypt toward the entrance.

Liv grimaced. "You cannot hold me against my will. I will finish this."

Erik stopped and faced her, his grip tight on her forearm. "I cannot let you go now that I have found you again. I will not live without you again."

"What will you do with me?" She asked again, a nervous twitch eating her arm as he continued to pull her to the entrance in his firm grasp. His eyes explored their surroundings at the entrance to the cathedral.

He rolled his eyes back to face her and huffed. "Keep you," he whispered as his eyes glowed. His face clenched up, and a voice came out of him that was not Erik. It was dark, sinister.

Liv leaned away from him, her arm still in his grasp. "I knew you would say that."

The hillside across the road erupted into a roaring flame, and rocks and dirt blew into the street. The explosion shook the air at the cathedral as boulders, bushes, and trees melted into it. The mushroom cloud kaboom shook the city, vibrating through the sky. The stone building next to the hill cracked in half, and fell into the street. The cloud of smoke and debris catapulted high in the air around them.

Erik let her go for a moment to lean away from the heat of the blast as they blasted back against the doors. People screamed at the altar and rushed outside, and the city filled with panic and moans of shock.

Liv turned to run down the steps, but Erik lunged into her and missed, slipping at her feet. She pulled her gown up to her knees and ran the opposite direction of the blast in the street. She still needed the relic Erik had taken from her, but she would have to figure that out. Another explosion rattled the city, and screams and hollers erupted behind her in chaos.

As she neared the end of the street, she noticed Halfdan sitting in a wagon with a donkey pulling it. His eyes were wide and bright. When he opened his mouth to speak, Liv turned as Erik rushed her. He lunged her up by her waist and plopped her over his shoulder. She grimaced in his grasp, but Erik was right; he was always stronger. She would have to use her wits to beat him.

"Here we go again." Halfdan sighed.

"Halfdan, what are you doing!" She hollered at him, even as Erik tossed her into the back of the wagon and climbed in to hold her there.

Halfdan swished the whip, and the donkey pulled the wagon away from the rubble and the screaming masses. "I take it your pirates are creating a diversion, no? Well played!"

Liv growled at them both, her eyes wide. She pressed atop Erik in the back of the wagon and straddled him, her hands craning his pockets. "Give it to me!"

Erik pulled her fists away and rolled on top of her, pinning her down by her arms. "No."

He smiled at her face, his eyes back to normal. "I have missed this position, you beautiful, stubborn woman."

Liv gasped. She smiled at him and then froze. "Damnit, Erik!"

Erik smiled wide. "Damnit, indeed. You are beautiful." Erik gazed at her face.

Liv growled, sneering. "Erik!"

Erik laughed. "What, Liv." He toyed with her, his laugh echoing.

Halfdan sighed, singing, "I grow tired of this, so tired of this, so tired," He hummed as they left the city for the rolling countryside. "What is it with you and fire anyway? Last time I witnessed an all-out war between the knights and pirates."

"It was just an explosion!" Liv hollered back at him, struggling with Erik's grasp.

Halfdan leaned back on the seat and shook his head, his eyes wide. "You women are mean."

As Halfdan pressed further into the country, Liv gave up and lay still under Erik for endless moments. Shrieks of screams and vibrations of the hillside collapsing stopped ringing in their ears. He did not take his eyes off her, but his breath was as calm as the night sky. She wanted to kiss him. She wanted to make love with him again.

All she could do was lay under him and see memories of them making love in the pool, and then on the shoreline atop the ferns. As if Erik sensed what she was thinking, he raised off her and pulled her up. They both sat up and stared at one another in the wagon. He met her face with longing but a pain lingered in his eyes.

"How did you find me?" She raised her long arm and stretched it, squinting.

"I feel drawn to where you are." He turned his face and sighed. "Like a damn plague."

Silence ate at them.

"Do you?" Erik asked her.

She met his stare. "What?"

"Do you regret those times." His face shadowed with pain.

"No. I do not regret any of the times." She swallowed. "I need you." She belted out.

"I can no longer do this, Liv." He stared at her.

Liv swallowed. "I love you." She whispered, her heart aching.

Erik leaned to stand up and kiss her. He stood up and stepped toward her.

"I want you for the rest of my life." She told him as he stood over her to meet her lips.

Liv held her breath, waiting. Erik was catapulted away from her out of the wagon. The blood spray hit her cheek and forehead. He fell head over heels onto the road onto his back, the boom echoing. She lunged up to jump out of the wagon. Halfdan stopped the donkey, the color draining from his face.

Through the olive groves among the trees, she heard a whistle and whistled back. She jumped down and stared at Erik's body, a fatal heart wound with a Wheellock Rifle. Her plan worked. She bent down, dug through his pockets, and found the key.

Halfdan turned to face her. "Well, that is unfortunate." Not surprised.

She stuffed the key down her bosom and shook her head at Halfdan, turning to march up the hill. "Why did you show him the year of the relics?"

Halfdan huffed at her. "I had no choice! You try dealing with a vigorous Viking for hundreds of years, okay? He is stubborn and in desperate need of you!"

She stopped in the grass, pulling up her gown to walk through the woods. "I have less time now! Next time, he will not let me go, and you must help me!"

"That is also unfortunate." Halfdan glared at her, shaking his head.

"I mean it, Halfdan! You are the only one who can stop him next time." She warned.

Hafldan called back at her. "Liv! You must bring the cylinder relic and all the relics back to the abbey. You must come back home to finish this. You cannot destroy them by yourself!"

She froze her back to him, her whole body tense.

Halfdan huffed. "Do you understand this? Because if you do not listen to me, I may be unable to stop him. Liv." Halfdan warned her, his eyes fiery crimson. "Or me." He waited for her response, his eyes piercing her backside.

She turned her head to face him and saw his fiery crimson eyes. She froze staring at him, her heart beating wildly. The color drained from her face. She swallowed and closed her eyes as the truth hit her heart. "Of course, it would be there, wouldn't it? Of course we must go back to Scotland." She grimaced.

"Liv!" Halfdan sneered. "You cannot break them. Promise me!"

Liv did not promise. Halfdan watched her race up the hill to meet shadows moving in the woods, and then she was gone. She had planned this so that she could get away when Erik did find her. Halfdan knew she was racing against time, because when Erik awoke again, it would not end well for her. He jumped from the wagon, glaring at Erik's body, and sighed.

"I hope this plan of yours works. I did warn you. I did." He rolled his eyes. "Damnit."

At the top of the hill, Liv met three men dressed like peasants and two women, and she smiled at them. They all held their gold trimmed Wheellock Rifles. The decorated gunstocks were inlaid with panels of ivory, the carved walnut wood depicting hunting scenes. They followed one another until they reached horses tied up in the woods, and Liv raced away with them to the mountains.

When Liv and her pirates reached the mountain village an hour later, the stone townhouse community brimmed with life. The road opened to show markets and lanterns lit it like the sun had kissed it at night. Liv smelled the bread baking, and the Polenta fritta's appetizers filled the street vendors. She climbed down, her stomach growling for Pici.

This town meant something to her as a haven for the pirates she continued to converse with. Throughout the many years, it remained a safe place for her to have silence, and unwind from the travesties of all the lives she had lived. She melted into her townhome at the end of the street and marched up the stairs to her room. The house was a continual bright light from her oil lamps, and the warmth of the Tuscan walls was a calm reprieve for her.

She plopped down on her knees in front of the picture window. Her gaze fell to the views of the street and valley rolling out before her, the olive groves kissing the sloping plain like fingers rising from the earth. She took a deep breath, clutching her heart, put her face in her hands, and cried into her palms. A tickle itched her palm with the runes, and she wiped her face and held it up, sneering at it.

"You will die today inside us. Or I will. I will go no further with you carved into me."

She wiped her face and pressed down on the plastered wall where the small hole beckoned her. She stuck her finger inside it and yanked, and the panel under the window pulled off. She pulled out the silver cylinder she had stolen from Halfdan.

She did not care what he had told her. She knew they would all end up back in Scotland, but not today. Today, she needed to do something to move the curse along. She had no choice after seeing the darkness begin to take Erik. And Halfdan's eyes also showed signs of the curse. She could not let it continue because it haunted her day by day, as she knew Erik would fall to the darkness spawned by the chaos.

She pulled the key out of her bosom, and shifted the cylinder around to match the runes on her palm. She pressed the small golden key into the section with no runes, a perfect fit. They key melted onto it as if it had come alive, and runes emerged, filling in the gap that once was there. She clenched her teeth. The runes erupted inside of it into a raging crimson-like fire. It wafted to a glowing blue, the same blue she had seen in Erik's eyes. Her palm burned, her stomach churned, and her head ached.

She grimaced in pain as runes were pulled off her palm and absorbed back into it. Her arm shook like it was caught in the grip of no escape, and she watched her palm burn against the cylinder. The runes on her hand swelled and then sloshed off like liquid. She clenched her face as the pain seared into her as if her hand was on fire, and she screamed in pain. She held the shaft tight until her vision became blurry, her head fuzzy like a shroud had been pulled over her.

And then the light was gone. As she sat on her hip breathing deeply, the cylinder blasted out a shock wave. The blast pushed her back out her door, and she hit the wall by the stairs. The wall cracked atop her as she fell. The ground vibrated under the mountain. The people celebrating and eating in the streets froze, gazing up at the mountain, waiting. The air rumbled around them.

H alfdan felt a rumble that shook the sky, hitting him under his feet. The sonic blast catapulted him and Erik straight up from the road into the air. Halfdan landed in the wagon flat on his back. The blast pushed a mushroom cloud out from their bodies. The road collapsed into cracks and dust flew high around them. The sonic boom vibrated throughout the air like thunder from the ground up.

"No, Liv!" Halfdan hollered, but it was too late. "Noooo!"

Erik landed on his feet when he dropped back down. He hunched over to brace himself with one hand, his arms and back flexed, his body stiff. His eyes flew open as if something had flipped inside him. His eyes were on fire like the bluest heat burned him from the inside out. He growled as his face clenched under narrowed brows. He pulled his palm up to see a line of the runes were gone.

He belted out a rageful moan, his hand shaking in pain. Erik clenched his face toward the mountain as the dust settled around them. His chest heaved to get Liv, calling him. A breath of fervor filled his aching bones like a fire from hell's core had lit him up, ravaging his soul. He stood there breathing hard, seeing in his mind exactly where Liv had gone.

Halfdan lay on his back in the wagon sprawled out, his trousers and robe twisted up high around his pale, hairy legs. Part of his robe was hanging over the side of the wagon, and the donkey cried at him. He gazed into the sky, the dust still settling, and gripped his heart, a dull ache taunting him. He could not go after Erik as he wanted to, because Erik was now filled with the curse. His strength would be hard to break.

"Why, Liv!" He moaned. "Oh, Liv what did you do..."

Liv would have to use cunning to be free of him now, and she would need help. Halfdan swallowed, his eyes staring into the dust around him. Erik raced back to town to steal a horse as if his legs were on fire and a great wind was taking him there. Halfdan understood where Liv was coming from. He wanted to get this over with too. But this may end up killing them all to do it anyway.

"This is the part of the curse I do not like. Damnit." Halfdan moaned, rolling over. "You damn Vikings will be the death of me."

L iv rolled over to her hip, her heart beating hard as a migraine throbbed between her eyes. She rolled over to her stomach, pressing her shaking rune hand to her face. One line was gone. She rolled over to her back, planted her palm to her face and cried in her hand for endless moments. Then she pushed herself up and picked up the shaft that had rolled out of her hand down the hall. She rushed into her room and fell to her knees again, melting to the wall under her window where the other relics lay.

She reached in, pulled out the dagger, and pulled out the rune stone. It fit in the palm of her hand, and the runes matched. It was smooth and burgundy, and she gripped it in her palm and sighed. She closed her eyes and pressed the shaft into her rune palm again, holding her breath. Tears rushed down her cheeks as the shaft burned into her palm again while the stone melted into it. She screamed, the pain filling her with mountains of pain. She used the dagger to press the stone into the shaft, shaking all over.

Thunder roared over the mountain.

E rik had taken a horse from the village. He pressed his head into
the horse's mane as his eyes sparkled in malice. His heart busted
through his chest as if some unknown hand clawed into him. It pulled
him to her as if time existed no longer, calling him to her presence. He
pushed the horse hard, and pebbles and dirt flew high behind him. His
burgundy cloak spilled in the air like a mountain of blood.

His palm burned, and he clenched his teeth. He belted out another
moaning growl in pain as the blue embers ate another line of the rune
off his hand. "Aughhh!"

He clenched his jaws breathed in pain, lunging down further and
pushing the horse harder. As Erik neared closer, Liv pulled out the
final relic she had from under the window. Her face was red with tears
as her hand seared in pain, but she had to hurry. This was going to hurt
the worst. It may even kill her.

She lunged into the wall and pulled out the ruby stone. It was rich
and dark like blood. When she held it up to the oil lamp, she saw the
shadows of runes inside the gem. She swallowed, her hand still shaking
in pain. She pressed the shaft into her palm again, pushing the gem
against the shaft stone, and took a deep breath.

She closed her eyes as tears fell down her neck, her mouth twisted
in pain. Memories of the many years past plagued her. She saw Erik
bent over in his shop making shoes for horses. His muscle-riddled
body bent over working, covered in sweat, his long blonde hair braided
down his back.

She saw his handsome smiling face laughing with her before they
raided the abbey. She saw his long, blonde braids spilled down his

broad shoulders over his pelt. She saw him standing on the shores before getting on that ship. He pulled her face in his palms and kissed her, and the sunrise caressed their faces as they melted into one another.

She screamed again, but this time, her whole body jerked.

She saw herself lying on the floor of the prison, and Erik came and loomed over her, picking her up in his strong arms.

"*I have you now.*" He told her.

And then the most painful memory of all hit her. Her memory went to the village where they first made love. And then she remembered Estonia and her and Erik's bodies entwined in passionate embraces. Their open kisses were wild upon each other, their hands pulling each other's bodies closer in.

I have loved you deeper than your desire to keep running from me...

It kissed her soul alive. Her heart ached, and her stomach burned for him, jumping like bugs were eating her alive inside. As the third rune line absorbed into the shaft, the earth moved under the village and her house shook. The walls cracked, the ceiling beams vibrated, and dust fell like snow.

A sonic blast erupted under Erik as he raced on, and the sky around him filled with dust as if the world had exploded. He closed his eyes and pressed the horse through it, even as the blast slung them into the air. He pressed his feet into the horse's side even as it neighed out protests. It landed on its legs and Erik burst through, opening his eyes on the road up the mountain, his face hard.

As another line of runes burned off his hand, he grimaced, belting a roar of pain. "Livvvvv!" He screamed into the air. His ponytail flipped behind him, and his hand seared in pain. He floated atop the horse as his legs clenched into the stirrups. His butt was in the air, his face into the wind, and his eye on the prize.

T he shaft burned from the inside out, and the floors cracked under Liv's knees. A rush of weakness overcame her just as her eyes caught a dark shadow on horseback throttling up the street through the chaos the town had turned into. Dust from the road blew behind him as his cloak belted his rage into the air.

She had the sudden urge to run, but it was too late. Erik had found her. She knew this may happen, but did not know Erik would be so strong and fast. She fell back, her body riddled with pain. She craned her neck as the door burst open, flying off the hinges. Tears fell down her face still.

She turned her head to her open palm stretched out from her body, and watched the rune line dissipate. It burned off her palm, leaving only two left. She screamed in pain as it filled her body with convulsions, and her face filled with tears hitting the floor. She writhed in agony, her body lunging up and down on the floor.

Erik lunged in at her, his face in torment. Before the terror of him could make her react, her mind saw blackness. There was nothing she could do, but she managed to destroy all the relics. All but two. It would be a miracle if she could get Halfdan to do it now.

As she lay there weak and in pain, going in and out of consciousness, Erik breathed on her face. She took a deep breath as he fell to his knees and leaned over her. He put his face against hers, breathing so hard into her his soul sucked inside her. He pushed his arms around her and under her, cradled her in his arms, her head limp. A sudden pain shot through him, too, and he pulled his palm up where the runes had gone. Erik hollered in pain, his body in agony even as he held her.

"Aughhh!" He hollered.

He took a deep breath and closed his eyes. After a few moments, when the pain had gone, he lifted her from the floor, his face clenched. He paused with her in his arms, his hot breath of desperation upon her face as a deep, familiar voice called to her.

"Liv." It was Erik calling to her.

She opened her eyes for a moment to see his handsome face. "I have loved you greater than the time between us," she moaned, grazing the side of his face with her fingers, crying.

Erik gazed into her as his chest heaved, but then he changed, and Erik was gone. He took a deep breath, his face clenched into hers. His eyes bored into her face, and shadows filled them.

This time, it made her shiver in fear as Erik was someone she did not know anymore, just as she feared. Her heart beat wildly as she was helpless against his grasp. His whole body was a surge of power like a storm had carried him to her.

As she blacked out for the last time, she heard the curse speak to her deep inside. "You are mine nowwwww." It spoke. Its dark echo was edged in desperation and filled with malice.

The three of them would continue dying over and over in their misery, never truly living. Whoever this Erik was would never let her go. She could not stop him anymore. A part of her did not want to.

28

Mountains of Vengeful Desires

I *have you now. You are mine. You will never leave my side. I have hunted you long enough. Liv. Liv. I need you.*

Livvvv Runnnnnn from meeeeee!

Liv took a deep breath and squinted her eyes as she woke up, her head still throbbing. Erik screamed in her head, and she pressed a weary palm on her forehead and sighed. As she craned her eyes open, she met Erik. He stood over her, blocking the light. She raised her eyes to his eyes and froze.

His eyes were flaming blue, and raging into her face. "You are not Erik," She whispered. "I want my Erik back." She demanded.

She swallowed and pushed herself up on her elbows, waiting. Erik huffed, shaking his head. "I hunted you all over the world. You eluded me many times. I never stopped loving you, and now you are mine."

Erik's voice was echoing and deep. Liv pressed against the wall on the bed, her eyes froze at his face. "Erik?" She wondered.

He leaned away from her, his face hard. "Yes, Liv." He responded, but it was not him.

She sat up, her heart racing. "Where is Halfdan?"

Erik scoffed. "Could not keep up with me."

"He is coming?" She hoped.

Erik shook his head at her, his eyes exploring her body. "I hope not. I need time with you first. A lot of time." He rolled his eyes up and down her.

Liv held her breath and swallowed. "Is this the part where you ravish me until our immortality dies?"

Erik licked his lips and clenched his jaws, his eyes meeting hers. He breathed heavily like a summer storm had filled him up inside. "Yes."

Liv stood and faced him. "And then we kill one another?"

Erik stared down at her. "You have killed me over and over, Liv."

Liv leaned against his lips. "Yes, but now I do not want to. Now, I just want you." Her breath was hot on his lips. "You know only two relics are left, and we are standing here."

Erik held his breath at her face. "Take your dress off." His eyes were as hard as his voice and cold as his eyes.

"Even though we are the last two relics?" She wondered.

Erik's eyes lit up. "My relic needs your relic." He bent against her lips again. "Take your dress off."

Liv took a deep breath, watching his eyes shimmer in the blue fire. "Will you make love to me until dawn?" She inquired, stalling him. "Or until tomorrow night? Will we make love until starvation takes us? Or exhaustion?"

Erik sensed her stalling him. He undid the buckle at his waist and jerked his tunic off. He slung it to the floor and she held her breath at his perfection. Liv gawked at his muscular chest and big, strong arms for a moment. She rolled her eyes over him and sighed inside. He was nearly naked as his trousers fit his frame perfectly. She wanted him, but this was not Erik.

"Erik," She moaned, wanting him. "Damn this curse."

She stepped back, but he lunged at her and grabbed her waist. He gripped her back and pulled her tight against his chest. "Where do you think you are going?" He breathed against her lips.

"What?" She asked, a twinkle in her eyes. "Handsome Viking."

He kissed her lips, and she met him back. He stopped kissing her, breathing on her face. "You stall meeeee. I will rip this dress off you, Liv. Like we did at the village. I will make hard love to you until we have no strength left." He belted out.

Liv thought a moment, her heart racing against his chest. "Wonder when that will be?"

Erik leaned his face up, narrowing his brows. "What?"

"I can feel your strength. I wonder how long it will take for me to wear you out in the bed." She raised her lip in a half smile. "Erik, the mighty Viking," She whispered.

Erik smiled against her lips, his groin hard and pulsing against her. "Let's find out." He gripped her back harder, roving his hands to her buttocks while his heart raced against her chest.

Liv closed her eyes and leaned back as Erik dove into her neck with open-mouthed kisses. He pulled her dress off her left shoulder and kissed her neck. He gripped her waist hard in his palms, his arms quivering.

"Erik," She moaned, wanting him. "I love you."

She craned her head further as he gripped the front of her dress in his palm to pull it down. "I know you are in there somewhere, Erik, and you love me." She moaned as his lips were a fire on her skin, and his hands groped her hips. "I know you would never hurt me."

He paused, turning his neck to glare out the window, his eyes afire. He gripped her tighter, his grasp desperate. Liv held her breath as he glared at her again. His eyes flipped to his normal sea blue, and his face clenched at her as if in pain.

"Liv," Erik met her face.

Liv gasped. "Erik?!" She moaned, seeing him.

"Run." He whispered, released her, and lunged backward, removing his hands from her body.

He closed his eyes and fought the curse, belting out angry moans. "Go, Liv!" He pleaded with her. "To the abbey!" He yelled.

He seethed inside, and Liv saw him fighting it. She had mere moments to get away. As his eyes burned in fire again, he scowled at the pirates filling the road with torches. Erik's face seethed and lit up in fury.

Liv crossed her arms as tears flooded her face, and turned to lunge down the steps. She yanked a thick rope from the ceiling against the wall on her way down. The rope stretched tight into the ceiling and pulled the beam in the bedroom against the sawed-off wood.

The ceiling beam fell upon Erik as he turned to go after her. The window broke, and glass shards hit him, spraying blood down the hall at Liv. She rushed down the stairs and out the door, just as the floor collapsed behind her and took out the stairs.

She met her pirates on the road. They had saddled horse ready for her and were prepared to stall Erik so she could get away. But they risked their lives doing so. Liv turned to face the townhome as it collapsed atop Erik, crying.

"I'm sorry!" She cried.

The street echoed and roared as the home fell against the hillside, and the dust from the fall quaked at their faces. She pulled her horse to jump on and then froze at the saddle. She craned her neck to the rubble, lunging onto the saddle just as sections of stone from the home shimmied. The ground cracked to the horses, and the pirates stared as the rubble slid out of place.

A rumble quaked the sky and Erik catapulted straight out of the rubble, his piercing, fiery blue eyes on Liv. He took a deep breath, his chest heaving as he watched her. His sculpted muscles twitched as he clenched his fists into balls, staring at her.

"Liv!" He moaned at her.

"Shit!" She gasped. Her knees went weak.

Erik stood there bleeding and half naked for endless moments, his slashes and cuts healing over in seconds. Liv widened her eyes and held her breath. There was no stalling this cursed Viking anymore. The pirates flanked Erik, surrounding him. He eyed their long swords and clenched his face. There were around fifty of them, but that did not matter.

Erik met them as if a swift wind had bred him. He flew into them, disarming their swords and running them through with their weapons. Even as blades ran Erik through, he pulled them out and continued killing them. Death would no longer take him. The pirates flailed onto the road, screaming in pain.

Erik was too strong. As he was killing them, Liv panicked. She lunged up the road to leave the village. Where was Halfdan? Now she was all alone facing Erik and could not defeat him, not like this. She had one chance left to drive the curse from him or stall him, and it would be painful.

Behind her, the pirates were dying for her again. Behind her, the village she loved would fall to ruin because of this curse. The man she loved would kill them all. She bent her head into the horse's mane and clenched her face in pain. She had not listened to Halfdan but had to destroy the relics.

She stopped the horse, her heart racing. "Oh no!" She left the cylinder relic in the village. "Aughhh!" She was angry at herself.

But now the house was rubble, and Erik was coming. She craned the horse around in the olive grove and gasped as Erik met her there in the darkness. His head stared at the ground, and when she turned around, he raised to face her. His eyes glowed in the dark at her. He held up the cylinder, huffing. He flexed his naked torso and stretched his muscular shoulders, twisting his neck. Liv gasped at his power.

"You forgot something." He glared at her.

Liv froze as chills darted up her spine.

"Come and take it." He spit.

"I cannot take it. You will overpower me." Liv moaned at him, clenching her face.

Erik huffed, a half-smile on his face. "I will do more than that."

"We will not die to this damn curse!" She yelled.

Erik raised his chin at her, his blonde beard blowing in the breeze as a distant storm blasted in. "You are filled with it, Liv. Your eyes are silver and powerful and as brilliant as mine." He held out a bloody palm to her. "Come to me, beautiful."

The silence filled her with dread before he spoke again.

"Do not make me come to you," He warned her. "You will not like it," He whispered and then smiled. "But I will make you like it."

Liv's lips quivered. "This is not you, Erik. I need you to fight this!" She begged, her eyes filling with tears. "I love you!" She yelled at him. "You have already been fighting it!"

Erik took a deep breath. "I love you too. Come off that horse and come to me, my beautiful Viking."

Liv glanced around, craning her neck. "No." She stared at his trousers, and her eyes fell to the knife in the sheath at his knee.

Erik sighed. "That horse cannot outrun me. Let it go."

Liv held her breath and stayed in the saddle. "No."

Erik sighed at her, his face firm. "Your village is destroyed. The fires are finishing it off now." Erik warned her. "Shame. It was a beautiful place."

Liv widened her eyes as glowing crimson filled the horizon behind Erik, and her heart shattered. She seethed.

She took a deep breath and rolled her eyes. "So, this is where it ends?" Her lips quivered. "So be it. You give me no choice, Viking."

She let the horse step closer to him. She eyed him up and down and rested her stare at his eyes. His eyes were burning and sharp like a sword. The Erik she knew was not there, but this curse writhed within him and fought the Erik she knew. She led the horse to step closer and sighed at his face.

"You are still my people, Erik." Liv slid from the saddle.

Erik belted out a yell, his eyes twisting from the Erik she knew back to the curse. "Augghhhh!" He screamed.

Her eyes focused on his eyes as torment ate him up inside. She let the horse go and stopped feet away from him. "I love you more than the time passed between us."

He moaned. "Liv!"

He lowered the cylinder to his side and glared at her, his chest heaving. He twitched his eyes and sighed, his arms flexing. Liv dropped her head to her feet and closed her eyes. Then she held her breath, raised her chin to the stars, and stared at them as if Erik was not there.

"The world is a big place. I am sorry we did not get to explore it together," Liv said as she stepped closer to him. "Or live together," Tears fell down her cheeks.

She stepped closer.

"Or love together and stay together," Her lips trembled. "If you can hear me, Erik, I am sorry I have hurt you. This is all my doing." She cried. "This is all my fault."

Erik's face was drawn and grieved as he stood there silently watching her. He kept closing his eyes and opening them again as if a battle was being fought deep inside him. He froze in a state of seething madness, and Liv sensed his pain.

Liv met his chest and sighed at his face, tears falling to her neck. "I will never love like I have loved you." Her voice broke.

Erik watched her, his chest heaving, his face twisted. He clenched his jaws and closed his eyes.

"I will die in peace knowing I loved you with all I am and that you loved me for me. You truly loved me, Erik."

Erik stepped back as Liv lunged her hand to the sheath down his leg on his trousers. She jerked out the relic knife and twisted the blade toward her chest. Erik grabbed her wrist to stop her, pressing his fist around the hilt over her palm. Liv plunged herself into the blade at his chest. She shoved it through her heart, pushing her firm grasp over Erik's on the hilt to make him kill her. Erik gasped. Liv fell.

He fell with Liv, his eyes roaring back to normal, his heart breaking. He pulled the knife from her chest and moaned. "Noooo!"

He kissed her face, his heart busting. "You will always be my people, Liv." He whispered.

From the darkness of the groves, Halfdan slithered up to them. He was still in the wagon, and the donkey paused at Liv's horse. He huffed, shaking his head, his eyes a fiery crimson.

"I liked my plan better, but noooo. You had to let yourself kill Liv while possessed with this damn curse." He rolled his eyes. "I knew she had the relics!"

Erik scowled at him, wrapping his strong arms around Liv's body. "The curse killed her, okay? I could never do it."

Halfdan gasped. "She has killed you many times. What does that make her?"

Erik leaned his head against her forehead and sighed. "Brave."

"Come on, Viking! We have a short time before the curse takes you again, and I must murder you both in Scotland." He rolled his eyes. "That will be fun and unfortunate." He huffed.

Erik lifted Liv's body in his arms and walked with her to the wagon. "This is almost over. You will be my wife soon."

Halfdan narrowed his brows as Erik climbed on Liv's horse. "How did she know about the relic knife?"

Erik froze. "I thought you told her."

"Why would I tell her that?" Halfdan met Erik's stare, and they turned to look at Liv's body in the back of the wagon. "She let you kill her with it. She pushed the curse along, freeing you of its grasp for now."

Erik swallowed. "True. The curse did not fully take me. I did not imprison her. I fought it. I heard her."

Halfdan eyed him. "Yes, but you truly love her." He paused, a headache looming over him. "We must realize this has not gone how it was meant to because of your true love for her."

"The last piece of this curse is that we must die at the abbey, and you destroy that silver thing." Erik huffed.

Halfdan nodded. "Time to go. We have a ship waiting." Halfdan and Erik eyed one another as they journeyed to the shore.

The curse had not done what they expected. It had always been a step ahead of them, and there was a great loss of life because of it. Halfdan leaned into the seat on the wagon, but a pang of chaos grew inside him as his heart ached. A wind blew around them and whistled through the grove.

Something was still coming that was not written in the stories about the curse. The curse was still coming for them all. It hunted them, and Halfdan feared it would be their fall.

Halfdan turned to Liv's body again, eying the knife in Erik's hand. "Put it back in." His eyes raged crimson. "One of you must stay down until we reach the abbey."

Erik swallowed, his face contorting as realization hit him like a dead weight. He shoved the knife back into Liv's chest.

29

Where the Curse Breathes

A fire breathed like it had been emptied into a vast chasm, writhing in silver flames and whispering. The whispers trickled from a gentle ping and then roared into a raging storm. The raging storm pried a dark veil in half, ripping it like parchment. A loathing power lunged from that open rip, and it tore through Liv. A devious laugh echoed inside her, and Liv hid in a dark corner of the vats of her mind.

Liv gasped for breath as Halfdan jerked the knife from her chest. She lunged her back straight up as the shock of the pain chased her backbone. She opened her eyes, and Halfdan paused at her face, looming over her. Liv rose, grasping her chest, eying him with suspicion.

"Did it work?" She gasped.

"Did what work?" He narrowed his brows.

"Erik? Where is he?" she pleaded. She gazed around, realizing she was on a longship. "You brought me back to Scotland," She gripped her sore chest, gasping. "How long did you keep that in me?!" She stood up, appalled. "Weeks?!" she feared.

Halfdan melted to the steps, turning his back to her. "Long enough for the curse to not fully take Erik," Then he froze, gripping the railing, his back still turned to her. "How did you know about the knife he needed to get to kill you with?" His voice was edgy.

Liv held her breath. She inched against the wall by the cot she had been on, eying him. Halfdan craned his head to her when she didn't answer and clenched his face. "Liv?" He demanded an answer, but Liv could not give it.

"Where is Erik?" Her face grieved as Halfdan turned to face her. "I must get to him," she pleaded, her voice shaky. "I need Erik."

Halfdan paused.

"Take me to him, Halfdan." Liv sighed, stepping closer.

Halfdan turned away from her and marched up the steps, and as Liv emerged from the hull, her eyes widened. Erik stood on the rocky, sandy shore, his eyes wide and bright at her. He clenched his face as she emerged, and she held her breath at him. To her left, the abbey loomed on the hill. Shadows from torch lights stretched over the hill and rested on the shore, where Erik stood. The ocean sparkled like diamonds, and shadows slithered in the darkness, edging closer to them.

Halfdan stepped to lead Liv off and froze as longboats loomed around the bend at them. Twelve ships filled the horizon from the shoreline opposite the abbey. "Curonians. Bad timing." He turned his gaze to Erik, but Erik craned his neck toward the open sea at his left as Viking longboats also coasted in to meet them. They filled the horizon, too, and a silent dread raged as night fell upon them.

Liv gasped, watching the ships surround them slowly, her gaze glaring at Erik.

"I prepared for this day." Erik nodded, sure of himself. His eyes met Liv's, but Liv was not there. He held his breath and swallowed, waiting.

Halfdan rolled his eyes. "Damnit." Then he hollered at Erik, "You and Liv cannot die by them today!"

Erik gasped, "What? You said we had to die!"

"Yes, but by me! Meeeee!" he yelled. Halfdan turned to stare at Liv, but she stood wide-eyed, glaring at the ships coming to face them off.

Erik narrowed his brows and blinked his eyes at Halfdan, shaking his head. "Going to be hard, then." He stared at Liv, then glared at the young pirate on the bow coasting toward their longboat. The young man's face was clenched and hard. He was dark-skinned, with long, black hair and eyes as dark as the night. His eyes lighted upon Liv, and he scoffed. "The cursed one!" The ships became a mass frenzy of warriors as they coasted closer.

Halfdan turned to face Liv, but it was too late. She stiffened and took a deep breath. Her blazing, silver eyes rolled to Halfdan's face. "I will not be taken," she whispered, her face clenched. "I am never taken. I am the one who does the taking."

Halfdan gasped, "Liv?"

Liv growled, her face hard. "Did you and that Viking think I would let you get away with my demise by using Liv's pirates? I can live and breathe now through my heir." She breathed heavily. "I've been following her for sometime now."

Halfdan stepped back, "I knew the curse would breathe in you, not Erik. You." He shook his head, "You fled from me. This whole time. You were the living, breathing curse while I lingered at Erik's side and he died over and over because of you."

Liv breathed through her nose and closed her eyes. "I needed room to breathe, monk," She seethed, "the tales were wrong about me," She sighed, "I killed that man because he didn't love me. I let my sister live, but she twisted the story. Everyone dies who does not love me."

Halfdan widened his eyes, stepping off the boat and meeting Erik on the shore. "How did she twist it, seer?" He held his breath. "Erik does love you, though." He mumbled. "True love always remains."

Liv laughed, her eyes meeting his, "He loves Liv, not meeee." Liv popped her neck, "You kept me down for weeks, but now I am strengthened. Erik will die, and I will continue breathing." She stepped closer, "These Curonians will die, along with your Vikings. I know they have hunted me for ages. They seek to take me today and let Liv go to this Viking lover." She took a deep breath as if a deep chasm awakened within her, "But I will not go. And you will all die."

Halfdan lunged off the ship and ran toward Erik. "I was wrong!"

Erik glared at him, his eyes on the ships filling the waterway, "What?" Then he glared at Liv again, sighing. "Liv."

"The curse endowment! It's Liv, not you! Run!" Halfdan screamed. "Run to the abbey! She is going to kill you! We will lure here there."

Erik widened his eyes, "Well, shit." He turned to follow Halfdan as Liv lunged off the side onto the sand and followed them up the rocky hill. "And the times I had it?" Erik seethed, lunging toward the abbey.

Halfdan huffed, "She said she didn't like you as much! Let's get inside to begin the end of this curse." He breathed heavily.

Erik huffed, "I'm offended."

Liv followed them up, her face raging, and then stopped as the Curonian whistled at her. His whistle was condescending and grated her nerves. She turned to glare at him, and he widened his eyes at her raging silver eyes. "Ah! Cursed pirate queen! We have come to ensure you die today!" He laughed, "We are done with this curse!" He sneered at her. "It is time to meet your demise."

Liv took a deep breath and turned to the shoreline again, growling. "You pirates will meet the demise today."

When Erik and Halfdan nearly reached the abbey doors, they turned to find Liv had not followed them as they had hoped. "Damnit!" Halfdan cursed, his eyes craning over the hill to the water. "She is after you, but,"

Erik squinted his eyes in the dark, "Looks like she changed her mind and is going after the Curonians first," He raced back down the hill with Halfdan on his heels. "Ah, this isn't going to plan at all!"

Halfdan agreed. "Because she is a stubborn Viking!"

Erik clenched his face, "Yes, but she's my stubborn Viking." He lunged down the hill toward the rocky incline, even as Liv pushed the longboat off the sand back into the sea. She glared at the Curonians, her face tense. Liv was powerful as the curse empowered her.

Erik reached the rocky slope as the ship melted into the water and jumped over the sand onto the boat to face her. He landed on his feet and pressed his sword toward Liv's neck. As she turned, she met him with a blade of her own. "Viking." She seethed at him.

Halfdan followed Erik back down, but it was too late to jump. "This is not part of the plan!" He complained, his eyes roving to the small row boat next to where Erik had been standing. "I hate boats. I'm so tired of boats." He waded out and jumped in, rowing to them as they coasted into the fray of the oncoming ships looming in to get Liv. "I can't even kill them properly because of a stubborn woman."

The boat coasted deeper, and behind them, hollers of rage and high-pitched screams echoed in the air. The Curonians and Vikings readied to face off, all the while, the pirate leader's eyes roared upon Liv. He nodded at several pirates behind him, and they readied their matchlock guns. The burning slow match would take moments before it smoldered into the flash pan and ignite the powder. The Curonians aimed at Liv's back and held their breaths, waiting.

Liv met Erik at his throat, and they stood one another off in silence. Liv's eyes were shimmering silver at his face, even as Erik met her hatred with his fiery blue ones. Their blades pressed against one another, and Erik clenched his face at her eyes.

"I see you, seer." He bit. Erik narrowed his brows, wondering if this was how Liv felt when the curse took him at the village. "You can't have her. She is mine." Erik warned. "She has always been mine."

Liv laughed. "I've had Liv her whole life. I was roaming in your head too, Viking," She sneered at him. "When you killed her with the knife, I knew that was my opportunity to take her." Then she laughed again, "Once these pirates kill me, you and that monk fail at saving Liv. She will be gone forever, and I will live forever."

She craned her eyes toward the ships coming at them, smiling.

Erik pressed the blade harder against her throat, and Liv grimaced. "Careful, Viking. You don't want to decapitate the woman you love."

Erik pulled back, grimacing at her. "You've had your time, seer! You could have loved someone else. You cannot have my Liv!" He yelled. "I love her!"

Liv flexed her arms and met his face, "I am Liv, Erik. I am living, breathing, Liv."

Erik scoffed. "You are a pathetic, desperate woman to have killed a man who never loved you and then to take the woman I have cherished for ages now. I will not let you have her," He clenched his face and pressed his blade harder against her throat, but she pushed against it with her blade. As Erik's blade pressed on her throat, blood seeped down. He was killing her whether he wanted to or not, but he had no choice but to keep her focused on him.

Behind them, the flammable cords of the matchlock guns simmered, and the Curonians waited.

They coasted closer to the ships flanking them, and Erik held his breath. His raging eyes melted upon the woman he loved, but Liv was not there. Erik's lips trembled, and his voice broke. "I love you deeper than the forests I have tracked our enemies through,"

The Curonians pulled the levers.

Erik swallowed, "I love you stronger than this drive we both have to keep going, even when you run away from me."

The Viking longships slowed as they met the Curonians, and Liv and Erik coasted between them. The Vikings gripped their double-edged swords, their broad blades shimmering under the moon. Three Vikings stood and jumped to the edge, pivoting their swords to fling at the ship.

A tear fell on Erik's cheek, "I love you harder than the pain of dying."

Liv met his face, but her eyes roared in flaming silver and she would not be swayed. Erik held his breath as his tears fell, clenching his face and gripping his hilt with every strength he had in him to keep her fast. "I love you." He cried.

The Curonians released the levers, and the barrels fired. Liv and Erik fell opposite of one another, moaning against each other. Erik met Liv's eyes and yelled in pain as blood poured from their arms. Liv grimaced, scooting away from him on the deck.

The Vikings slung their swords, lodging the blades in the mast beside Erik. As Erik and Liv flailed in pain on the deck, Halfdan lunged between them. He pulled a sword from the mast, grimacing, his eyes flaming crimson. He turned to Liv first, and she roared in anger at him. Halfdan lunged the blade through Erik's chest, and then raised it to face Liv. He pulled a second blade from the mast as she eyed him, leaning over to grasp her sword.

She met Halfdan's rage in her face as he shoved the blade through her chest and fell to his knees in agony. He closed his eyes, moaned in frustration, and raised his chin to the starry night. A wind blew over them, and the waters moved like something breathed beneath them. The ships coasted against Halfdan, bumping into each other.

Halfdan opened his eyes and stared back and forth at them, shaking his head. "You didn't listen, pirate!"

The pirate sighed, raking his long fingers through his beard. "Hey, monk! My great ancestor Rait left explicit instruction that the cursed one was to take a hit to knock her down first, okay?" Then he rolled his eyes. "Worst love story ever, and he was right."

Halfdan sighed and turned to the Vikings. The warriors shook their heads at him, too, and sighed. "Come on, monk! We will bring the bodies into the abbey."

H alfdan stood over Liv and Erik, their bodies on the ground where they first touched the cylinder relic. He placed it between them and pulled out the dagger. They were still bleeding out and pale as Halfdan pressed the dagger against the stone, and it cracked to pieces.

He craned his neck to stare at the monks, Curonians, and Vikings who assembled to watch. They stood in eerie silence, their eyes as wide as their weapons. Halfdan sat back on his knees between them, and tears fell. He closed his eyes, and the ground shook beneath them. He jerked his eyes open to face the cylinder relic, writhing in the air at his face.

It twisted and seethed as if it were alive, and the air became heavy like a stone. A roar rumbled over the abbey, and the sea shook and raged, pushing the ships against one another on the shore. Halfdan held his breath and watched it writhe in pain. Liv and Erik's eyes burst open, and a misty veil pulled itself off of their palms. The veil moaned, and for a moment, Halfdan saw it scream into a woman's face. The woman wailed in agony, ripping herself apart like parchment.

"Die, seer." Halfdan clenched his face.

He gripped the dagger tightly and plunged the blade through the stone as the relic turned at his face. It slid inside it as if the relic was flesh, and the runes shimmered flaming blue and silver. It blasted raging shimmers and doused the abbey courtyard in light, even though dawn was coming. Halfdan let the dagger go, and the cylinder tore apart, writhing like snakes. He raised his chin and watched it dissipate over the abbey, and as the night took over, his eyes were normal again.

Halfdan closed his eyes again and sighed, gripping his heart.

Behind him, the pirates and Vikings raged and roared at the revelation. Halfdan watched Erik and Liv, lying still. He turned to the monks lingering around the pillars and nodded. They came and lifted the bodies up and carried them out, and Halfdan swallowed. He stood up slowly and marched out of the abbey to the edge of the rolling hill, and faced the sea until dawn.

30

Where the Hearts Live Again

Dawn arose like a crimson tide, blasting the hillside and the sea at the abbey in a serene hope. This hope did not wail or die. It breathed liberation because it kissed their soul alive with it.

Erik sat leaning against the wall, watching Liv. His tunic was still drenched in blood, but his heart was whole. The sun rose at his face through the window, and he breathed it in as Liv turned on the bed to face him. Her eyes flew open like something flipped inside her, and she gasped at Erik's face.

He sighed. It was heavy and deep, and tears filled his eyes. "Hello, beautiful." Tears fell on his face. "I see the woman I have loved my whole life returning to me." He breathed heavily, his eyes lingering over her face, "Finally."

Liv bolted up, gripping her heart. Her lips quivered as tears fell. "We're free!" She cried, "I love you!" She fell off the bed into his lap. They clung to one another in desperate grasp and cried on each other's faces. "We're free. We're free." She cried against his lips, their mouths quivering on each other, their breaths hot on their lips.

They cried against each other as grief melted off them. They cried in each other's breaths as their hope roared inside them. And they shivered in each other's arms as the years of pain and anguish tore at their hearts, but it breathed to life again.

The curse had broken.

Erik gripped her tight against him and held her face in his palm as his chest roared against hers. "We're freeeee."

They gripped one another like they were on a slippery slope, their hands strong and desperate. Erik lunged against her lips, and Liv met him there. His mouth roared over her face and down her neck, and he pulled her against him tighter. Liv met his face with open-mouthed kisses, and wiped his tears with her shaky fingers. She met his eyes, her lips quivering.

Erik's voice broke against her lips, "You are the most beautiful hope I have ever seen. You are the love of my life."

"Forgive me." She pleaded. "I love you."

Erik pressed his forehead against hers and smiled. "Forgive me," he pleaded. "I love you."

They roared into one another until they heard voices out in the hall. Erik pulled Liv out by her hand, and they walked out of the abbey to face the rising dawn and Halfdan. The monk was on his knees, staring over the sea, still and quiet. Erik and Liv melted on their knees on either side of him, and Halfdan took a deep breath and smiled. He gazed at them with sparkling eyes and nodded, turning to face the dawn again.

The silence of the morning filled them with peace.

Liv lunged down and grabbed Halfdan's hand off his lap, pressing his palm into hers. She leaned her head on his shoulder and smiled, her lips still quivering. Erik took Halfdan's hand, too, and they sat there, staring into the dawn, holding one another. Halfdan squeezed their palms tight, smiling as he sniffled. "This is the beginning of the end of our lives." He sighed. "Finally."

Liv met his face and Erik smiled at him, laughing. "I am so ready." Erik's voice was deep and joyous.

Behind them, the monks had gathered around the abbey to take in the miraculous events they had witnessed. The Curonians and Vikings had slept on their boats but were moseying about the shores as dawn kissed the rolling hills. Halfdan held his breath as a voice sounded behind them, but did not turn to acknowledge it.

From behind them, the monk belted out. "Excuse me, Halfdan, but I have discovered this obsidian relic,"

Halfdan, Liv, and Erik craned to stare at the monk. He was young, with a head full of curly black hair and wide brown eyes. He held a black stone tablet carved with runes, some of which were missing. Liv and Erik eyed one another, their backs stiff, but Halfdan calmly huffed at the monk.

Halfdan sighed. "You know where the well is?"

The monk cleared his throat, nodding. "Yes."

Halfdan turned back to the sunrise. "Toss it in there. Do not tell the others."

Erik and Liv watched the monk rush back to the abbey to do Halfdan's bidding. They stared at Halfdan briefly, but he had closed his eyes again, still gripping their hands tight in his palm. As they turned back to the sunrise with him, Halfdan burst out laughing. His laugh was thunderous and resounding, and Liv and Erik could not help but join him. They sat on their knees, holding hands and laughing into the sunrise. Their laughter carried to the abbey and rolled over the hill.

Erik pulled away from Halfdan when they finished laughing and lunged to get Liv. She watched him loom over her, and she took his hand as he pulled her up to face him. She gripped his back with her arms and melted against him, and Erik swayed her back and forth in the sunrise. He wrapped his arms tight around her, pressing his head against hers, breathing on her lips. Halfdan stood smiling, watching them slowly dance in the sunrise, his heart lighter.

"Will you be my wife for life?" Erik asked her. "For the rest of whatever time we have, will you?"

Liv kissed him, moaning against his lips. "Til death do us part, my handsome Viking."

Halfdan cleared his throat. "Glad you mentioned that,"

Erik raised his head, his eyes wide, "What now? What, Halfdan?!"

Liv gasped. "Halfdan! Nooooo."

Halfdan stepped back, holding a palm out to calm them. "What? I am happy to officiate the wedding." Then he sighed, "But where will we live?"

Liv laughed, but Erik met her face again, smiling. "I know a perfect village that needs some work. It is a happy place."

Halfdan laughed at them, turning to face the dawn again, his heart at peace.

Erik held Liv tight against him, and they danced together on the hill outside of Iona Abbey. They danced in the morning light, their lips upon one another and their hearts bursting with joy. They held one another close, their smiles breathing hope. Erik and Liv swayed slowly like a gentle tune played in their souls, kising without fear of being ripped apart again.

And they lived happily ever after.

The end.

When the curse breaks, immortality is spent. When death's malicious grip finally takes them, the one who was stricken with grief finds rest, and the one last to fall has peace they will never forget.

Made in the USA
Columbia, SC
28 December 2024

48739860R10164